The Man Test

AMANDA ✦ AKSEL

ISBN: 0996028609
ISBN-13: 978-0996028608

Cover Design by: Amanda Aksel & Mona Lin

Edited by Lauran Strait
http://www.linkedin.com/in/lauranstrait

For Chantell

CONTENTS

The Man Test

1

Love and Las Vegas

THE TRUTH WILL SET YOU FREE. And yet, people have a tendency to keep secrets from those they love. As a therapist, I observed this occurrence regularly. Even now. My patient had spent the last forty-five minutes attempting honest communication with her husband. But I can tell by the way she averts her eyes, she's been holding back. She's hiding behind her tactful words. And just when I thought we were getting nowhere, she parted her lips.

"I need more passion in our sex life!" She blurted the words like they'd been trapped inside her for years. Her husband flinched. "There's no spontaneity with us. You're always asking me, 'do you want to have sex?' I want you to stop asking and just do it! I want you to pick me up and throw me on the bed. You know, just really give it to me. How come you never pick me up?"

He shrugged. "You're too heavy."

I shot him an incredulous look, unintentionally of course. She did the same.

"I'm not too heavy. You're not strong enough!"

Their insults ensued, each nastier and more spiteful than the last. Every second increased their volume and pace and quickly spiraled out of control. I grabbed the whistle from around my neck and blew hard. Their heads whipped in my direction.

"Time out," I said calmly. "Let's not criticize each other." They turned spitefully from one another and each rolled their eyes like spoiled children. I looked to the husband. "I understand this can be difficult to hear, but your wife is trying to be open with you about her needs. How do you feel about her suggestions?"

"I'm not into what she is into. Is that so wrong?" He offered, and his chin drifted down.

Her eyes fixed on him. "It's not wrong, but we always do it your way. I'm just asking for you to do it my way sometimes."

He remained silent, so I leaned in. "You love Abby, right?"

"Of course." He lifted his head.

"Does she make you happy?"

"Yes," he answered.

"You want her to be happy too, right?"

"Well, yeah."

"Then consider having an open mind. Who knows, you two may discover something you really enjoy." He gazed into his wife's eyes and took her hand. Fifteen minutes later, they left my office with smiles on their faces and hope in their eyes. Progress not perfection.

My father used to say, "Those who stand for nothing fall for anything." The only thing I could ever stand for completely was love. I'm not talking about the butterflies, can't eat, can't sleep kind of love, but the morning breath, movie night in, grow old together love. My affinity for love can be traced back to my childhood obsession with happily ever after fairy tales and witnessing the deep love between my parents and even my grandparents. It gave me a sense of believing, of knowing that there was a great love out there just for me. Not just me, but I believed this to be true for everyone. Standing up for real love gave me a purpose and a passion for my profession. It was my mission to remind couples of the heartfelt reasons they got together and to help them stay together. I won't be so bold as to say I'm a relationship expert, but I've helped absent men become present husbands, set wandering eyes straight, and fueled fire back into sexless marriages.

I glanced at the clock. Time to collect my things and head home to finish packing for a weekend-long bachelorette party in Vegas for my dear friend, Rachel. Diana, our office assistant, sat at the front desk typing with only her index fingers. For the most part she was a wonderful assistant, except for one thing; she had a way of making short, simple answers unnecessarily long and drawn out. Not overly informative or longwinded, she just spoke too slowly, which was fine if you had an hour to kill. I didn't have minutes to spare.

"Diana?" I tried to look rushed as I approached.

"Oh, hellooo, Marin . . . how are you?" she said sweetly as she stood with her fingertips touching near her chest, a classic move that always preempted long conversations. I needed to be quick.

"Great, thanks. I wanted to remind you that I'm leaving for a long weekend and will be back Tuesday. If you need me, call my cell, okay?"

She smiled, but it quickly faded into her conversational entrapment look again.

"Oh, okay . . . You have a message. Would you like me to read it to you?"

"No, that's okay. Can you email it to me?"

"Oh, um . . . yes. I guess I can do that. Okay."

I thanked her before rushing out of the office and around the corner to the elevator, which was as slow as Diana's speech. Its open doors seemed to wait patiently while my least favorite associate, Andy, gabbed on his phone inside.

"Hold the elevator!" I hurried forward, clutching my oversized purse to my side. He glanced at me, still talking on his phone, but did nothing as the doors began to close. I managed to wedge my body between the doors at the last second. As I squeezed in, I tumbled to the ground. My poor shoe, lodged between the steel teeth, completely detached from my foot. The elevator began to move. I pushed my hair out of my face and rescued my Ralph Lauren pump.

Andy hung up. "You all right?"

"I'm fine, no thanks to you," I said, catching my

breath.

"Sorry," he said, not taking his eyes from his phone. I gave him a sour look, and held up my beloved navy pump, after noticing a decent scratch on the heel.

"Look what you made me do."

"Me? I'm not the one who made a mad dash into a closing elevator."

"It wouldn't have closed if you'd held it open," I said through clenched teeth as I continued to put myself back together.

For the few years I had known Andy, there had always been a rift between us. Something about his east coast arrogance made me defensive. Andy was a cynic and some of his ideas about human relationships were appalling.

The shoe eaters reopened as we arrived on the first floor. Andy stepped out.

"Run faster next time." A sarcastic grin spread across his face before he walked away with his usual haughty stride.

Once I made it outside of the building, with both shoes on my feet, I breathed in the warm San Francisco air. I was looking forward to the long weekend escape with my friends. Barely beginning my six-block commute home, my cell phone rang. I reached into my purse touching everything except my phone. The call was moments from going to voicemail. *Gotcha!* And just in time.

"Hey, it's me," said my best friend, Telly, a divorce lawyer who lived and worked in the city. I'd met her in passing after her client became my patient. Needless to say the client didn't need her services after I was through with her and her husband.

"You excited about Vegas?" I asked.

"Yeah, after the day I've had, I'm most definitely ready for Sin City."

"What happened?"

"Ugh, it's Grayson. He's being such a whiny bitch." Grayson was her lover, one who mistakenly started saying things like *love* and *marriage*—two red flags to Telly. "I'm like 'what do you want from me, kids and a white picket fence?' I don't think so dude. Get yourself a wife and give me some ass." She cackled.

I laughed too. "Is that what you said to him?"

"Yeah, right. He'd probably start crying. I just told him that it is what it is. I never gave him any reason to believe it would be more. I didn't lead him on, and if he can't handle it then I'm sorry."

"At least you were honest." I shrugged, poor Grayson.

"That's right! I am honest. He's the one who said he could handle it. Now he says he has to think about it. Pfff! No, I'm done."

"I guess another one bites the dust," I said.

"You know I don't sugar coat anything." It was true. Telly was brutally honest, and never neglected to put in her two cents, especially when it was unsolicited. Some called her coarse, but I appreciated that about her. I could always count on her to tell me the truth.

Five increasingly steep blocks later, I arrived at my building and climbed the stoop. Mine was the first apartment on the right, number 102. True to San Francisco real estate standards, it was "cozy." I loved everything about it from the dark stained hardwood floors to the close proximity to work and the park. But what I loved most about coming home was coming home to someone, my fiancé Chad.

Since we were only months away from getting married, we decided it was time to share our living space. Mounds of Chad's half-empty moving boxes blocked my path as I made my way through the living room.

"Hey, Babe!" he said, smiling from the kitchen as he fed vegetables into a juicer. Yum. Chad's toned, personal-trainer body that is, not the veggie juice.

"Hey." I ran to him with open arms. He held me tight and kissed the top of my head, making a sweet muffled kissing sound.

"Are you all packed?"

"No, I still have more to do, and I don't have much time."

Chad sat with me while I crammed more outfits into my already overstuffed suitcase, his eyes gazing at me as if he had to have me. I wanted him too. I struggled to lift it from the bed.

"Let me do that." Chad moved it to the floor.

"Thank you. It's gonna be nice having a man around the house."

"Well, now there's more room on the bed." His eyes set on mine a moment before he grabbed me and kissed my neck. With his body pressed tightly against mine, he laid me on the bed. Our lips were locked and I wedged my hands between us to undo his belt.

The sophisticated sound of Telly's 7 Series BMW car horn beeped outside of my apartment.

"She's here." I lifted myself onto my elbows and pouted my lip. "I have to go."

"Can she wait five minutes?" he asked.

"Five minutes?" I laughed. "We'll finish this when I get back."

"Promise?"

"Cross my heart." He gave me one last long kiss. I took a moment to stare into his sweet brown eyes, wanting to stay.

"I'll miss you," he said. "Don't get into any trouble."

"I won't." I smirked.

Telly popped the trunk, and Chad placed my bulging suitcase inside.

"Love you!" I said one last time before getting into the car.

"Love you too."

I opened the passenger door to find Telly dressed in a short, skin tight, black DKNY dress with matching four-inch stilettos and big dark designer sunglasses. Already tall, her heels made her legs go on for miles. She was a stunning Latina goddess with amazing breasts. She was never in short supply of eager men and their compliments.

Telly was definitely the pretty one, the one who was asked out first at the bar, the one people stared at whenever we went to a party. Though I never begrudged her, I did wish I had been born with some of her physical genes. I was shorter and lacked her curves. We did share similar long locks, as I was fortunate enough to inherit my Chinese-born mother's thick Asian hair. But it was wavy in all the wrong places, which I got from my American father. Not to say I was unhappy with my appearance, I was perfectly pretty with my big almond-shaped hazel eyes that reflected specs of green, brown, gold, red, and blue. The one unique physical feature I had over Telly.

We met up with the girls at the terminal bar, and from the looks of it, the bachelorette party had already started. Rachel, the bride-to-be, wore a hot pink sash that read *Bachelorette* and a plastic tiara with a white tulle veil.

Rachel was one of those girl next-door types, a schoolteacher in her mid-twenties with a sweet naivety about her. She probably still kept a stuffed teddy on her bed. Beyond her Sandra Dee good-girl image, there was also something elegant and enchanting about her. It was most easily seen in her eyes, big and beautiful with long thick lashes that gave the illusion she had the secret to perfect mascara.

"Marin, Telly, you're here!" Rachel hugged us. "I want you to meet my bridesmaids. This is Denise, Jamie, and Sonia." She pointed to each of the cute twenty-somethings.

"Hi!" the girls said in unison.

"Where's Holly?" I asked Rachel as I looked around for her sister.

"She went to the bathroom. She'll be right back."

There was still a half-hour before boarding so I asked Telly to order a cocktail for me while I went to find Holly. In the ladies room, I found her leaning against the wall near the sinks reading a newspaper.

"Hey," I said, stealing her attention.

She looked up at me beneath the brim of her khaki cap and smiled. "Marin, how are you?"

"Good, what are you doing in here reading?"

"I got caught up in this article, and it's quieter here."

"Are you excited about your sister's bachelorette party?"

She scoffed. "Partying in Vegas with a bunch of drunken twenty-six-year-olds? No, I wouldn't exactly say I'm excited."

"Come on, everyone's waiting for you," I pulled her in, and we walked out to the terminal.

Holly was my oldest and dearest friend. I'll never forget the first day of second grade in Mrs. Smith's class when a little frizzy-haired girl came up to me at recess and asked if I wanted to help her pick up litter after school. I didn't know what litter was, but I knew that I liked her right away.

As we grew into our early thirties her hair became less frizzy, but her passion for the environment increased. She worked for a company called EcoWorld and traveled the globe promoting eco-friendly initiatives.

We found the girls still sitting by the bar enjoying their cocktails. Telly handed me a Malibu Bay Breeze, a favorite of mine. Rachel's bridesmaid Sonia gave us a run-down of the weekend's events and it wasn't long before we were on our ninety-minute flight to Vegas. The plane was packed and lively, everyone engaged in conversation and seeming to have a good time. When we landed at

LAS, the pilot sang to the tune of *Barney*.

We love you. You love us.
We're much faster than the bus.
We've got style and personality.
Marry one of us and you'll fly free.

Everyone applauded and laughed. True story.

After baggage claim and a cab ride, we made it to the MGM Grand Hotel. Telly, Holly, and I shared a large suite with a view of the Vegas strip, thanks to Telly's frequent stays and reward status.

"I can't believe my sister's getting married," Holly said while she examined her figure in the full-length mirror.

"You mean getting married before you?" Telly smirked as she carefully put the finishing touches on her mascara. I rolled my eyes and smiled at Telly's reflection in the bathroom mirror we shared and imagined Holly had done the same.

"It's not that, just that she's so young. She's my baby sister. She'll have her own family soon," Holly said.

"A family? You mean Rachel's pregnant?" Telly leaned over the counter to finish her make-up, cleavage spilling from her iridescent gray dress.

"I didn't say that!" Holly sounded mad. "All I'm saying is she's growing up."

I moved toward her. "I know what you mean." Our reflections side by side in the sleek, black-framed wall mirror, my thoughts flashed back to when we were eight, the beginning of our awkward phase right before hitting puberty. We were so young then and Rachel was just a baby. Looking at Holly was the same as when we were kids, even though we're much older and less awkward.

"Do you remember when Rachel said her first word?" I asked Holly.

Her face lit up. "Yeah, we were looking at my mom's baby magazines when Rachel came over and pointed at the baby."

"Then she said, 'baby' and you nodded and said, 'yeah baby.'"

Holly smiled with a slight laugh. "It took us a minute to realize she said her first word."

I put my arm around her. "I guess the baby's all grown up."

"Ugh, you sound like a bunch of old sentimental grandmas." Telly grimaced. "Can we not talk about Rachel as a baby? She's a grown woman and tonight she's a Sin City bachelorette. I don't want images of her innocence when a hot male stripper grinds on her later."

"You ordered a stripper?" Holly sounded appalled to say the least.

Telly shook her head innocently and shrugged. "Maybe."

"We gotta go, guys." I ushered the girls to the door, while Holly ranted about why strippers are disgusting. After passing the casino downstairs, we made it inside the Tabu Lounge. We were led to a special bachelorette booth adorned with a confetti of martini glasses.

Rachel raised her glass, compelling our attention. "I want to say something," she began. "I want to thank you all for coming all the way here to celebrate my last days as a single girl. It means the world to me." Two of the twenty-somethings ahhed. "There are no other six ladies I would rather be with. I love you guys!" We raised our glasses and leaned in for a toast.

Telly wrapped her hands around her martini glass, clutching it like a warm cup of coffee, and bouncing in her seat with a grin. "Okay, who's my crush for the night?" Her eyes wandered around the lounge, scoping out the men like a lioness on the hunt. I'd seen it many times before. She stopped, grinned, and sure enough stunned her first prey. He made his way over to us, which always made me uncomfortable because I knew what would come next. He was attractive, built like a football player. Eligible looking enough except his hair was spiked with a tad too much gel.

"Hey," too-much-hair-gel-guy said to Telly, ignoring the rest of us.

"Hi," she said.

"Can I buy you a drink?"

Telly curled her lip. "I already have a drink." He raised his eyebrows in a sigh, almost admitting defeat, but tried again.

"You wanna dance?"

"I don't know." Telly paused and ran her eyes down his body. "Can you dance?"

"Only one way to find out."

Telly raised an eyebrow. She walked toward the dance floor, hips moving to the beat with each step. He, of course, followed eagerly.

It wasn't long before the seven of us were throwing back cocktails and shakin' it on the dance floor. Denise created a list of dares for Rachel, like rub a bald guy's head and ask random guys to take off their shirts for pictures. Rachel exhibited her low tolerance for alcohol as she crossed through each fulfilled dare on the list.

At one point she looked over at me. "You're next." She was right. My wedding was only four months away, and it wouldn't be long before I was rubbing bald heads and asking for men's shirts. She was the first of all the girls there to get married and, having known her since her diaper days, I was incredibly happy for her. We were both so lucky to have found great guys who wanted to spend their lives with us as much as we wanted to spend our lives with them.

The girls spread throughout the lounge, Holly was chatting with the bartender, Telly had moved on to bleached-blonde-surfer-guy, and Rachel was enjoying herself in the crowd on the dance floor. I made my way over. When I reached her, she stumbled and bumped into a dancing couple. I grabbed her to keep her upright.

"Are you okay?" I shouted over the booming music.

"Yeah, I think I need some air." She looked like she was going to be sick. I led her into the hotel corridor.

"Do you need to go to the ladies room?" I brushed her hair away from her eyes.

"No, just air."

I nodded.

We walked through the casino and outside to a nearby bench under the walkway escalator. Rachel took deep breaths as I lightly rubbed her back.

"You okay?" I asked again.

"I think so. I feel panicky all of the sudden." She put her hand on her chest, her breathing became shallow.

I kneeled in front of her and looked onto her face. "Rachel, what's going on?"

"I'm scared."

"Scared of what?"

"Getting married. It's such a huge thing, you know. It's like . . . forever."

"That's the thing about marriage, honey," I said with a smile.

"And I love David, I do. He's great, but he has a past. And what if he hasn't grown—"

"Rachel, listen."

She held her breath.

"The past is the past. David's a great guy, and he would not have asked you to marry him if he wasn't ready to make that commitment, okay?"

"You're right." She nodded.

"It's normal to get cold feet, and if you're not ready, then it's okay. You can postpone the wed—"

"No!" She jumped to her feet with conviction. "I'm marrying David."

"Good," I said and brushed her cheek. I stood up ready to head back inside when she grabbed my arm. Her concerned expression returned.

"I have to tell you something." My heart jumped at the severity of her tone. Maybe she was pregnant.

"Okay."

"This might sound crazy, but a month after we got engaged . . ."

"Yes." I took a deep breath.

"I lost my engagement ring in a parking lot." I studied her left hand, which glistened with two carats worth of shiny diamonds. I held it up.

"I don't follow," I said.

"I got the ring back, thank God, but I didn't tell anyone because of the superstition, you know?"

I shrugged. The only ring superstition I knew about involved wearing a used ring from a broken engagement.

"Lose your ring, lose your spouse," she said as if it was as common as *step on a crack and break your mother's back*. "That's crazy, right?" She bit her lip. It did sound crazy, but as a therapist I did not encourage such terms.

"Of course not, but your ring isn't lost. You got it back. I would call it no harm, no foul."

"You're right. I'm getting married, and it's going to be great."

"It's going to be great." I nodded and smiled. "Let's go back inside."

The next day at the casino we handed chips to the black jack dealers and spent the evening mesmerized by the latest performance of Cirque du Soleil. By Sunday morning we were in need of some R&R. Telly, Holly, and I spent our time at the pool, soaking in the sun and cooling off in the water. Rachel and her friends opted for massages and facials at the spa.

After an hour of sunning and reading a few articles in *Psychology Today*, I put my head back and closed my eyes. The sun felt good on my face, and I thought about all the fun I had the past couple of days. Then, I thought about

Chad and how much fun I would've had if I'd been home helping him move into my apartment, our apartment. I missed him.

"Hey, guys?" I said turning to the girls who were resting on their lounge chairs next to mine. Their heads turned in unison. "I think I'm gonna fly home tonight and surprise Chad."

"You're leaving?" Telly asked.

"Yeah, I really miss him. He's been working a lot, and I haven't seen him much lately. Do you think Rachel will be upset?"

"No," Holly said. "She'll understand. I'm sure she's itching to get back to David too."

Before leaving for the airport, I found Rachel at the salon and said good-bye. She thanked me for coming and for our little pep talk the first night.

The flight was as quick as the one before, but it felt longer still. I was antsy to surprise Chad and finish what we started a few days ago. By the time I got to our apartment, I was almost giddy at the idea of surprising him. The doorknob turned easily as I carefully opened the door and dragged my suitcase behind me. The space was dark except for a hint of light spilling out from the bedroom.

2

The Catch

I SHUT THE DOOR WITHOUT A SOUND and tiptoed through the living room and down the hall. I stopped short of the bedroom and just stood in the doorway.

A naked woman wrapped up in my once pristine white Egyptian cotton sheets laid alone in my bed. My mind didn't register anything about her other than that she had no business being there.

"Who the hell are you?" I yelled. Before she could answer, Chad came out of the hall bathroom wearing nothing but his boxer briefs.

Heart pounding, hands shaking, a stabbing pain of betrayal warmed my face. How could this be? My perfect fiancé was having an affair, in our apartment, in our bed. I fought to hold back the tears.

"Marin." He started as if to explain.

I held up my hand. It was my turn to speak, though I

didn't know where to start. He was having an affair. How could he do this to me? We're getting married. What a lying, cheating, son-of-a-bitch.

There were no words. I heaved and covered my mouth. "I'm going to be sick," I said, heaving again. I pushed Chad out of the way and locked myself in the bathroom. My complimentary Southwest cocktails spewed out of me as I hovered over the toilet and my tears spilled out like an opened floodgate.

Chad banged against the door. "Marin, let me in!"

"Go away!" I shouted.

"Let me explain," he said, still banging against the door.

"I don't want to talk to you. Just go! Take that whore with you."

"I'm not going anywhere until you open this door and let me talk to you." I broke from my tears long enough to tell him I would call the cops if he didn't leave.

"They won't do anything, Marin. I live here, remember?"

"Not anymore. Now get the hell out." I sobbed.

"I'm sorry," he said in a lower, defeated tone. I remained silent, sitting on the floor with my head against the wall. Waiting. A minute later, the front door closed and he was gone. The sorrow was so overwhelming that I breathed in and tried to cry out, but the cry stuck in my throat until it released a second later. Hours later and still lying on my bathroom rug surrounded by balled up tissues, my eyes were parched. I felt numb, thoughtless, speechless, and even breathless. At some point during my dismal daze, I fell asleep.

I was disoriented the next morning until the base of my toilet came into view. The whole thing came back to me like a bad dream. Except it wasn't a dream. Chad, my fiancé, was having an affair. The man I had spent two years with had betrayed me in the worst way.

I splashed cold water on my face, then left my grief chamber to investigate the empty apartment. There was nothing but silence. My memory flashed back as I entered my bedroom and stared at my bed. An unsettling urge to scratch my skin off came over me as my new reality crawled under it. I shifted that urge to the bed, clawing the white sheets soiled by infidelity. Minutes later they tumbled down the garbage shoot. When I returned to the room, my running shoes appeared in my peripheral vision. I knew exactly what was needed: a good run.

There was something peaceful about the sound of my feet against the pavement and the steadiness of my breath. Running allowed me to clear my head, gain perspective. It was my version of therapy, helping me through grad school, tension with my family, and the pressure of being single in my late twenties. I hoped it would get me through the trauma with Chad.

One question hounded me. What should I do now? In my professional experience, many couples combat infidelity with success. I always encouraged people to work it out if they could. Now that it had happened to me, I didn't feel so willing. For starters, Chad and I were not married, and in that moment I was thankful for that. If I wanted to get out of my relationship, I could easily do so. The truth remained that I loved him, but was love enough? I wouldn't have agreed to marry him in the first place if I hadn't thought we could face the hard stuff. My rose colored view of love never imagined infidelity plaguing our relationship.

How could I ever trust him again? Cheating can make people crazy with jealousy and suspicion, and I didn't want to be the kind of person who second-guessed him all the time. Plus, I didn't know the nature of his affair. Was it a one-time thing or a long-standing relationship? Would it matter either way? The whole thing made me sick.

Chad was waiting for me in the living room when I got back. He jumped to his feet at my entrance.

"What are you doing here?" I asked sternly, crossing my arms and trying not to cry.

"I came to see you." He walked toward me, and I stepped back.

"I told you I don't want see you."

"I know you're mad."

"Mad? You think I'm mad? You cheated on me. You lied to me. You betrayed me. I'm not mad. I'm furious, and hurt, and confused. And more than any of that I feel like a fool that I believed you loved me."

"I do love you." He sounded earnest.

"You don't do this to someone you love."

"It's not that simple, you should know that."

"What I know is we're supposed to be getting married.

You asked me to be your wife. Now what am I supposed to do?"

"I know. I messed up," he said, head down.

"Yeah, you did."

"Once I moved in I realized what a big commitment I was making. I realized I would never be single again, and I thought I could have one last hurrah before I said forever. I didn't want to go into this thinking, *what if?*"

He may have intended to sound sincere, but all I could hear were lies. "That doesn't justify what you did."

"I know, but it's the truth."

I shook my head. Now he wanted to tell the truth?

"Why didn't you talk to me? We talk about everything. We could have found another way." I wanted to understand how he could have been so deceitful. How I could have been so blind.

"I didn't think there was another way."

And there it was. The man I had given my heart to didn't think there was another way to go into a marriage with me other than to do something that would break my heart. If I hadn't come home early, then we would have gotten married, and I would have been none the wiser. But he was caught red-handed, and that situation gave me a choice. It wasn't going to be easy, but it was for the best.

"I don't think there's another way either. I can't do this." With that affirmation, I slipped the round, one-carat diamond, Tiffany style engagement ring off of my finger and placed it in his hand.

"Please, don't end it like this, Marin."

"I didn't, you did."

I grabbed my keys and headed for the door.

"Where are you going?" Chad called.

I looked back at him, hoping it was the last time I would ever see him. "I'm leaving. I can't stand to look at you. Get your stuff out before I come back." And before he had the chance to say anything, I slammed the door.

I spent the rest of the day walking around the city, visiting the park, the coffee house, the deli for lunch, and a few shops. Considering everything, I felt okay, but I knew enough to realize that it was the calm before the storm. In an effort to stay out as long as possible, I paid my office an unexpected visit.

"Oooh, Marin, you're back early," Diana said, greeting me warmly.

"I'm not staying. I just need to see Katie. Is she free?" I leaned on her counter while Diana checked the calendar. After almost a minute of her repeating, "well, um," she finally said, "Yes . . . she's available."

"Thanks." I headed toward Katie's office.

"Come in," Katie called after I knocked on her door. Slowly, I made my way inside before shutting the door.

"I thought you weren't coming back until tomorrow."

"I had a change of plans."

She frowned. "Is everything okay?"

"No. I need to take some time off. It's sort of a family emergency," and by emergency I meant my wedding was off.

"What happened?" She walked over to me. As a possible patient going through a personal crisis I wanted to open up to her, but as a partner in the practice with an excellent handle on my patients' relationships, I couldn't admit that I had suffered a major failure. I glanced briefly into her eyes.

"I don't really want to talk about it yet."

"Of course," she said, placing a hand on my shoulder. "I'm always here if you need to talk."

"I know. Thank you." I conjured a little smile.

"Take as long as you need. Don't worry about your appointments, we'll take care of everything."

"Thanks, Katie. I really appreciate it."

Smiling, she wrapped her arms around me. It was hard not to break down crying when she showed me affection. A small tear escaped, but I smiled through it.

I headed to my office for some quiet alone time. Before I made it, Andy, the not so supportive partner, caught me.

"You all right? You look like shit." Andy chomped his gum and stared at me with obvious disdain.

"Nice, Andy. I'm fine."

"If you say so. I can't chat, I have another nut case to see now." He turned toward his office.

Charming as usual. Thank God he was gone. I increased my pace down the hall avoiding every other possible run-in. I shut the door and leaned against it, then flipped the lock. So much for feeling *okay*. I hadn't let myself cry the whole day, but I couldn't stop it any longer. The love seat and box of tissues were all the provisions I needed for a good cry. I let it all out. Tear after tear, tissue after tissue, until I had all the symptoms of a cold—feverish skin, stuffy nose, aches and pains. Only it wasn't a cold I was suffering, but a broken heart.

I eventually left my office and ended up at the local market to stock up on some over the counter broken heart relief. After liberating fifty bucks from my purse in exchange for wine, ice cream, and tissues, I walked back to my dark and empty apartment. Neither Chad nor any of his things remained. His key rested on the kitchen bar. It was the best decision he'd made in the past twenty-four hours. The lonely silence pushed me to call Holly and Telly. I gave them the quick version of what happened. They were shocked to say the least, and agreed to stay the night.

While I awaited their arrival, I poured a glass of white wine and walked around my empty apartment. I looked through the rooms to see what was missing. His computer was gone from the office and his toothbrush was gone from the sink. It was like he was never there.

He did put a fresh set of sheets on the bed and made it up really nice. A considerate gesture, but in light of the circumstance, it didn't amount to much. I saw myself in the mirror that hung on the closet door. My face appeared tired and worn. I squeezed my cheeks, but was unable to get any color back into them.

Behind the closet door hung a half empty rod. A box sat just inside the closet. I sat my glass on the dresser and knelt to open it. My wedding dress. The sight of it broke my heart more as I mourned the wedding that would never be. *I will never get to wear this dress.* I felt the need to put the dress on one last time. A bad idea, but with an empty stomach I was already tipsy and didn't care. I slipped the dress on. It was a strapless, trumpet-style wedding gown with a lace overlay, and it fit me like a glove. Admiring myself for the moment, I thought of what a beautiful bride I would be. But this would-be bride had just been jilted. My stomach sank. Would I ever get to have my special day, with a special man, in a special dress like this?

Self-pity made me feel even worse. There I was standing in my wedding gown only hours after I had called off the wedding. It was pathetic and humiliating. In that moment, I felt the magnitude of everything that Chad had taken from me: my love, my trust, my dignity, but most of all, he took the hope that I could ever love and trust again. Tears rolled down my cheeks as I dropped to the floor. Holly found me in my room and ran over to console me.

"Marin, I'm here." Holly held me tight. "It's going to be okay. I promise."

I looked up at her, my eyes flooded with tears and buried my head in her chest.

Holly helped me out of the dress and instructed me to take a long hot shower. The water felt good on my tired, sore muscles that I forced into walking around the city all day after sleeping on the bathroom floor. I felt drained, like I had been through a war. Only the war wasn't over. It had just begun. In all my experience dealing with broken hearts I knew this was going to take time, and I'd have to be patient.

I dressed in clean pajamas and found Telly and Holly

in the kitchen. Telly wrapped her arms tightly around me. She wasn't much for showing affection but never neglected to when it really mattered.

"I'm so sorry." A pity-filled smile covered her mouth. I tried to mirror it, but was too sad and too tired. She smiled bigger. "I brought Chinese. Your favorite!"

The three of us sat in the living room eating pork-fried rice and spring rolls. Well, they ate and I just pushed my food around with my chopsticks. They listened intently to the full story and offered encouragement at all the right moments. Afterward, Telly put on a movie. She was trying to cheer me up, and for that I was grateful. But I was beyond cheering up now, and my mind couldn't focus on anything other than the fact that my engagement was over.

I tossed and turned most of the night with thoughts of Chad and my ended relationship. Finally, around six in the morning, I fell asleep. An hour later, Holly came in to check on me. She shut my curtains to darken the room and kissed my forehead.

"I'll call you later," she whispered.

I closed my eyes again and tried to forget the unforgettable.

3

How Can You Mend A Broken Heart?

MY BED BECAME A PERMANENT fixture to my body. Food, communication, and even bathing were of little interest. I wanted nothing more than to be swallowed by the darkness of my room.

Lights started to flood my apartment with Holly's arrival. I managed to open my heavy eyelids and lift my head from the pillow.

"What are you doing?" she asked.

"Nothing,"

"Have you been here all day?" She settled next to me.

"Pretty much."

"Telly and I got worried. You didn't answer our calls." I remained silent while my worn eyes blinked in the light. "I brought you a sandwich. Are you hungry?"

"No."

She lay down next to me and brushed the hair out of my face. Her eyes peered steadily into mine. When she received no telepathic insight she asked, "What's going on in your head, Mar?"

"Emptiness," I said.

"Emptiness?"

"My head, my heart, my body, my life feels empty. I don't know how else to explain it."

"You know that's not true, right?" Her warm voice cooled at my ears, failing to comfort me.

"I don't know anymore. I loved him, Holly. I thought he loved me." My voice cracked. "I thought he was the one."

I broke down crying, curled up on my side like a baby. Holly held me and stayed until I was silent and fell asleep again.

A pounding ache in my head forced me to stomach a few crackers and aspirin. I walked a lap around my apartment, stretching my legs to avoid possible atrophy. When I returned to bed, I summoned the television with my remote. I flipped through commercial after commercial before settling on a movie channel. Fitting, the movie was a tragic love story. As much as I wanted to change the channel to something lighter and more cheerful, I couldn't. I was hooked. Within an hour, I was crying inconsolably for the heroine who lost the love of her life in a plane crash and never recovered after his death. My sad state was exacerbated by the prospect of being like her and living out my days in mourning. I didn't want to believe that Chad was the only chance I would get at lasting love, but I couldn't see myself taking a chance to be fooled again.

I thought about everything that had happened and wanted to blame something, someone. Chad was the obvious choice, but I started questioning my responsibility in all of it. Had I pressured him to get married? Was the idea of marrying me so bad that he had to have an affair to kick-start our marriage? Was there something I could have done to change things? All I could conclude was, *why me?*

Then I thought of my past relationships. There were few to recall, and yet there was one common theme. I always got dumped. My first boyfriend, and high school sweetheart, was Von. Before him, I had no experience with boys. My parents kept me busy with AP classes, tennis lessons, and the track team. Von was the crush of all crushes. Not just to me, but to most of the girls in our class. I'll never forget the first time I saw him. It was love at first sight. Really.

After a year of nothing and out of nowhere, he asked me on a date. I couldn't believe it. To me, a seventeen-year-old girl, it was a miracle. Our romance was brief, but nonetheless magical. We ended things that summer when he went away to college, and I never saw him again. It was the first time I felt the pangs of a broken heart. My dating life was scarce in college, but that changed in medical school.

Jack Ashbury was a first year med student like me and had all the makings of a great doctor. He was smart, charismatic, and incredibly caring. For a long time I believed he was the love of my life. Our relationship took a turn when I dropped out of med school and moved to the east coast for grad school. Jack had no desire to keep up a long distance relationship and began dating someone new almost immediately. It took me years to get over that one.

Grad school and my internship kept me too busy for anything serious. My mom began to worry that I might never give her grandchildren as I was twenty-eight and still single. Then, I met Chad and subsequently lost him too. For some reason I could sense my breakups with Von and Jack before they happened. The signs were always the same. One day they started acting strange and distant. The glow in their eyes disappeared and my gut felt uneasy and nauseous. Both times it happened they convinced me that nothing was wrong, until days later when they got the courage to tell me it was over. No warning signs with Chad though. His deception came as a complete surprise.

My mind raced with memories from that night and tears wet my worn-out eyes. I studied myself in the mirror, hoping it would reflect some explanation for the sudden turn of events. Was I not pretty enough? Was my ass too fat? Were my boobs too small? What was so wrong with me?

I threw myself on the bed and sobbed one of those intense cries that start off about one thing, but end up about something different. My father called it a *good cry*. Oh yes, I thought about every bad thing that had ever happened to me, allowing myself any reason to be sad.

"Why, why," I cried out. The pity party was in full force and lasted the entire day. Heartbreaking love songs filled my apartment while tear filled tissues littered the floor. I needed it and wanted it that way. I wanted the sorrow to consume me like a flame so I could be reborn from the ashes like a phoenix. And that's what I did for days, a pathetic routine of sleeping the day away, eating little food, and doing nothing useful. My professional mind advised me otherwise, but the idea of leaving the apartment, exercising, and being with other people felt like a harder burden than the depression.

By the weekend, my friends were so concerned that they showed up to execute an intervention. I awoke from another nap to find Telly and Holly standing over me. Holly knelt down to face me. "You ready to get out to-day, sleepy head?" she asked in her sweet, maternal way.

"No. I don't want to go anywhere."

Telly knelt next to Holly and in the same tone said, "There's a big sale at Nordstrom today. Half off select shoe wear." Her words a bribing tactic no different from the kind a mother uses to get her child to eat his vegeta-bles.

"I don't care about a shoe sale, Telly." I turned my head in the other direction thinking that if I didn't see them they wouldn't be there. Telly did not accept that. She stomped over to the other side of the bed and bent down so I could see her face. Her maternal tone was re-placed with an attitude of disbelief.

"Don't care about a shoe sale?" She gaped at me for a moment, looked up at Holly, then back at me. "Honey, when was the last time you brushed your teeth?" She tried to smile, but it turned into a cringe. I pulled the pillow over my head, but could still hear them whispering to each other in the hallway.

Ten minutes later they returned. Holly stole the pillow from off of my head. "Telly drew you a nice warm bubble bath. I think it'll help. You wanna take a bath?"

"No," I said, firmly covering my face with my hands and curling into a ball.

"Come on, Marin. It's just a bath. You'll feel better," Telly said.

"I appreciate it guys, really, but I just want to be alone right now." How could they not get it?

"That's it!" Telly said, pitting my hardwood floors as she stamped over in her stilettos and tore off my comforter. "You can't just lay here day in and day out. If you want to start feeling better you have to get out and do something. This isn't you. You're stronger than this. Don't let that selfish son-of-a-bitch do this to you. Take your life back."

Surely deep down I knew she was trying to help, but it wasn't very apparent in the moment. Why couldn't they leave me alone and let me deal with my heartbreak my way?

"You can't lay here forever," Telly said.

Tough love was definitely her tactic, and it pissed me off. I stomped over to the bathroom and slammed the door shut. I brushed my teeth rashly and stepped into the tub still dressed in my three-day-old pajamas. The girls came in after me and stared from the doorway as I sat fully clothed and soaked in bubbles.

"Is this what you want?" I shouted with tears in my throat. "I'm taking a bath and I'm brushing my teeth. Do you feel better now? Because I feel the same." I rose from the tub, my pajamas saturated and dripping warm bath water. I looked onto Telly's pity filled face.

"Telly, I'm sorry I don't care about bubble baths and shoe sales right now. And Holly, I'm sorry I don't want to leave the house or eat anything. I'm sorry, but I don't." I broke down and sunk back into the sea of bubbles. My eyes filled with tears, blurring my view of them. "I can't. I just can't."

Holly wrapped a towel around my shoulders with few words and they left me alone. They helped me to my bedroom and into dry pajamas. My point was clear to them, and so they let me be. I fell asleep, and when I awoke I felt a wave of embarrassment over the way I acted. Yes, my fiancé cheated on me. Yes, my wedding was over. And yes, I was sad. But that was no reason not to bathe, change clothes, or eat.

Those five days had been such a blur, and I recalled it like one incredibly long and painful day. Even with all the sleep, my body and mind were still so tired. My friends were right, the only way to feel better was to get up, and that's what I did. After a long, hot shower, I put on some jeans and a tee-shirt and made a PB&J. I wasn't quite ready to leave the house, but it was Saturday night, and I had slept enough for the next month.

Just as I was about to sit down with a new magazine, I heard a knock at the door. I was sure it was Telly with cocktails, or Holly with dinner, or both. But I was wrong on both counts. It was Chad standing in the hallway. His head hung, and he barely looked at me. I froze.

"Hey, Marin," he said. I remained stiff not knowing what to say, what to think, or what to do. "Can I come in?"

I took a deep breath and stiffened.

"Sure."

He entered the living room. I remained by the door wanting to reopen it.

"How are you?" he asked.

"How do you think I am?" I said.

"You're right. That was a stupid question."

"What do you want, Chad?" I was surprised by my emotionless persona.

"I miss you, and I'm so sorry. I can fix this. I can make it right." *Make it right?* His face was desperate. I considered every possible couple's counseling trick I could think of to move on from something so devastating, but nothing seemed viable.

"I don't think this is going to work," I said. His face became desperate.

"Marin, please." He gently took my face in his hands and I fought the urge to cry. In that moment, as I inhaled his cologne, I missed him. I wanted things to go back to the way they were, lock the door behind me, and never let him go. But I couldn't. The truth was that deep in my heart I knew it was over. "I love you," he said.

"I know, but I can't do this." My voice choked on a lump in my throat and a tear escaped. He wrapped me in his arms, and I squeezed my eyes shut, fighting like hell not to cry on his shoulder. Whatever strength I had was no match for his touch, his smell, his voice.

"I'm so sorry," he said, holding me tightly to him. After a minute, my eyes dried, and I pulled away. For the last time, I gazed into his brown eyes, the ones that once filled my life with love. I searched for something I might have missed, but found nothing.

"I need you to go now," I said.

With a regretful sigh, he covered his face. I thought for a moment he was crying too. He pushed the hair out of my face. "I'll never forgive myself for this, for what I've done. I'm sorry I let you down. Take care of yourself, okay?"

I nodded. A second later, he was gone. I closed the door behind him and placed my forehead against it, tears streaming down my cheeks and dripping off my chin. I had mourned my loss for nearly a week, but the sting of severed ties felt as fresh as an open wound. I will never know how my body expressed so many tears in such a short period of time. It was over. My heart was broken. The end. At the same time I felt a sense of relief, relieved that I could move on.

When I was done crying, I glanced around my apartment planning my next move. The most appealing option was to return to bed for another week of sadness and despair, but I had finally made progress and didn't want to regress. Instead, I channeled it into something useful; cleaning. When I got to the bathroom I realized what a mess I'd made. It was one of the only rooms I had used during the week, and given my depression, I didn't bother to clean up after myself.

I snapped on some yellow rubber gloves and got down to work, which included scrubbing the tub, the toilet, and the sink. I also polished the mirror and the faucets, then swept and mopped the floor, wiped down the baseboards, and reorganized the cabinets. *Whew*, I thought wiping the sweat from my brow and smiling with accomplishment. The freshness of the bathroom transformed my spirit. It was the best I'd felt in days.

Following the same protocol in the other rooms of the apartment, I dusted, scrubbed, and organized. I rearranged the furniture in my bedroom and in the living room. On a whim, I took down my drapes, and then decided to put them up again. It was three in the morning when I finished and admired my work in every room. Everything was so clean it was like new. It felt almost like a fresh start. I was a firm believer in changing your space to change your life, and here I had done it without even realizing it. My cleaning venture exhausted my mind enough to stop thoughts of Chad, and so I slept like a baby.

Determined to get back to my normal routine, I opened the drapes and let in the morning sun. My newly cleaned apartment looked even better in the daylight. I let out a peaceful sigh as I sipped my coffee and picked at a blueberry muffin. Then, there was a knock at the door.

I jumped up to look through the peephole fearing Chad's reappearance. This time it was only the sweet face of my wavy-haired friend. She greeted me with a caring hug as I let her in.

"This place looks great!" Holly said, noticing all of my hard work. "You even rearranged the furniture." She looked closely at the arrangements in my living room and spotted my half eaten muffin.

"Are you eating?" she asked.

"Yes, I'm eating," I said, rolling my eyes though her astonished tone was completely justified.

"How do you feel?"

"Better. I'm going back to work tomorrow, trying to get back to some kind of normal." I was feeling better, but I wasn't sure if I would ever be normal again.

"A new normal," she said.

A new normal, I thought. What would that mean for me, a series of half-tried relationships or a dozen cats? Then again, I would have more time to focus on my career. Maybe it was a good thing. I hadn't even considered the idea that my break-up could be helpful. Only time would tell, and so I would have to push through.

"I brought you something," Holly said. She revealed a small bookstore bag. I reached inside and pulled out a square-shaped hardback titled, *Daily Meditations for a Broken Heart*. A scripted font and a peaceful picture of an ocean with birds flying into the sunset adorned the cover.

"I know you've been in a funk, and I thought this book could help. It got great reviews online."

I smiled and gave her an appreciative hug. "Thank you."

"Listen, I need to tell you something important." Holly sat on the couch.

"What's going on?" I sat next to her, my heart beating a little faster.

"I have some really good news."

"What is it?"

"You're not going to believe it."

Out with it already!

"Remember when I started the initiative to build vegetation roofs?"

"Yeah, the Thailand Project, right?"

"Well, we finally have the funding we need. We're gonna build fifty thousand green roofs!" She squealed with excitement.

"Oh, my God, that's amazing." I gave her a congratulatory hug. She had been working on the project for over two years. Her eyes welled with tears and her voice quivered as she replied, "I can't believe it, ya know? It's been a long time coming."

I wiped the tears from her cheeks as she had done many times for me those last few days.

"There's a downside," she said.

"What?"

"I'll be in Thailand for six months."

My heart sank. *Six months?* I wasn't prepared to be without her for six months, especially after my catastrophic break-up. *Be supportive*, I told myself.

"When do you leave?"

"A week after Rachel's wedding."

That would mean she was leaving in . . . "Two weeks!" I shouted. "You're leaving in two weeks?"

"I know it's bad timing, but I have to go. You understand, right?"

"Of course, I want you to go. It's just I'm gonna miss you. We've never been apart that long before." It was true I had never been away from Holly for more than a couple of weeks since we were kids. She even got an internship in the city where I moved for grad school.

"Well, you have Telly and you know Rachel's here for you too."

"Yeah, that's true." I sat for a moment trying to imagine the next six months without Holly. "Well I guess we can still talk on the phone," I said, reassuring myself that her absence wouldn't be so bad.

"Actually, no." She cowered as the words left her.

"What do you mean?"

"I won't have phone or internet access most of the time. Even if I did, we're going to be working sun up to sun down. I'll be in touch as much as I can, but it'll be sparse."

Sparse contact? Sounds like no contact. My heart couldn't take any more surprise bombs. The little bit of solace I was able to generate was lost and replaced by an itch to crawl back into bed to sulk. It may have sounded dramatic, but it wasn't. The thought of being away from her for so long was almost as depressing as my newly ended relationship, but she had been supportive of me. Always supportive. I needed to do the same.

"I'm sure it'll be fine," I said. She smiled, placing her forehead against mine.

"Thank you," she said.

Holly stayed a little while longer, but when she left the silence became uncomfortable. I needed to keep busy. My chick-rock Pandora station resounded throughout the apartment while I went through my bills. When the bills were paid, I organized my computer files, and when that was done, I cleaned off my DVR and my Netflix list. The to-do list I had compiled for months was nearly complete and there was little left to do at the apartment. Then, I stumbled on the book that Holly brought me and opened it to see what it could offer.

After reviewing the stages of grief with fresh eyes, I found the section on visualization and breathing techniques to help with heartbreak. It incorporated mostly meditations, but some affirmations and yoga too. I attempted the first meditation in the book, which was only twenty minutes. The scent from my lavender candle filled the room as I sat crossed-legged on the floor. The book instructed me to take deep breaths in through the nose and out through the mouth, with eyes softly closed, then to visualize myself surrounded by family and friends. Then, it said to repeat in my mind, "I am not alone." For twenty minutes I thought, *I am not alone, I am not alone, I am not alone.* I came out of the exercise and looked around at the empty room. No one around. No one to smile for. No one to hold. No one to love.

"I am alone," I said, getting upset all over again. In an attempt to rescue myself from falling back into my rut after I had begun to climb out of it, I flipped the page to the next exercise. It was an affirmation, look in a mirror and say, *I am a strong woman and I deserve love.* I went to my all-knowing mirror, which annoyingly reflected my recent state, and stared at myself for a few minutes. To my surprise, I couldn't make the words come out without tears, so I started slow.

"I am a strong woman." I repeated about fifteen times. "I am a strong woman and I deserve . . . love." I said over again until it felt better. I wasn't sure I believed it wholeheartedly, but I hoped eventually I would.

4

The Book

THE SUN PEEKED THROUGH the window blinds early Monday morning, alerting me to get up. When I remembered that I would be returning to work, my stomach knotted in anticipation like it was the first day of school. I lay there for a few minutes internally debating whether or not I was ready to go back. How could I possibly help people with their relationship problems if I could barely help myself? What kind of expert doesn't spot a cheat until it's too late? I felt over anxious, under qualified, and dizzy. I reached for the meditation book on my nightstand and opened it to an exercise for anxiety.

The exercise consisted of a yoga pose I was familiar with, the child's pose. With my knees on the floor, I bent forward and rested my forehead. I breathed deeply and repeated *I am safe* over in my mind. I even repeated the words aloud. The exercise was supposed to be calming, but instead I started to feel claustrophobic and my sinuses pained. It wasn't working, and I was going to be late for work. *Perhaps my humbling heartache will give me greater compassion for my patients*, I thought trying to see the silver lining.

The moment I saw the revolving doors of my office building, I turned around to go home. Going back to work was a bad idea. About half a block later, I stopped and told myself I was being ridiculous. Then I turned back and walked on, making it inside and all the way up the elevator and to the doors of the practice.

Diana greeted me with a thoughtful smile.

"Oh, hellooo, Marin." She stood in her usual stance.

"Hi, Diana."

"I hope everything's okay now."

I was silent for a moment, unable to conjure any appropriate words, not even a polite lie to say that I was fine. She must've gotten the hint, because she began updating me with appointments and messages.

It was nine o'clock when I was able to shut myself in my office. I tried to remember the last time I was there. It was such a blur, as if my life before was a dream. So much had changed, and I was braving a new world. Chad and I smiled inside a frame that sat on my desk. The memory of that sunny day in Cancun flashed, an easier time to say the least. Tears threatened, but I shook myself out of it and hid the picture in my purse. After a minute of deep breathing, I got to work. I was sorting my files and notes when someone knocked on the door.

"Come in," I said. Katie came through the door with a big smile, her red hair fastened in a bun with a pencil. She carried a bouquet of yellow flowers.

"Hi, Marin!" she said.

"Hey."

"These are for you." She handed me the bright flowers. Their fresh aroma pleasantly welcomed me back.

"Thank you."

"I don't want to bug you, but we want you to know that we all missed you and we're glad you're back," Katie said with a hesitant hug.

"I'm glad to be back." *No I wasn't.* Hey, I could politely fake it!

"That's great. Call if you need anything," Katie said and left my office.

It was time for my nine-thirty. I braced myself. Unsure of how it would go, I wanted to give it my best shot.

Rochelle and Chris, a couple in their late thirties with two teenage kids. They began seeing me almost two years before when they had hit a "rough patch." Their kids and jobs took up so much of their time that they became distant and nearly divorced. A friend recommended counseling, and they took it on as a last attempt.

The two sat close together on the couch, holding hands, which was a far cry from the first time I met them. Back then they could hardly look at one another let alone sit on the same side of the couch together. Yep, their progress was solid, and I was hopeful it would be an easy session.

"Dr. Johns, we have something to tell you," Rochelle said.

"Go ahead."

"Chris and I have decided to renew our vows this spring." They gazed at each other like little lovebirds.

"That's wonderful," I said, forcing a smile. With my help, they chose recommitting over divorce. It was the entire purpose of my work. I should have been jumping for joy, but all I could think was, *I want that.* I watched as the two of them hung on to their marriage with only a small hope. They put in the time and the work and realized they had a great thing the whole time. All they needed was a little help to remind them how to be together, see the good in one another, enjoy and support each other. That's real love, not giving up when the road gets rough.

I thought about Chad. Had I given up too quickly? I loved him. Yes, he cheated, but he wanted to make things right. Did I make a mistake turning him away? Tears surfaced at an unstoppable rate, and I was unable to stifle my cry.

"Are you alright?" Chris asked.

I lowered my head to my knees for a second, thinking it would help me pull myself together, but it only made me cry harder. How embarrassing. Crying over my breakup when I should've been embracing the couple's newfound happiness. *Happiness*, I thought. That's a good cover. I lifted my head and looked at Rochelle and Chris.

"I'm just overwhelmed with happiness for you both," I said, weeping. "I mean you've come such a long way. Despite all the odds you made it. You really made it." The two smiled with relief. Yeah, they bought it.

They spent the rest of their session updating me on

their progress. I congratulated them one last time and told them they could come see me anytime, but that my work with them was done. It should have felt great seeing them graduate into their new life together. Instead, I grappled with the notion that I could work so hard for them and give up so easily on my own love.

Somehow I managed to make it through the rest of my appointments, but not without a tear here and there. My excuses became more creative: seasonal allergies, eyelash in the eye, bad contacts, and tears of joy or sorrow for any obvious crying. All in all the day was pretty . . . terrible. I struggled to hold myself together in those sessions with the consistent doubts about my decision to send Chad away without giving him a real chance to work it out. After all, I was about to commit forever to him. Did I give up forever for a mistake that could have been forgiven with a little bit of time and work?

I poured myself a glass of pinot noir immediately when I got back to my apartment. The silence in the room grew more evident with each sip of wine, and I wondered how long it might stay that way.

I didn't want to be home, but I didn't want to be at work either. I was dreading counseling my patients. I doubted my ability to restrain my emotions in session, because I felt like a hypocrite. Maybe I returned to work too soon. As my worries developed, I called on one of my own.

Katie agreed to meet with me before her first appointment.

"Morning, Marin," she said behind the piles of paper

and files that towered around her. I handed her a cup of coffee from the shop around the corner, her favorite.

"You like scones, right?" I asked, handing her the small box.

"I love 'em, but you didn't have to do that," she said, taking two blueberry pastries.

"I really appreciate you meeting with me."

"What's on your mind?"

I waited for a second, then took a long sip of my coffee. Katie didn't know what happened or why I had been out for a week. I thought of the different ways I could manipulate the words, but in that moment I forgot all of them. So I opted for pure candor.

"Chad and I broke up," I said. Her eyes flew open, and she dropped her scone on the desk. I reinforced my words with a nod.

"Oh, my God, what happened?" She stared at me with gossip hungry eyes.

"I caught him with another woman when I came back from Vegas. Early."

"You're kidding!"

I shook my head and looked at the floor. "So I called it off and kicked him out."

"That's why you were out?"

"Yep."

"I had no idea. Is there anything I can do?" she asked. If only there were.

"Make him not a heartless bastard," I said, crossing my arms and wishing she really could. Katie frowned and remained speechless. "I don't know if I made the right decision. I help people patch up broken relationships all the time, and I threw him out. I do love him, but he hurt me so badly. How can I trust that he won't hurt me again?"

"I don't know," she said and sat in the chair next to mine. "Trust is a fragile thing. When it's been damaged it's hard to put it back together the way it was before. It's a lot of work, you know that." I nodded and she continued, "The question is—is it worth it to you?"

"At first I didn't think it was and that's why I let him go. But I'm not so sure anymore. Did I make a mistake?"

Katie put her hand on mine and looked me in the eye. "You already know the answer to that."

"And what's that?" I asked.

"You know."

What I knew was she had just pulled some shrink trick on me. I had done it many times before. The truth was she didn't know the answer, but apparently I did. Only I didn't! Or, one part of me wasn't letting the other part in on the secret. In any case, all that was left was to mull over whether or not I thought it was worth it to work it out with Chad.

For the rest of the day I sat through appointment after appointment, partially participating, but mostly absent-minded. Just before I shut down my computer for the day, Andy appeared in my office. He had a habit of walking into my office unannounced to unload his cynical bullshit. What is it this time Andy, a smug comment? Unsolicited advice?

"How are you doing?" Andy asked.

"Fine," I said, crossing my arms.

"Sorry to hear about what happened," he said. "It's not an easy thing." It was strange, his genuine tone. I mean, I couldn't ever remember him being so nice to me.

"What do you know about what happened?"

"Katie told me you called off your wedding. She didn't say why."

He didn't know the circumstances of my newly ended engagement, but I was curious about the conclusions he had come up with. I wasn't in the mood for a discussion, so I gave him a solemn look, hoping it would deter him from inquiring.

"Stand up," he said.

I hesitated, but he urged me to stand. When I did, he wrapped his arms around me. A hug? It was a first. I definitely couldn't remember compassion from Andy, but he was offering it. I'm a bit ashamed to admit it, but it felt good to be in the arms of a man, even if that man was Andy. The scent of his cologne reminded me of Chad. Tears surfaced, so I pulled away.

"I'm sorry," I said as I wiped my wet cheeks.

"Sorry for what? Crying about your ended engagement?" I gave him a half-smile, unable to compose myself. "You're gonna be fine, Marin. I'm here if you need to talk."

That was it. No discussion, no bullshit, just genuine kindness.

On the walk home that evening, I analyzed my situation and my feelings about Chad for what seemed like the millionth time. There were no clear answers, so I decided to try another exercise from the *Daily Meditations* book.

I sat cross-legged on the floor, candles lit, soft music playing, and a glass of vino by my side, trying to listen to my "inner voice." After forty-five minutes of nothing, I gave up. The only thing my inner voice said was how ridiculous the exercises were. I pushed the book across the room. "This is so stupid!"

I stomped over to the kitchen with my glass of wine and slammed it on the counter. My skin was hot and itchy. I did the only thing I knew to do in a moment like that. I had a hissy fit. I mean I did some weird, frustrated dance by moving my legs in a flash dance fashion and whaling my arms around and whining like a spoiled four-year-old. I was possessed by a violent urge to hit something or throw something. I had lost control, control over my feelings, control over the situation with Chad, and control over what to do next.

It was still daylight, and my inner voice told me to run. I grabbed my shoes and my iPod and headed out the door. With each step, my mind began to clear. I still didn't know the best thing to do about Chad, but I was determined to let it go for the night and deal with it later. That is, after I returned that stupid *Daily Meditations* book to the bookstore.

I took *Daily Meditations for a Broken Heart* and its gift receipt to the bookstore during lunch. It was one of those popular bookstore chains with a coffee shop in the center. I waited in line as students and stay-at-home moms lined up to purchase new books. While I waited, I looked through an endless display of bookmarks and stumbled upon one that read *Where to Look When* with different verses from the Bible. When I made it to the counter, I handed the young cashier my book and receipt.

"I'd like to return this please," I said.

He studied the book, then looked back at me. "I'm sorry, but this book appears to have been read. It's no longer returnable." He handed the book back.

"What! I've had this book less than a week." I pushed the book back across the counter.

"I'm sorry, but the jacket is creased and so are some of the pages. I can't take it back." He pushed the book back again, this time with attitude. Despite my better judgment, I wasn't giving up. I didn't care about getting Holly's money back or getting rid of the book, I wanted to make a statement; *this book sucks.*

"I want to speak to the manager," I said, and put my hand on my hip. He glared back at me for a moment, his lips puckered and brow furrowed. I raised my eyebrows and motioned him to run along to get his boss. He left without a word. I peered through the piles of discount books at the front of the store. *I bet Daily Meditations is in the mound,* I thought as I sifted through them to see if any caught my attention. There it was again, the same bookmark I had seen earlier. *Where to Look When.* Maybe it was some kind of sign to pay attention to, or a sign the store had overstocked the bookmark. I looked over the bookmark again before noticing the words *Secret* and *Men* among the book rubble. I moved the books to reveal the full cover, *Unspoken: The Secret Lives of Men* by John Su-omynona. The cover was designed like a top secret FBI file. I picked it up and turned it over to read the jacket description.

Warning: This book contains the truth about the unspoken, secret lives of men. Whatever you thought was real or sacred in your most intimate relationships is false. It is time that the truth is uncovered. You will hear stories from men everywhere and how they live as loyal lovers by day and playboys by night. You won't believe your eyes in this tell-all, and why would you want to?

The wheels in my brain turned rigorously. My breathing quickened. What was this book?

"Excuse me, Miss, you wanted to see the manager?" a voice came from behind and startled me. I turned and dropped the book at the man's feet. He wore a blue oxford shirt with a nametag that read *Frank Manager.*

"Ma'am?" he said.

"Uh, yes, I changed my mind on the return." I picked *Unspoken* off the ground and held it close to my chest. "I'll take this one."

He nodded and walked away. I took my place back in line and checked out in a flash, avoiding eye contact with the annoying cashier. Armed with both books, I headed out of the store. *Daily Meditations for a Broken Heart* didn't make it farther than the store's trashcan, while *Unspoken* was tucked safely in my bag.

That night I settled in with a glass of riesling, a few lit candles, and some comfortable clothes. I curled up on the couch and opened *Unspoken: The Secret Lives of Men.* I held my breath as I read through the first few pages, captivated by the words. It was as if I was discovering a secret no woman had uncovered until that moment. I was Columbus and the book was America. But this discovery wasn't going to be positive. By page ten, I needed a break. I slammed the book shut and stood at a crossroads.

Was I ready for the truth if it, in fact, could be found in the book? I paced for a few minutes and tossed over whether I should read further or pitch it with *Daily Meditations* and be none the wiser. Part of me felt it was wrong, but another part of me felt it was right. The book was intriguing to say the least. After years of being an advocate for love and honest relationships, I deserved to know if what I believed was real. I took a deep breath and lifted the book from the table. It was going to be a long night. I opened the cover and began to read.

Unspoken took off like a freight train, with page after page of enthralling stories. In essence, it was a confessional from different men in different situations with one common theme; all men lie and all men cheat, and they will do and say anything so their significant other does not find out. No exceptions. These telling men worked normal jobs, had normal lives, a wife, kids, and a mortgage. It was as if they were living a second, secret life. A life that was commonly understood by their fellow men and kept secret from the women.

My attention was diverted only slightly when I refilled my glass of wine. I heard riesling dripping off of the coffee table from my over-poured wine glass. Shit! Keeping my eyes on the book, I sopped up the spill and took intermittent sips from the brim of my glass.

I read a story about a married pharmaceutical rep in his thirties with two kids. He admitted to cheating on his wife regularly, explaining that men are primal when it comes to sex and women are emotional. His theory . . .

Having sex with your wife is like eating spaghetti. Spaghetti is good, but after a while it gets monotonous and you really just want a steak dinner. If you eat spaghetti every day and all of a sudden someone offers you steak, you're going to take a bite if not devour the whole thing.

I read on.

In truth, cheating only exists when it's discovered. When I cheat, I do it in a way that leaves my wife clueless. There's no way she would ever know. Even if she did find out, I would lie through my teeth to the bitter end. Deny, deny, deny!

I finished the final page, then closed the book. I pushed myself back into the couch, full of information and trying to digest it all. It was true, all men were liars and cheaters. Not just Chad, but every man. I hadn't been singled out. Chad's affair wasn't about me. It wasn't about something I did or didn't do. It was his nature, his true nature, and I had uncovered it.

"It all makes sense," I said. "I get it now." I stood tall with my arms stretched out and shouted, "It all makes sense. I get it now!"

The affirmation sent me running around to each room to look through drawers, shelves, under the bed, and all over the apartment for anything that reminded me of my ex. Chad paraphernalia piled high on the living room floor. My fireplace blazed and I watched as the flames danced for my new liberation. I blasted my favorite fuck-you break up song, poured another glass of wine, and sang along while I pitched the items into the flames. Old pictures, notes, and clothing wilted in the fire until there was nothing more than ashes and dust.

Amazing. It felt amazing to purge my apartment and my life of anything Chad. Though he had hurt me, I finally understood why. And for that reason I knew I would be able to move on.

5

The Wedding

MY ROSE-COLORED BUBBLE had burst, but I felt refreshed and exhilarated. Liberated. For the first time since I returned from Las Vegas, I was actually happy. The sun was brighter, my coffee tasted better, and I think my skin glowed.

Now that Chad was out of my life permanently, it was time to cancel all the wedding arrangements. I spent the afternoon on the phone with all of the vendors including, the DJ, the caterer, the florist, and the reception hall, telling them all the same thing, "The wedding is off!" Most of my deposits were gone, but I started to think the whole experience was worth it.

Then, right when I thought nothing could get me down, my phone rang. It was my mother. I slumped down in my chair and remembered I had yet to tell my family about my recent events. It was no accident. Yes, I loved them, but I spent much of my life trying to live up to their high standards. After awhile, it became too much. My oncologist father pushed my brother and me to be excellent at everything we did and somehow I always came up short. Even though I had a PhD and a successful practice, I still paled in comparison to my brother, Michael.

No doubt they would see my breakup as yet another failure. The thought of announcing it to them made my stomach churn, but it had been almost two weeks since the breakup. I needed to come clean before they heard it from someone else.

"Hi Mom."

"Oooh, is this my daughter?" Her words were coated with her heavy Chinese accent.

I knew she was fishing about my two-week absence. She would learn soon enough.

"How are you?" I asked.

"Fine. I wanted to let you know your father and I are not going to make it to Rachel's wedding this weekend."

"How come?"

"Our Beijing flight cost too much to change."

My parents had been planning a big three-week trip to China. I guess by the time they learned about Rachel's wedding, which changed dates a few times, it was too late to cancel. The notion of being spared my parents over the weekend was a relief, but I replied with a disappointed, "Oh, that's too bad."

"I know. It would've been nice to spend some time with my daughter and my future son-in-law."

There it was. My cue to tell her the truth, or at least a version of it. I hadn't thought about what to say, or how to say it, so I gave her the simplest version I could manage.

"I have to tell you something."

"Okay."

"Chad and I called off the wedding. We broke up."

"WHAT!" she shouted, her already loud voice amplified. "What do you mean the wedding is off? Since when? Why did you break up? Marin, answer me!"

"Mom, please calm down."

"Calm down! How can you be so calm? What happened?" She continued to yell questions at me. It was exactly why I didn't want to tell her. She had a habit of accusatory reactions to my bad news.

I sighed and rolled my eyes.

"Once he moved in, we decided it wasn't right, and it would be best to go our separate ways." I crossed my fingers hoping she would accept my answer as satisfactory. Silence hung on the phone, and I held my breath for her response.

"Did he see you bleach the peach fuzz on the side of your face?" she said. "Is that what happened?"

Figures. Typical that she would think an embarrassing beauty routine would be reason enough to break off our engagement.

"I always tell you not to reveal those kinds of habits to a man. You have to remain mysterious," she said.

"No, Mom. It's nothing like that. And I only did that one time! Will you please stop bringing it up?" I raised a fist in the air thinking that it would soon be full of freshly pulled hair.

"Yes, okay. I had to ask." I shut my mouth and let her go on. "Isn't there a way to work it out with him? You were getting married. Now it's over? Just like that?"

"Yeah, Mom, it's over."

"Well, I'm sorry to hear that, Marin. I suppose you want me to tell Dad."

"Yes, please. I really don't want to talk about it anymore."

"Okay, but we'll talk about it when we get back from China."

"Okay. Have a good trip."

By the time we said our good-byes I was dying to hang up. It was painful, and that pain turned into self-pity. My own mother thinks I'm incapable of keeping a man. My ability to keep a man wasn't the problem. Maybe I should've told her the whole truth. She probably would have reacted the same way regardless of truth or story. The truth was that I had nothing to do with the end of my engagement. It was all Chad, Chad and his man disease of deceit.

Since discovering the profound truth, I was compelled to share it with everyone, which was why I ordered ten copies of *Unspoken: The Secret Lives of Men* for overnight delivery. If I wanted to convince other women of the uncovered secret, I'd have to become an expert on the subject.

Over the next couple of days, I spent the sum of my spare time researching facts to support the book, facts I had conveniently ignored before. I diligently researched psychology journals dealing with infidelity and searched the internet for forums, blogs, and classified ads, trying to find other people who knew the same truth. In that short time, I gained a wealth of information and still only scratched the surface. The facts I uncovered were shocking, but nonetheless helpful.

Rachel's wedding day came quickly, and I couldn't wait to tell Holly and Telly everything I had learned since I last saw them. I had buried myself in my newfound truth, and I was ready to come up for air and shout it from the rooftops. It was the kind of day that outdoor brides pray for, clear, sunny skies, warm, but not too warm. I took the morning to dress in my spring wedding best, a simple yellow, cap-sleeved dress. When the cab arrived, I grabbed my oversized purse and stuffed a copy of *Unspoken: The Secret Lives of Men* inside.

I made my way toward the ceremony at the Botanical Garden. Flowers and hedges rounded out the area in the middle of the sunny garden. Tucked away at the far end was an arbor decorated in white lilies and sheer, flowing fabric. There must've been over a hundred and fifty guests seated in white chairs. Through the sea of guests, I spotted Telly standing among them in a fitted, sleeveless, midnight blue dress with her long, lush curls and huge dark sunglasses. She waived me over and I scooted in her direction, hoping to avoid seeing any chatty classmates or neighbors from San Jose.

I settled in next to her. She leaned over and said, "The wedding is going to start any minute now." I looked at my watch to see I had made it just in time. Telly leaned back as if to evaluate me. She stared inquisitively.

"Where've you been the last few days?"

"Working on a little project," I said with a smirk. She lowered her sunglasses to look me in the eye.

"Oh really?"

Before I could say another word, the bridal music began. Telly and I turned to the aisle as David and his four groomsmen sauntered down. The bridesmaids followed one by one. Step and pause, step and pause. Holly was first. The chiffon fabric of her lavender dress flowed in the wind. Her hair was hoisted in a prom-like hairdo with tight curls that framed her face. She looked so lovely, probably the most done-up I had seen her. Ever. Denise, Jaime, and Sonia followed in matching dresses and hairdos, like a uniformed army of beautiful bridesmaids. Everyone stood as Rachel's father escorted her down the aisle. She was truly stunning in her white A-line princess gown with beading from the sweetheart neckline to her waist, sparkling in the sunlight like a thousand diamonds.

Even though I had just called off my wedding and discovered the unspoken lives of men, I was touched at the sight of Rachel. I had watched her grow from a tiny, curly-haired baby to an exquisite woman. She would eventually have to accept the truth about her very soon to be husband, but in that moment I wanted to believe that somehow she could be immune to it.

The ceremony took no time at all. Rachel and David

were married and dancing in a soul train fashion to a cheesy seventies song. We were directed to a large white reception tent on the other side of the gardens. Paper lanterns floated from the tent's roof, while elegant pale purple flower arrangements sat on freshly pressed white linens. Telly and I drank our cocktails at our assigned table and waited for Holly to finish posing for pictures with the rest of the wedding party. Telly chatted on about clients and idiotic associates and consistently asked if she was hogging the conversation. She was, but I remained patient, waiting to break the news of my discovery.

The DJ announced the wedding party, couple by couple. All were gleaming with smiles. David and Rachel immediately took the floor for their first dance as Mr. and Mrs. It was simple, lovely, and choreographed for our entertainment. Soon after, plates of chicken and fish flooded the tables. As the alcohol flowed, the guests loosened up and started moving to the dance floor. Everyone appeared to be having a fabulous time, celebrating love and new life together.

I felt unsettled amongst all that joy. It seemed so fake in the light of the truth. Just an expensive party to keep up the appearances set down by society, while underneath was a terrible lie. I regretted not tackling Rachel on her way down the aisle and taking her far, far away. Thailand maybe, so we could be with Holly.

"This is sad to watch," I said under my breath.

"I know. I hate weddings," Telly said.

I watched the bride and groom dancing closely, gazing into each other's eyes. She was having the time of her life.

"She has no idea that he's going to break her heart one day," I said.

"Is that bitterness talking?" She called me out.

"No."

She shook her head unconvinced and looked back at Rachel. "Well, you're probably right. Men are only good for two things—household maintenance and sex."

"I completely agree," I said with my glass raised. We toasted.

Holly waved from across the room and made her way over.

"What are we toasting too?" Holly asked as she sat down next to us.

"Men," I said.

"Oh, that's nice." She picked up a lonely glass of champagne from the table and clinked it against mine.

"You look gorgeous, by the way," I told her.

She blushed and looked away, giving me a dismissive wave. "Thank you. I'm so glad you came, I wasn't sure if you felt up to it."

"Actually, I've been doing great."

She blinked a few times and focused in on me.

"You know, Marin, you look great. Even your skin is glowing. What's going on?" She stared at me wide-eyed, waiting for my answer, and Telly leaned in.

"Well, I've been doing some reading." I tried to control my excitement. Before I could continue, Holly interrupted.

"Oh, the *Daily Meditations* book I got you!" She seemed so pleased, but my smile quickly frowned.

"No."

"Then what?" she asked.

I retrieved my special book from my bag and handed it to her.

"This." My excited grin returned.

Telly leaned over to get a glimpse. "What is that?"

Holly examined the cover of the book with a puzzled look. "*Unspoken: The Secret Lives of Men.* Marin, what is this?" She rustled through the pages perplexed.

"I was at the book store a few days ago and stumbled on this book. Something told me to take it home. So I did. I spent the night reading, and let me tell you, this is the best ten dollars I've ever spent in my life."

"I still don't understand." Holly's concerned expression worsened.

"This book saved me. It explains what happened with Chad and me. It reveals the truth about men, all men."

"And what's that exactly?" Holly asked.

"They're all liars and cheaters, every last one of them. They can't be faithful. It's not in their nature. But since it's against the nature of society they have to lie about it. Believe me, they will do and say anything so that you don't find out. It's like they're leading double lives and we're clueless. Men don't want women to know and women don't want to believe it. It's the world's most unspoken arrangement."

Telly leaned back. "I believe it."

"I don't, and I can't believe you brought this to my sister's wedding!" Holly said in an angry whisper as she pressed the book against her chest, trying to shield it from the wedding.

"Actually, I brought that for Rachel. Can you see that she gets it?"

"Absolutely not! What are you thinking?"

"After I found out about Chad, I spent days in bed wondering what happened, what I did wrong, how I could've prevented it. You saw me. I was a mess." They nodded. "Our relationship seemed like a text book example of a healthy one. I'm a couple's therapist for God's sake! So what happened?"

I paused and watched their faces as they thought up possible conclusions for Chad's affair.

"Nothing." I said. "That's what I learned from this book. Men are made this way. They can't help it."

"You can't be serious? Not every guy fits into one category of pricks," Holly said. I knew she'd have trouble digesting the information. "Not all men are cheaters. That's the most ridiculous thing I've ever heard."

"No, I think Marin's right," Telly interjected. "I mean why do you think I haven't had a serious relationship since I was twenty-five? It's inevitable that they'll break your heart into a thousand pieces. One way or another."

Telly's positive reaction reinforced my enthusiasm. She understood what I was talking about long before I did. I nodded vigorously, "See, we should've listened to Telly to begin with. She's had it right this whole time. Meet a guy, have some fun, and then send him home."

Telly lifted her glass and gave a modest smile. "Here, here, sister."

"I can't believe what I'm hearing from you, Marin, of all people. You two may have converted to this belief of perpetual infidelity, but I'm not falling for it." I should have known Holly would not subscribe so easily to an idea that was so damning. She was blessed with eternal optimism, or in this case, cursed. It wasn't exactly my intention to burst her bubble, but it was time she heard the truth.

"Listen to this," I started, "I was on Craigslist the other day in the men seeking women ads. There were thirty-seven ads from married men looking for an affair. They all said the same thing, I don't want to end my marriage, just looking for that something."

"Just looking for my next blowjob," Telly said.

Holly rolled her eyes at this detail prompting me to continue. "But, in the women seeking men ads there was one married woman and she said, 'I'm married and I want out.' How much more proof do you need?"

Telly and I stared at her, hoping she would budge at least a little. Instead, she crossed her arms and gave me a stern look. "It's gonna take a lot more than a craigslist census to convince me."

Holly needed hard evidence. She had a tendency to be easily swayed due to her open-minded and gullible nature, but she also had very strong morals and convictions about seeing the good in all people. If I wanted her to get on board with the truth, I couldn't express statistics. I'd have to show her irrefutable proof. Most of the information that I had gathered was strong, but it could be vulnerable to skepticism.

Then, in the midst of my quandary, it hit me like a bolt of lightning. It was pure genius. The next words to come out of my mouth would change my life forever.

"Okay, then I'll prove it to you," I said.

"How?" Holly asked.

I hoped the idea sounded as good aloud as it did in my head.

"Easy, I'll start a fictitious relationship with the next guy who asks me out, and I will show you that he is going to lie, he is going to cheat, and he is going to break my fictitious heart. Then you will know that it's true."

Before she could respond, the music stopped and was replaced by the sound of a fork clinking against a champagne glass. We turned to the cake table where the best man, James, joined the bride and groom.

"If I could get everyone's attention please. It's the duty of the best man to say a few words. So here it goes." He paused and gave a humbling smile. The room silenced.

I had never met James before, but Rachel and Holly mentioned him several times. He was good looking, tall with sandy blonde hair, and one of those bright smiles seen on toothpaste commercials.

"David was my roommate in college," he began. "For those of you who knew David back then he was a little . . . extreme." The guests laughed, and James turned to David with an apologetic look. He continued, "especially to a small town boy from Montana. He was a great friend to have, and he taught me a lot. In those days he was a notorious bachelor, and I never thought that would change. But something did change when he met Rachel. I'll never forget the first time he took her out. He told me he was actually nervous. This was big, because we all know David doesn't get nervous." The guests ahhed at this admission, except for Telly who motioned a gag. I stifled a chuckle.

"After that, he stopped the hunt. He found one special thing that we all hope to find. You two are incredibly lucky, and I'm confident you will have a long, happy marriage. To the bride and groom!"

Everyone raised their glasses and repeated, "To the bride and groom."

The reception proceeded with Rachel and David stuffing each other's face with cake. Holly was pulled away for pictures, and the crowd dispersed around the dance floor and mingled among the tables. Telly downed her champagne and adjusted her dress to reveal the perfect amount of her perfect cleavage. She refreshed her lip gloss. "Time to prowl."

She strutted out to the dance floor, swaying her hips seductively, and letting off pheromones like a cat in heat. I sat quietly, observing the guests at the reception, while I finished my champagne and wondered if I would meet my new fictitious boyfriend soon.

6

The Hunt

I COULDN'T WAIT TO START MY FICTITIOUS dating experiment, so I started looking right away. Holly was leaving in a week, and I didn't want to waste any time. Realistically, I knew I couldn't complete the task before she left, but I was sure I would have every ounce of proof I needed by the time she returned. She would have no choice but to believe me.

My first opportunity to find someone came when Telly and I joined Holly for her yoga class. Usually, I'd show up with no makeup and my hair thrown together in a messy bun. In light of my new mission, I waltzed into class with natural looking makeup, a fresh pout of lipgloss, and my hair secured in a sleek ponytail. The yoga studio was one large suite, sectioned off by an Asian-style screen. Light colored bamboo floors led to a Buddha statue at the far end of the room, and rows of yogis conversed on their mats waiting for class to start. The girls were already doing some pre-yoga stretching when I laid my purple mat on the floor. I surveyed the men in the class for any potential candidates.

"You look pretty today," Holly said.

"Thank you." I smiled, then realized Telly was looking rather pretty herself. She was by far the most stunning woman, or person for that matter, in the room.

"Psst, Telly," I whispered. "Can you put on a hoodie and mess up your hair or something?"

"Why?" She looked confused and possibly offended. I leaned in over Holly to get closer. "I'm cruising this place for potential boyfriends." I winked a couple of times, hoping she'd remember what I was referring to.

"Here?" she said, louder than I would have preferred. Those surrounding us turned in our direction.

"Shh! Yes, here," I said in an exaggerated whisper. Telly shrugged and nodded. She covered herself with my hoodie and fixed her hair in a messy half up, half down ponytail. It wasn't her best look, but even with those efforts she still looked amazing. For a second I thought about asking her to leave, but figured that would cause more of an issue than was needed.

"Are you really going through with that ridiculous fake boyfriend idea of yours?" Holly asked, frowning.

"Of course, how else can I prove it? And it's not ridiculous. I think it's a brilliant idea. Don't you think so Tell?" Telly continued to stretch, but nodded.

"Please don't, Marin—" Holly started when the instructor demanded everyone's attention. My attention landed on the cute guy directly behind me. He had a boyish face, dimpled cheeks, and a really cute cleft chin. We exchanged smiles, and I spent the rest of class trying to look graceful and sexy in my yoga poses.

"Great class, huh?" I asked as we rolled up our mats.

"Yeah, definitely. You must be new, I don't think I've seen you before," he said.

"I come every now and then. I'm Marin, by the way." I offered my hand and he took it. "Nice to meet you. I'm Alex. You should come more often. I noticed you have great form." Great form, huh? I was pretty sure that was code for *you have a nice ass.* So far so good with cute-dimples guy, Alex.

"Maybe I will." I flirted with a smile, then bit my lower lip. Alex looked up ahead of me.

"Hi, Derek," Alex greeted the instructor. With a kiss. On the mouth! They turned to me.

"Derek, this is Marin. She's new to the class," Alex said.

"Great! Hope you come back next time," Derek said, holding Alex by the waist.

"Absolutely, I will." I said with an over exaggerated smile that strained my mouth. "Nice to meet you both." I waved good-bye and walked away.

Well, that figures. Who would've thought the guy I was checking out in a San Francisco yoga class would be gay? I usually had a knack for knowing who was gay and who was straight, but my impatience was clearly clouding my judgment. Telly and Holly stood near the entrance. I hung my head and dragged my yoga mat behind me.

"Tough break, Marin," Telly said.

"I think it's a sign," Holly said.

"A sign of what?" I asked.

"A sign that this thing you're doing is a bad idea. You can't go into something like that with bad intentions. It'll blow up in your face just like that." Holly was really on her high horse about my quest. I couldn't tell if her resistance was because she wanted to protect me or if she wanted to protect herself from the risk that I might be right.

"Let me take you out tomorrow night to find some real prospects," Telly said.

"Okay, yeah." I grinned. The search was still on.

Telly's offer to take me out to meet some prospective lab rats gave me a sense of excitement that helped the workday fly by. I slipped into a tight black dress with a plunging neckline and gave my eyes a smoky look. A spritz of my favorite perfume on my wrist and neck and I was ready to go.

Telly took me to Bleeker, a bar I'd never heard of. Men in suits and women in minis conversed on leather seating, served by bartenders in crisp white shirts and black ties. Music echoed off the vacant dance floor. I immediately scoped out the room. Telly bounced with excitement.

"Do you see anyone?" she asked.

As I looked at all the eligible bachelors, I became overwhelmed.

"Yeah, I see a few," I said, noticing a guy sitting alone at the bar. He was dressed like a stockbroker, but with a face of a bad boy. Sexy and dangerous. After a long sip of my martini, I mustered the courage to go talk to him, but Telly gripped my arm.

"Don't look now," she said.

"What?" I froze.

"There's a guy over there checking you out." She glanced in the direction behind me. I wanted to look so badly, but I decided to play it cool. Besides, he was probably looking at Telly anyway.

"Oh, oh, he's coming over here." She tried to contain her enthusiasm and looked down.

"Seriously?" I asked in a panic. Was this it? Was I about to be hit on? Asked out? Was this my guy?

He came around as sly as a fox, foxy all right with his light brown skin and piercing green eyes.

"Hi," he said in a casual kind of way.

"Hi," I said, trying to imitate his demeanor.

"I saw you from across the room, and I wanted to introduce myself." My heart raced. I spent the last two years blowing off any advances that didn't come from Chad. The act of picking up men was so foreign.

"I'm Anderson Harper." He lent his hand. I took it and smiled.

"I'm Marin Johns."

He kissed my hand the way gentlemen do in old movies.

"Marin, that's a beautiful name."

Get a load of this Casanova. Yes, I was on a mission, but I had to admit, I kinda liked the attention. "Thank you," I said. No doubt I was blushing. Telly stepped away from the table and Anderson took a seat next to me. I kept his gaze, which was easy since his eyes were so beautiful.

"So, Marin, what is it that you do?" he asked.

"I'm a psychologist."

"Oh, wow, Dr. Johns."

I giggled, not that it was particularly funny, but I was deeply falling in his schmooze. "What about you?" I asked.

"I'm a general surgeon at the UCSF Medical Center."

Impressive. He was a doctor. A surgeon! Hmm, surgeons work long hours, odd shifts. It sounded like the perfect recipe for a cheating boyfriend. A great choice for my project. I wasn't sure if he was the guy, but he was definitely in the running.

"That's exciting! There's a couple doctors in my family," I said, practically batting my eyelashes at him and definitely sticking my breasts out. The truth was I didn't want to talk. It had been weeks since I last had sex and there was something about the way he looked at me that made me want to jump on him. Antsy and on the rebound, I wanted to take him home with me. I'd never done anything like that before, but with my newfound freedom it was a good opportunity. There's a first time for everything, right?

"Are you attached?" he asked, lightly grazing his fingers over my newly bare ring finger.

"Nope. You?"

"No." He gazed into my eyes. No one had ever been so bold, or maybe I just never allowed anyone to be.

"So are you part Chinese?" he asked. Hmm, questions

about my background? Maybe this was the guy. He did seem really interested or maybe he just had an affinity for Asian American girls.

"Yeah, how'd you know? Most people guess Japanese or Korean."

"Your cheekbones are a clear giveaway and your eyes." He leaned in and whispered in my ear, his breath tickling me. "Your eyes are really beautiful."

His words sent a shiver down my spine, and I breathed in his cologne. Telly gave me a discrete thumbs-up from across the room. Anderson offered to buy me another drink when I realized that he didn't have one.

"Don't you want a drink too?"

"I can't," he hesitated. His smile quickly frowned.

"Oh, are you a recovering alcoholic?" I asked.

"No, nothing like that. I'm on call at the hospital." He chuckled and showed me his pager.

"Oh, of course." I let out a nervous laugh. It was an embarrassing assumption. I took a long sip of my drink hoping to recover quickly.

"I guess the psychologist in you goes right for a mental illness, huh?" he joked.

I nodded. "I believe everyone's dealing with some kind of neurosis."

"Oh yeah? What's yours?" His gaze was intense.

I leaned into him. "Do you really want to know?" He paused for a second and shook his head.

"No." We laughed. "Not yet anyway."

Anderson and I kept the conversation going for a good hour. I learned he was from Arizona, but did his residency at UCSF, where he got a permanent position. He liked merlot, sushi, Jazz, and late night sketch comedy.

The DJ played one of those sexy R&B songs and Anderson invited me out on the dance floor. He held me close, keeping my gaze while we swayed to the rhythm. I couldn't take my eyes off of him even if I wanted to. Though I knew that he was going to lie, cheat, and "break my heart." I was ready. He may have charmed his way in, but I was the one in control.

He squeezed my body tightly against his, and I could feel that things were going to get hot very soon. His fingers tickled the side of my face as he moved a loose strand of hair behind my ear. He traced my cheek down to my chin and pulled me in for a kiss. Not just any kiss. This was sexy, steamy. The kind that means I have to have you now! I came up for air. He leaned his forehead into mine, and in a sexy, deep voice asked, "Do you want to get out of here?"

"Yeah. Can you give me a minute?" He pulled me again and my mouth met his.

"I'll meet you out front," he said.

"Okay." He walked away, turning back around every few steps. I let out a deep exhale, trying to catch my breath. Telly rushed over to me.

"He's super hot! Who is he?" she asked, and our eyes followed him.

"Anderson Harper, a surgeon."

"What happened? Where'd he go?"

"He's waiting for me. I'm going home with him." I fanned myself in an attempt to lower my rising temperature.

"Go, Marin!" Telly gave me a playful pat on the back.

"It was so easy, Telly." Then a sobering thought, what am I doing going home with some guy I don't even know? "I've never done this before," I said.

Anderson was a complete stranger. Well, not a total stranger. I did spend the past hour or so talking, and not talking, to him. That's enough, right? Besides, there was a task at hand, and if I wanted to be like one of the boys, I'd have to play like them too.

"Don't worry. It'll be fine. Just text me the address and call me when you get home."

"Okay." I held my breath and headed toward the door.

"Hey, Marin," Telly called. I turned back.

"Yeah?"

"Just have fun." I gave her a playful grin and strolled out. Anderson stood on the sidewalk checking his phone. He looked so cool and sexy in his suit and open collar. Just looking at him turned me on. His arm was wrapped tightly around my waist as we walked the few blocks to his place. He squeezed me into him and whispered sensual innuendos in my ear.

Everything was tidy in his upscale condo. Light colored wood floors led to his dark brown leather seating. Asian accents like Buddha statues, gongs, and scrolls adorned the space. Too bad I wasn't into him for real. He had style.

"I love your place," I said with excitement as I glanced around.

"Thanks," he said. "I had a decorator help me."

"Did your decorator shop primarily in Chinatown?" I asked.

He chuckled. " Looks like it, huh?"

His keys hit the table and moments later his body was pressed up against my back. His soft breath tickled my neck as he pulled my hair away, kissing up to my ear.

"If you like this, you'll love the bedroom," he said.

"Can you show me?"

"Uh huh. That's not all I'm gonna show you," he said between kisses.

"I just need to powder my nose first." Powder my nose? Do women still say that?

"The bathroom's down the hall." He pointed through the kitchen. Once safely in the bathroom, I sent a quick text to let Telly know where I was. It was a little unreal, but there I was in his bathroom, touching up my make-up, spritzing myself with perfume, and adjusting my dress for better cleavage display. I forgot my mini mouthwash, so I sifted through his medicine cabinet finding only aftershave, toothpaste, a razor, deodorant, and a pink lady bic? Why would he need two razors, one of which was a lady's razor? Red flag. I searched for other women's paraphernalia, but I couldn't find anything except for a questionable bottle of Clinique moisturizer. Maybe it was his ex-girlfriend's. Maybe it belonged to his sister, or maybe he liked women's razors and quality creams. True, it was suspect, but it wasn't enough to sabotage the night.

He met me in the hall and directed me into his candle lit bedroom. Though the evening had an element of risky romance, the addition of candles tipped it to the sleazy side. I took a moment to refocus before he came up behind me and softly kissed the tops of my shoulders. He grabbed my waist and turned me to face him. My heart was pounding, echoing loudly in my ears. My body stiffened. Chad was the only man I had been with for so long.

"Are you okay?" he asked.

I nodded and swallowed my nerves with his kiss. Our mouths moved with intensity. My fingers loosened the buttons on his shirt and revealed his defined abdomen and amaretto-colored skin. I kissed his smooth chest and he brought me over to the bed where he laid me down. He sank on top of me, kissing all over my face and neck. The weight of his body felt good. His kisses trailed past my neck and he pulled my dress down to reveal my black lace bra. "Mmm, you taste so good," he said. His words muffled between his mouth and my thigh. Beep, beep, beep.

"What's that?" I said. He dropped his head and sighed.

"It's the hospital." He picked up the pager from the nightstand and turned it off.

"I'm sorry, Marin. Rain check?" I lifted myself up on my elbows and nodded. "I'll call you a cab."

I left him my number and kissed him goodnight. He paid my cab fare, which was a chivalrous gesture. It was disappointing to end the night without my expected finale, but what could I do? Anderson would probably be saving a real life instead of resuscitating my libido.

The late night resulted in too much hangover and too little sleep. A recipe of Excedrin and coffee got me through the workday. Exhausted from the previous night's events, I settled in early with my latest infidelity research, *See the Signs: How to Catch a Cheater*. I was finishing a section about the kind of opportunities men will go for, when my phone rang.

"Hello?"

"Hi, Marin, it's Anderson," he said in a low, sexy tone. I didn't feel like sleeping any more.

"How did everything work out at the hospital?" I asked.

"Good, my patient's been stable since last night. Thanks for asking." I smiled and waited for him to carry the conversation. "I'm sorry we had to end things so abruptly."

"Life of a doctor, I guess," I said with a sigh.

"I'd like to make it up to you. How's dinner Friday night?" he asked.

"It's a date."

"Great, I'll see you then." I could hear him smiling on the phone.

"Good night, Anderson," I said softly.

"Sweet dreams, Marin," he replied, making me blush. I tucked my phone away and fell asleep contemplating all the ways I could bait and reel him in.

The week dragged on as I waited for my date with Anderson. Finally, Friday evening arrived. I heard a knock at the door and I quickly slipped on my nude shoes that matched my nude colored dress. I checked my makeup one last time before answering the door.

"Anderson," I said with a big greeting smile. He looked like James Bond in his black suit and white shirt.

"These are for you," he said handing me a bouquet of red flowers that had been hiding behind his back. I smelled their strong fragrance and faked enthusiasm as I cared little for red roses. There was something insincere about their cliché nature, but it was a thoughtful gesture.

"Thank you, they're beautiful," I said and took them to the kitchen.

"So this is your place, huh?" he said, looking around my apartment.

"Yep." I smiled at him as I filled the vase with water.

"It's nice, you even have a fireplace." I smirked, re-membering burning every last thing that reminded me of Chad. I placed the roses nicely on my breakfast bar.

"Ready?" he asked.

I nodded. He escorted me to his black BMW, the same model as Telly's. I took it as a good omen.

"Are you okay?" Anderson asked on the way to the restaurant.

"Yeah, I'm fine," I insisted.

I was being quiet, not as uninhibited as I was on Monday night. I let Anderson go on about his week at the hospital and an experimental surgery he took part in. We arrived at a sushi restaurant on the other side of town. It was small, dim, and somewhat empty.

Our conversation was casual—work, personal inter-ests, favorite places in Frisco. Anderson ordered a bottle of warm sake and after a few drinks I loosened up. He did too. We shared rolls and sashimi, all while inching closer to one another. His hand softly rubbed my knee and tickled my thigh playfully. Things were starting to heat up again. He leaned in and softly kissed my neck, shooting a tingling sensation throughout my body. I giggled and batted my eyelashes at him.

"Should I get the check?" he asked.

I nodded. He seemed anxious to finish what we started the other night and soon we were back at my apartment making out against the front door. I turned to unlock it while Anderson continually kissed and caressed my body. We stumbled inside, locked at the mouth. The door slammed, and we clumsily made our way into my bedroom, stripping off items of clothing on the way. I stood wearing nothing but my lace panties and heels. He stared down at me as I unbuckled his pants and dropped them to the ground revealing his rather well endowed . . . instrument. My eyes drew up his naked body from the definition in his abs, to his pecks, his chiseled jaw, and finally meeting his lustrous green eyes.

He backed me to the edge of the bed and passionately threw me down. He climbed on top of me, caressing my face with his hand and moving down my body until he reached my panties. He squeezed my thigh with his hand and slipped the lace off.

"Stay right there." He retrieved a condom from his pants pocket and returned ready. Then, a hard passionate kiss with an equally passionate thrust. The sex was hot, and new, and uninhibited. Oh, yes, to be with a man again. He made love to me with such fervor. I wanted to show him that I was an equal force to be reckoned with, so I pushed him down onto the bed and gracefully climbed on top. I rode him like a seasoned cowgirl, and moaned with each sensation of pleasure. All I could think was, I'm glad to be back in the saddle. He sat up and caressed my chest and breasts with his tongue, which threw me over the edge.

The feeling became more intense.

"Mmm, you're so sexy," he said in a low seductive voice. I threw my head back as I reached the point of no return. Waves of thunderous pleasure came over my entire body.

"Oh, Anderson!" I cried and he held me tighter and let out a sexual grunt. He had made it too. A relieved laugh left my lips as I stared into his eyes. He joined with an exhausted smile. I rolled over on my back and looked up at the ceiling. It was truly amazing. Never before had I been able to reach an orgasm with someone that I wasn't in love with. It was a liberating accomplishment. The same exhilarating feeling I had when I finished *Unspoken: The Secret Lives of Men*.

Anderson lay next to me. "That was great," he said, trying to catch his breath.

"Yeah." I looked over at him. The buzz from the sex was starting to subside. I wanted more. I traced my finger around his chest and looked into his eyes.

"Wanna go again?" I asked, lifting a single eyebrow.

"Now?"

"Uh huh," I said and climbed on top of him kissing his chest.

"Okay," he said and rolled me on my back as I let out a playful squeal. After a couple more rounds, he left my apartment. He said he had to work over the weekend, but would plan to see me again on Monday. That night, I slept like a baby.

The next morning I went for a power walk with Telly and Holly in the park. I was in a brilliant mood over the night's events and the prospect of starting my mission. Anderson was perfect. He was a gorgeous surgeon, and I had no doubt he would eventually cheat on me. Since I'd know it was coming, I could enjoy the other things about Anderson like the sex, and well, the sex.

"Anderson and I had our date last night," I said.

"How did it go?" Telly asked.

"Great! He's perfect."

"Did you sleep together?" Sex was among Telly's favorite subjects.

"Telly!" Holly said.

"Yep," I said.

"Really?" Telly asked. "And?"

"And it was amazing. He was so, ya know, grrr, about it." I tried to articulate the feeling.

"Marin, you barely know this guy," Holly said.

"I know him enough. He's going to be my new boyfriend."

"They're having a fauxmance," Telly said, holding her interwoven hands up to her face and batting her eyelashes.

"You know, when you start dating someone, even if it's fake, you have to play by the rules. If you give it up too early it won't last," Holly said.

"I'm not looking for it to last. I'm looking for him to prove my point."

"The only way he can prove your point is if he is really with you. Exclusively." Holly made an excellent point. Infidelity can't exist without first establishing fidelity.

"Don't worry. I sleep with all my boyfriends early on," Telly said, but her words only invoked panic.

Telly hadn't had a real relationship in four years. Most of her "boyfriends" were gone within a couple of months. She was a relationship nomad, never stayed with anyone too long. I always thought it was because she was afraid to get her heart broken, then I understood it was because she knew better. Holly on the other hand had one boyfriend in high school, another in college, and her last boyfriend, which ended about a year ago. She didn't have much of a desire to get married, but when she was with someone she was committed. Holly could keep a guy around for years. I had to heed her advice. The damage, if any, had already been done. I hoped that it hadn't set me back too far.

I tried to keep myself busy that weekend by spending as much time with Holly as I could. She would be leaving Monday night, and I knew she was feeling tense about being gone for so long even though she tried to hide it. Anderson didn't call, but sent a few sexy texts. He promised we would get together on Monday for another date. His interest seemed strong enough, but I wouldn't know for sure until I saw him again. I tried not to sweat it since I wasn't interested in him for real.

7

What Goes Around . . .

OUTSIDE OF A LITTLE BISTRO, Holly and I enjoyed iced tea and warm weather.

"When does your flight leave tonight?" I asked taking a bite of my panini.

"About nine o'clock," she said.

"Is it one of those flights you can sleep on?"

"Yeah, thank God. I'm exhausted from all the preparations."

I imagined her flying across the world not to be heard from for six months and felt the pangs of her absence.

"I'm gonna miss you, Holly."

She grabbed my hand. "Me too."

Afterward, we walked back to my office, our pace slow and our words few.

"Will you stop by before I leave tonight?" Holly asked as we approached the building.

"Sure."

"The cab gets me at seven."

"I'll be there." I gave her a big hug and waved good-bye.

I settled back into work with plenty of time to catch up on some paper work before my last two appointments. Then my cell rang. It was Anderson.

"Hey, you."

"Hey, beautiful," he said.

"Are we still on for later?" I asked.

"Actually, I have to cancel. I had an emergency surgery come up, and I'm not sure when I'll be able to leave tonight. Can we reschedule for Wednesday?"

"Of course," I said all the while thinking Holly was right. We moved too far too fast, and now he would probably put me off a couple more times before he stopped calling all together. Damn.

"Good. I can't wait to see you again. Especially after the other night," he said. His words were a little encouraging.

When my three o'clock appointment ended, I got the message that my four o'clock had cancelled. Relieved to leave early and spend more time with Holly, I hurried down the hall, then froze. Anderson? Could it really be him, I blinked my eyes for reassurance. Yes, it was definitely him.

Anderson sat in the waiting room next to a small-framed woman. She leaned close to him with her hand resting on his wrist, and flipped her shiny black hair. Her eyes flirted with him in a familiar sort of way. Only one reason for them to be sitting in my waiting room. Couples counseling.

Emergency surgery, huh? I tried to remain calm and not jump to conclusions. We had barely started dating, and already I was getting duped. I should've known with all the "emergencies," the lady bic razor, and the need to take me home so early in our fictitious relationship. He was trouble, and I knew better. Instead, I let my ambition get in the way of my judgment.

After cursing him ruthlessly to myself, I realized that a rare opportunity had presented itself. It was my chance to get even. I ran back into my office and called Diana's desk.

"Hellooo," Diana said almost in a yodel.

"Diana, that couple in the waiting room, who are they here to see?"

"Dr. Barrett," she said.

"Does she know they're here?" I tried to keep my composure, but the sound of a ticking clock echoed in my mind.

"No, I was just about to tell her—"

"Diana, don't call Katie. Make sure those patients stay put."

"Okay, but—"

I hung up and made a mad dash for Katie's office. My heightened adrenaline from seeing Anderson in the waiting room and my mini run had me gasping to catch my breath. I shot Katie's door open. She was madly filling out paperwork with folders and loose paper cluttering her desk. Her eyes glanced up at me for only a moment, then went back to her consuming task.

"You okay?" I asked.

"No, Cooper's going to a new private school. I have a million and a half forms to sign and it's all due tomorrow. Plus I'm behind on all my files because I was out of town a couple of days last week, and I feel like I will never leave this office again." She slammed her hands on the desk.

"Oh, okay . . . I just wanted to tell you Anderson Harper and the other woman, are out front."

"What?" she whined. "Is it four o'clock already?"

"Yep," I said.

"Shit," she said under her breath. "I really don't have time for new patients right now." She took a moment to think. It could not have worked out any better if I had planned it.

"Listen, my four o'clock cancelled. Let me take these two off your hands." Relief spilled over her face as the words left my mouth.

"Really?" she said almost in tears.

"Of course. That's what we do. We help each other out."

"Thanks, Marin, I really appreciate it." She smiled.

"Don't mention it," I said, and dashed to my office.

Diana brought me their file, and I told her I would be out to get them momentarily. I took a deep breath as I read the names, Anderson Harper and Miko Wada. Sounds Japanese. Boy, did he have a type. My hands trembled as I walked out to the waiting area. I paused to gain control and took a deep breath, relishing, and yet fearing, the potential outcome of the moment. Then, I strolled in confidently, smiling at them. Anderson looked up and his face turned alarmingly pale.

"Hi, I'm Dr. Johns. Dr. Barrett had an emergency come up," I darted at Anderson. "So I'll be seeing you today." I shook their hands.

"Nice to meet you, Dr. Johns. I'm Miko, this is my boyfriend, Anderson," Miko said, about a week too late. We were already acquainted. Three times in my apartment acquainted.

"Hi . . . Dr. Johns," Anderson shook my hand slowly, shocked to say the least.

"Anderson, have we met before?" I asked.

"I . . . um . . . don't think so," he stuttered, then cleared his throat.

"Are you sure?"

"Yep, I'm pretty sure."

"Oh, never mind. You just look so much like someone I know."

I asked them to follow me back to my office. As we walked, I overheard Miko ask Anderson if he was feeling okay. That he looked like he was going to be sick.

They sat down on the sofa, and I sat across from them in my usual chair with a note pad and whistle. I played my role as the uninterested third party couples counselor, while Anderson squirmed and fidgeted. It seemed like it was really getting to him, and I was glad.

"So, why are you here today," I asked.

"Well, we've been together for two years, and I feel like our relationship has hit a road block," Miko said.

"Wow, two years," I replied and raised an eyebrow at Anderson. He put his head down.

"Yes, and I would like to take our relationship to the next level and move in together, but he feels like it's too soon. I wanted to have a professional settle the argument for us and help us move forward."

I felt sorry for her. She probably had no idea he was a cheater, and likely a serial one. Not to mention the fact that I was actually the other woman.

"So, Doctor, do you think it's too soon to move in together?" she asked.

"Every relationship is different. It really depends on when the couple is ready. The time to wait before moving in is all relative."

"Oh," Miko said, pouting her lip slightly. Obviously, not the answer she was looking for.

"Anderson," I said. His head shot up as if he was startled out of a nightmare. He looked alert yet frightened and blinked intermittently. He was in the spotlight now.

"Yes?"

"Is there any particular reason you don't feel you're ready to move in with Miko?" He looked at her, then me, then her again. We stared at him, anxious to hear what he had to say.

"I just, um, I like to have my own space and privacy. Is that so bad?"

"Well that depends. Do you need all that privacy and space to hide something?" Like another woman, I thought as I stared him down. Anderson's mouth gaped for a moment, then he began to stutter. Normally, I'd never say something so accusatory to a patient in couples therapy on the first day, but I wanted him to squirm a bit. Miko shot impatient eyes at his hesitance, waiting for him to come back with a quick rebuttal.

"That seems like an inappropriate question," he said, deflecting my inference.

"Dr. Harper, are you questioning my ability to counsel and ask questions?" I gave him a severe look and so did Miko.

"Anderson!" Miko yelled. He looked at her then looked at me. He was outnumbered, so he slouched back into the couch and lowered his head.

"No," he said. A moment of silence created an unnerving wave of tension. I relaxed for a second and tried to think of how I could make Anderson's torture just a little more entertaining.

I snapped my fingers in recognition. "I know why you look familiar," I said. Anderson's eyes widened and the color drained from his face. Surely he thought I was going to blow him in right then.

"You look like this guy I dated. Geez, that guy was an asshole." They cocked their heads. "He had trouble committing too." Suddenly, Miko appeared interested in my paralleled tangent.

"So, what happened?" she asked.

"Oh, you're not going to believe it." Miko and I leaned in as I continued. "Turns out the reason he didn't want to commit was because he was already with someone else."

"No," she gasped.

"Yes." I nodded.

"How did you find out?" she asked. I smirked and looked at Anderson, who had sweat beading along his forehead. For a moment, I thought he was going to pass out.

"That's the worst part. I ran into him and his real girl-friend in this very building."

With wide eyes she asked, "Oh, my God, what did you do?"

"I did what any sane woman would do. I confronted him right there in front of his girlfriend. She was furious and totally clueless." I let out a deep sigh at the thought, "I don't think they lasted much longer after that."

"Did you ever see him again?" Miko asked.

"No, and I hope I never will." Miko's eyes were fixed on me, mine were fixed on Anderson, and his were on the ground. "Well, enough about me, let's talk about you two. That's why we're here, right? To talk about you and your two year relationship?" I faked a warm smile.

Miko sat up straight appearing eager to resolve her own non-committed boyfriend issues while Anderson remained stiff in his petrified expression.

"Are you alright, Anderson?" I asked.

"Yeah," he said and gave a nervous smile. "I'm fine." Miko took one look at him and grabbed a tissue from the box sitting on the coffee table.

"Why are you so sweaty. It's not even that warm in here," she said wiping the perspiration off of his head and neck.

"Let's get back on track. I want you two to try an exercise that I think will help with your communication on

94

this issue. We're going to do a little role playing." Anderson exhibited a bewildered face as if he was pleading with me to go easy on him. No doubt the afternoon had already been trying enough. Unfortunately for him, I wasn't in the mood to sympathize.

"Anderson, you'll be Miko, and Miko, you'll be Anderson. Now, Anderson, pretend that you're Miko, and tell Anderson," I said pointing to Miko, "what is on your mind." I smiled and sat back in my chair to watch the show.

"Anderson, I think it's time we get a place together," he said to Miko.

"Wait," I said. "Anderson, this is role-playing. I really need you to get into it. Sit up taller like Miko and talk in her voice, not yours." He looked frustrated, but I urged him to follow my directions. He sat up straighter.

"Anderson, I think it's time we get a place together," he said again. This time in a higher pitched voice.

"Anderson," I whispered like a director back stage, "more girly."

"Anderson, I think it's time we get a place together," he said again sitting up straight just like Miko and in a high soprano voice. He sounded ridiculous. I tightened my lips to contain a laugh.

"I don't want to," Miko stated in an Anderson sort of way.

"Why not? It's time we move forward." He kept up his ladylike tone.

"I don't want to move forward. I like the way things are now," Miko said.

"You're right. Things are pretty great the way they are now. We can see each other when we want and be away from each other when we don't," Anderson said with a smile. It was an out-of-character statement for Miko. Before I could blow my whistle to tell Anderson that he was not playing fair, Miko shouted in her own voice. "Oh, I see. This arrangement is convenient for you, isn't it?" She brought her lips and brow to the middle of her face.

"What's that supposed to mean?" he asked defensively in Miko's voice. He quickly cleared his throat and in his normal voice asked, "I mean, what is that supposed to mean?" I also leaned forward and asked, "Yes, what does that mean?"

"I mean you're out of touch a lot, even a little too much for a surgeon."

"Miko, you know I work crazy, unpredictable hours."

"Oh, there's a new excuse. What about Friday night, huh? Where were you?"

"Yes, where were you on Friday?" I said. I knew where he was on Friday night, but I had no idea what excuse he gave her. At the time he and I were going at it in my bed, I didn't know she existed. He looked appalled, stressing his eyes as if he hoped I'd get the hint to keep my mouth shut. I got the hint. Just didn't care.

"I was at the hospital," he said.

"No, you weren't. I went by the hospital and couldn't find you," she said shaking her head.

How's he going to get out of this one?

"What time did you go by?" He stalled, probably trying to think of a good excuse.

"I don't know, around seven or so." She started to retreat. It was probably an old trick he used and for whatever reason she fell for it.

"I must've left to get dinner." He looked up at the ceiling. "That's right, I went to eat sushi." He smiled with pride. Did it work?

"Sushi?" Miko asked. She stood and yelled, "Like you were eating some other girl's sushi!" She grabbed a pillow from the couch and started wailing on him. I kept my game face on, but inside I cackled like a villain. Revenge was sweet and Miko was right.

"This is good, Miko. Let out your frustration," I said. She stopped shortly after and threw the pillow in his face.

"Why can't you just want to be with me the way I want to be with you?" she asked, then tears fell from her eyes. My vengeance instantly melted into guilt. It wasn't her fault he was a cheat. Miko was probably a great girl who didn't know any better. I knew all too well what that was like. She hid her face in her hands and ran out of the room.

"Miko!" he called out as he stood, but she was gone. He turned to me.

"Looks like you have quite a mess to clean up," I said.

"She'll be okay. We've been through this before." I remained silent, glaring my two cents at him. Would he apologize or leave? He rested his hands on his hips and shook his head, then gave an inappropriate smirk. "Of all the counseling practices in San Francisco, I had to come into yours."

"So I guess this means our date's off?"

What an asshole. I gave him a chilly stare. "Good-bye, Anderson."

"Right," he said defeated, then vanished from my office and from my life. I threw myself back into my chair, letting out a long sigh. Of all the ways I imagined catching Anderson cheating, this was not one I had expected. It was an unsatisfactory end, but it fueled my belief about the unspoken side of men. I decided not to give up. It was only a matter of time before I found "Mr. Right."

Five minutes after five, and I had plenty of time to stop by Holly's before she left. I waited for what seemed like ages at the elevator. My phone started ringing when I arrived at the revolving doors of the building. No doubt it was Telly promptly calling for our after work chat. Considering the circumstances of the afternoon, it was going to be a long call. The phone seemed to be hiding in the depths of my bag among my wallet, iPod, business cards, and packets of spearmint gum. Right as I walked through the revolving doors, I looked into my bag, struggling to find it before it went to voicemail. Then suddenly, WHAM!

The door hit me, knocking me off my balance and sent me tumbling to the ground. My vision blurred and it took a moment to clear. When it did, I saw that I was lying faced down, smelling pavement, my knee stung in pain. Humiliation churned my stomach when I realized numerous, respected business people from my building would see what a klutz I was. I surveyed my surroundings. My purse and all of its contents had spilled out everywhere.

I heard a faint voice as I tried to pick myself up.

"Are you alright?" the voice called out.

And in only a second, I was lifted to my feet and handed the effects of my bag. Some nice gentleman had come to rescue me. The man put my arm over his shoulder and helped me over to a bench nearby. When he sat me down, I began to notice little details about him, his wavy, dirty blonde hair, striking blue eyes, and handsome face. He sat a large gym bag on the ground next to him and examined my knee. It was scraped and bloody, the kind a seven-year-old gets from a bike fall. The humiliation sunk in deeper. I must've looked ridiculous and in front of such a cute guy. I kept my head down, wishing I had the power to make myself disappear.

"You really took a spill there," he said as he reached inside his gym bag.

"You saw that, huh?" I said blushing.

"Oh, yeah." He took out a first aid kit and began to bandage my knee.

"Oh, no, you don't have to do that." It was very sweet, but could I feel any more like a loser getting my knee bandaged in the street like a helpless child?

"Sure I do. I can't let you walk around with a bleeding knee." He dabbed peroxide on my scrape with a patch of gauze. "This might sting a little." I tried to hiss silently not knowing if it was a reaction of the minor pain or the blaring embarrassment.

"So, are you a paramedic?" I asked, wondering about his handy first aid kit.

He smirked. "No, I'm a physical therapist."

"Wow, so you really do heal people." Suddenly, I felt a little better.

"Yeah, that's the idea."

"I'm a therapist too," I said with an anxious giggle. "Well, a couples therapist anyway."

"So you heal people, two at a time." He winked with a bright smile.

"Something like that."

"You work in this building?" he asked.

"Yeah, you?"

"No, just passing by on my way home from an appointment." He secured the bandage gently on my knee. "Good as new." He smiled. Then, the smile turned to puzzled recognition.

"Were you at David and Rachel's wedding?" he asked. I didn't recognize him at first, but then it hit me like lightning. It was James, the best man. Then came another inspirational bolt of lightning. This was the guy. He was perfect! Cute, sweet, and a modern-day hero, at least in this scenario. I decided I might want to play up the damsel in distress role that I had been serendipitously placed into.

"Yes! You're David's best man." I smiled, this time, with all my teeth.

"I'm James Young." He stuck out his hand for a proper introduction, and I returned it.

"I'm Marin Johns." We stared into each other's eyes, our handshake lingering a bit. The connection was made, and I knew instantly that my search was over.

"Well James, it looks like I owe you one."

"Hmm, you can pay me back by letting me buy you an ice cream." Ice cream! Isn't he adorable?

"Ice cream?" I asked, trying to hide my excitement.

"Yeah, that's what you do when you fall and hurt your knee. You get ice cream."

"Okay, sure. When do you want to go?" I couldn't wait for this ice cream date.

"How about right now?" I guess I wouldn't have to wait.

"If you insist," I said with a modest smile and a coy tone. He stood and offered his hand.

"I do." The pain in my knee was dulled by the moment and all the promises of the encounter.

We took the trolley to Baskin Robbins. Of the thirty-one flavors, I got strawberry cheesecake on a waffle cone and he chose plain chocolate. We enjoyed our cones in the warm, spring sun while we walked around a nearby park. It was a perfect random first date.

"I can't believe you got chocolate. It's called thirty-one flavors because there are thirty-one to choose from," I said, nudging him a bit.

"But chocolate is simple and classic. You know it's always a good choice."

"Oh, I see. You're unadventurous," I said with a smirk.

He laughed. "Okay, Freud, let's psychoanalyze you."

"What do you want to know?"

"Well, for starters, how do you know David and Rachel?"

"Rachel's sister Holly is my best friend."

"Ah," he uttered as if it all made sense.

"Yeah, we all grew up together. Rachel's like a little sister to me."

"So, you must be from San Jose?"

"Yep. What about you? Where are you from?"

"I'm from a small ranch town in Montana." His tone was cautious, as if I'd judge him for it.

"Really?"

Which I did. Not in a negative way. This Montana ranch boy was just the horse I was looking for. I bet he grew up with strong family ideals about marriage. Catching him cheating would be like finding the proverbial Holy Grail.

"Yeah. I also have two sisters, a horse named Kabob, and I was nineteen before I rode a rollercoaster."

"Wow," I whispered. "And what did you think of the rollercoaster?"

He stopped, and his eyes locked on mine. His smile was big and full of warmth. It was infectious and I felt my eyes sparkle back at him.

"It was a great ride." He turned to keep walking. "How's that strawberry cheesecake?" he asked.

"It's so good."

There I was with a bandage on my knee, an ice cream cone in my hand, and a handsome man of possibilities. What a crazy day.

We finished our ice cream and engaged in light, fun conversation. James was completely different from Anderson. No smooth one-liners or attempts to take me home. He was relaxed, friendly, considerate, a complete

102

gentleman. I spent most of the time observing him, the things he said, and how he interacted with me, trying to uncover even an ounce of liar, cheater, or mistreater. I couldn't see any. It was in there somewhere, and in time I would reveal it. Then, I could prove, without a shred of doubt, that all men were liars and cheaters.

In the middle of him talking about his college experience with David, I remembered Holly.

"What time is it?" I said.

He looked down at his watch, "Six-thirty." Uh oh.

"I have to go. Holly leaves for Thailand in thirty minutes," I said with haste.

"Can I call you sometime?" he asked. I rummaged through my oversized bag and found a business card.

"Thanks for everything. You really saved the day," I handed him the card. He smiled.

"You're welcome."

I hurried out of the park and hopped on the nearest trolley toward Holly's neighborhood before stopping by a local drug store to pick up a going away gift of mosquito repellent and sunscreen. A little impersonal, but I knew she would appreciate it. My knee and feet were sore as I rushed to Holly's on foot. The cab was parked outside and Holly loaded her suitcases into the car.

"Holly!" I yelled still a fair distance away. She looked over and waved.

"Are you okay?" she asked.

"Yeah, I got here as fast as I could," I said, panting and trying to catch my breath.

"What happened to your knee?"

"I fell. You know how graceful I am."

She laughed. "Oh, yeah, I'll never forget the time you broke your arm when we were nine. Do you remember?"

"How could I forget? I wore a cast for two months and you drew a big green peace sign that said, peace, love and—"

"Best friends," Holly finished and her eyes started to water. In that moment, it was like we were little girls again. It felt like one of us was going on a family vacation without the other for a week. When you're a kid, a week feels like forever and when you're an adult, six months feels like forever too.

"Oh, before I forget here's your farewell gift." I handed her the repellent and sunscreen.

She smirked. "Nice. I'm gonna need it."

I brought her in for a big hug. "Be safe out there."

"I will."

She kissed my cheek and said, "I have to go." She walked to the cab, but stopped before she got inside.

"Hey, Marin," she called.

"Yeah?"

"I know that you're going through a lot right now and you're searching for answers. But you're not going to find what you're looking for on this pursuit of yours."

"What are you saying?"

"I'm saying if you go looking for trouble, you're going to find it." My smile frowned. I didn't know what to say. "What I mean is let it go, Marin."

Holly rarely advised me on anything. That was usually my job. She always played the role of the supporter.

Whatever decision I made she was behind it simply on best friend principle. Needless to say her opposition was unusual, and a little part of me wanted to heed her advice. I could sense my cognitive dissonance, but the larger part of me wanted justice.

"I don't think I can." I looked into her eyes knowing that she was leaving, but needing to stand my ground.

"Then you'll only get hurt again. Trust me on this one, okay?"

I stood there silent for a second.

"Okay?" she said.

"Okay," I said, but I had already made up my mind. We exchanged reassuring smiles before she closed the door. I watched the cab drive away until it was far enough ahead that I couldn't see it any longer. On my own cab ride home, I quietly reflected on the bittersweet Monday. Anderson and I were done, Holly would be gone for six months, and already I had met someone new. I let out a sigh of relief, thankful that the day was finally over.

8

Zen and the Art of Fictitious Dating

THE EASTERN SUN POKED THROUGH MY curtains. My scraped knee ached a dull pain. I immediately recalled Anderson's astonished face when I introduced myself as his new therapist. It was the same look that Chad had given me when I caught him. Why would someone put themself in that situation if getting caught was so troubling? It would have to be a pretty damn good reason. Then, I remembered men's typical tendency to be impulsive, placing themselves in dangerous situations that were absolutely idiotic. Cheating is just one of them.

I thought about James and the look in his eyes when he told me about the rollercoaster. He seemed so honest, so genuine. But after everything that happened and all the information I was acquiring, I knew he was just a wolf in sheep's clothing.

Katie walked in my office as soon as I sat at my desk.

"How'd everything go yesterday?" she asked.

"Fine," I said with a reassuring smile.

"Good. Thanks again for your help," she said and walked out of my office.

"Anytime," I called after her.

After work, I looked forward to a restful evening at home. My phone rang as I left through the revolving doors. The memory of falling flashed back, and I wondered if it was James calling. That would be kinda freaky. When I was safely outside I looked in my purse to retrieve my phone. It was Telly.

"Hello?"

"What-up, sucka!" she said in an exaggerated man voice.

"Just left work. What are you up to tonight?"

"Nothing."

"You wanna come over for some Chinese and a movie?"

"Yeah, sounds great. Hey, can I tell you something?" Her voice quieted as if she were hiding a secret.

"Yeah."

"We got a new associate at the firm and he is super hot. I think I love him." Telly said this about every hot guy she encountered.

"Oh, yeah, what's his name?" I said with a sarcastic chuckle.

"Zack." She giggled.

"A normal name for once?" Telly often dated guys with names like Grayson, Cohen, and Shad. Seriously, Shad.

"Not exactly," she said, slowing her words.

"What do you mean? Is it spelled with a silent F?"

"His last name is Morris." I immediately bellowed a huge laugh.

"His name is Zack Morris?" I blurted the words loudly, forgetting I was in public. "Like *Saved By The Bell* Zack Morris?"

"Yep," she said.

"Remember the episode when Jessie was taking speed?" I said, picturing the scene as if I had just watched the show that was so beloved in our childhood.

Telly started singing "I'm So Excited", then let out a fake, dramatic cry. We laughed and joked about it until I reached the restaurant. It wasn't long before I was unpacking the hot Chinese food in my kitchen and waiting for Telly to arrive with the movie.

Knock, knock. I hurried over to let Telly in. She followed me inside. "Okay, so I know we were going to watch that new Denzel thriller, but I thought this was more appropriate." She quickly whipped out an old copy of *Wedding in Las Vegas*. I snatched it from her in disbelief.

"Oh, no you di'nt," I said in my best Queens accent.

"Oh, yes I did," she mimicked.

"Oh, my God, where did you find this?"

"It's a secret," she said, looking through the white greasy cartons of food while I served it on little plates.

We shoved noodles in our mouths with chopsticks and watched while Zack and Kelly battled one fiasco after another.

"So, what's going on with Anderson? Any news?" she asked.

"Yeah, about that," I said. Her brows rose in concern. "Yesterday I took this last minute appointment at work and guess who was sitting in my waiting room?"

Telly's eyes widened. "No," she gasped.

"Yep, Anderson and his girlfriend."

"What did you do?"

"I was completely professional," I said with a hint of arrogance. Telly stared at me, lips pursed. "Okay, I was mostly professional."

"Mostly professional?"

"Okay, fine. I screwed with him a little. He deserved it," I said throwing my chopsticks on the coffee table.

"Damn right, I would have slapped the shit out of him," she said.

"I'm pretty sure his girlfriend took care of that for me."

"Really?" she said, surprised. "I thought you might have gotten into a brawl with her by looking at your knee. What happened?"

For a moment, I considered telling her about James, but decided to keep it quiet. I wanted to see if it became anything first. Even though I knew it was inevitable, being cheated on by two men in a matter of weeks was a little defeating.

"I tripped when I was running yesterday." She gave me a sympathetic face.

"Now what?" she asked.

"Not sure," I replied. "I'll find someone else."

Telly left shortly after our chat, and while I was washing the dishes I got a call from a number I didn't recognize.

"Hello?"

"Is this Marin?" a male voice asked on the other line.

"Yes, this is Marin."

"Hi, this is James from yesterday." My heart leaped and I hushed the kitchen faucet.

"Hi, how are you?"

"I'm good. How about you? How's your knee?" I looked down at my bruised and scabbed skin.

"It's doing fine."

"That's good. Listen, if you're not doing anything this Friday night, maybe we can grab dinner." He sounded a little nervous. It was kind of cute.

"Okay, sounds fun." I tried to sound casual, not too excited.

"Do you like sushi?" he asked and I grimaced.

"Um, actually I'm kind of sick of sushi. Could we go for Mexican?" As soon as the words came out of my mouth I regretted them. Mexican food on a first date! I'd probably be bloated and gassy before we left the restaurant.

"Yeah, that sounds good. I'll call you Friday then," he said.

"Okay, talk to you then." I hung up and sighed. Another Friday night date. Fear settled in, and I tried to remember if James brought a date to the wedding. I didn't know if I could take an Anderson repeat. Then again, I guess that was the chance everyone took when meeting someone new.

James called again early Friday to confirm our date at a restaurant called Colibri Mexican Bistro. I dressed in a short, form fitting black dress with a high neckline and a matching belt. My hair pinned back on one side, letting my side swept bangs fall. I felt sexy, but very tasteful.

James was waiting outside when I arrived at Colibri. He wore dark pants and a buttoned up shirt with the sleeves rolled up showing his muscular forearms, and he wore it well.

His smile seemed to grow with every step forward I took.

"I hope you're hungry," he said.

"I am." He led me into the restaurant and we were seated right away.

"Thank you for inviting me to dinner," I said.

"The pleasure's all mine."

We looked over the menu while chatting about how nice the weather had been and sipping our drinks, a mojito for me and a draft Corona for him. The conversation slowed to an awkward silence. I got the impression he was nervous, which gave me a boost of confidence.

"So, tell me, why did you decide to become a physical therapist?" I asked.

"I played sports my whole life and was offered a full scholarship to play for the Golden Bears at Berkeley.

Then, in my second semester, I injured my knee during a game. I couldn't play for four months and had to have physical therapy. By then the team had replaced me and I wasn't able to come back. I wanted to stay at Berkeley, and I was really inspired by my physical therapist. That's when I decided to change my major from Economics to Sports Medicine, and here I am."

"That's too bad about your knee. Did you get to keep your scholarship?"

"Yeah, a partial scholarship."

"How's your knee now?" I asked.

"Not bad. It gives me trouble every now and then, but for the most part it works great. How's your knee?" At first I wasn't sure how he knew about my knee injury, then I remembered he was talking about the scrape that prompted our meeting.

"It's healing nicely, thanks to you." We smiled at each other and he let out a little laugh. "I know about bad knees. My right one was injured during a marathon a couple years ago. I used to run the US Half Marathon every year, but I haven't run it since."

"Oh, that's too bad," he said.

"Well, I've been training again. I think I'll be able to run it this fall."

"That's good. I guess it's a good thing you fell on your left knee, huh?" he said.

"Yeah." I smiled.

"I'd be happy to help you train. You know, make sure you don't put additional stress on your knee." His offer was kind and genuine.

"That would be great. Thank you," I smiled at the thought of having a professional help with my knee and that he offered to spend more time with me. Things were looking good with James. "Are you gonna charge my insurance for your services?" I asked.

He smiled. "No, you can be my charity case."

"Hey!" I said, but he just laughed. It was a warm laugh, not arrogant like Anderson's or obnoxious like Chad's. His was the kind of timeless laugh that would sound just as vibrant in his nineties as it did in his thirties.

"So, what about you? Why'd you become a counselor?" he asked.

"Well, my father is an oncologist, and so my brother and I were groomed to go to medical school. Michael, my brother, was first in his class and now he conducts cancer research at Berkeley. Me, on the other hand, I quit after my first year of med school. I couldn't take the blood and needles and tubes. I took the summer to think about what I wanted to do, what I believed in. That's when I decided on therapy. My father was disappointed, of course. So I moved to Boston for grad school, got an internship here, and I've been living here ever since. It worked out, because I love what I do."

"That's cool. Didn't you say you were a couples therapist?" he asked.

"Yeah, I primarily work with couples, but I work with women too."

"Why couples therapy exactly?"

"I got into it because I was an advocate for love," I said as if I had rehearsed the line a million times.

"You were an advocate for love?" he asked, placing the emphasis on the word *were*.

"Well, things change I guess." I should have bit my tongue because it was too honest of an answer.

"What do you mean?"

Why didn't I just say yes?

"After everything I've seen, I've learned to be more realistic about human relationships." I hoped my answer would be enough to end the conversation.

"So you don't believe in happily ever after?" he asked like a child asking if I believed in Santa.

"I believe it takes work," I said in my sensible tone.

"Well, I'd like to think it exists." As soon as he said it, I gave him my best scrutinizing lie detector stare. He stared back at me never losing eye contact. Hmm, this was definitely my guy.

Our food arrived as we closed the topic. We ate, talked, and enjoyed a couple more drinks. The bill finally came and I realized we had been there for two hours. James was easy to talk with, a little too easy. All in all we had a really nice time. We shared a cab on the way home and he walked me to my door to say goodnight. It didn't seem like he was trying to weasel his way into my apartment, unless the whole "hold the cab" thing was just a ploy.

"Thanks for joining me. I had a great time with you," he said, pushing his hands into his pockets.

"Me too." I smiled.

"I'd like to take you out again," he said, looking unsure of himself.

"I'd like that," I said and he gave a shy smile.

"Good, then I'll call you." I unlocked the door.

"Do you wanna come in?" I asked to gauge his reaction.

"I've got to head home, but maybe next time." He took my hand and gave it a gentle kiss.

"Good night, Marin," he said.

"Good night."

And then he turned to leave.

I shut myself into the apartment and leaned my back against the door. My stomach was aflutter, and I took a moment to reflect on the night. James was such a gentleman, kind, cute, just easy to be with. I started to blush. Then, I immediately shook my head. No! I couldn't let him fool me. James was a man, which meant he was a cheater like the rest of them.

The next afternoon, I went shopping with Telly. We sorted through clothes and discussed why stirrup pants are never okay. I decided to confess.

"So . . . I think I found a new lab rat," I said.

"Eww, for what?" Telly said, half paying attention with an arm full of outfits.

"Not a real rat, a new guy."

"Oh, wow, that was fast. So who is this poor bastard?" She continued to browse the racks, unfazed by my news.

"Do you remember the best man at Rachel and David's wedding?" I asked. Her eyes and mouth flew open.

"No way! That guy James?"

"Yep."

She drew nearer and lowered her voice, her face full of

intrigue. "Holy shit. How'd that happen?"

"It's kind of embarrassing. I fell outside of my office and he happened to be walking by. He sort of . . . rescued me and took me out for ice cream."

She raised an eyebrow at me. "Oh, God, that's so you with your prince and his white horse." She grimaced.

"Hey, I don't believe in fairytales anymore."

"Okay, so then what?"

"We went out for dinner last night and it went well," I said.

"Did you guys have sex?" she asked as if that was the most natural of follow-up questions.

"No, it wasn't like that."

"Boo!" she said, giving me a thumbs-down like a ten year-old boy.

"I have to play this one for real. If we don't establish a commitment, then it won't mean anything if he's unfaithful," I argued. Telly walked in the other direction to another rack of clothes. I followed close behind.

"Marin, that could take months, years even!"

"Yeah, but I have a good feeling about this guy." I smirked and she looked unconvinced. "Did you know that fifty percent of married men will cheat by the time they're forty? I mean doesn't that make you sick?"

"Not really. I don't believe in monogamy." I shrugged my shoulders and reluctantly agreed.

"I hope you know what you're doing. Holly would kill you if she found out you were playing games with her brother-in-law's best friend." Telly had a point.

"She's not going to find out. By the time she comes

back this whole thing will be over, and then it won't matter."

"I hope you're right. In the meantime, Rachel is going to have a field day with this. You just wait. As soon as she gets wind of it she's going to be calling you with double date plans and couples weekends away in Wine Country." I hadn't thought about Rachel and David's involvement before. It was going to be a bit tricky playing fake girlfriend with a close family friend around genuinely rooting for us.

Telly was right. Rachel called later that week.

"Eeekkk!" she screeched in excitement.

"Are you okay?" I asked holding the phone away from my ear.

"I'm great! Why didn't you tell me you were going out with James?" she said in a high-pitched, sorority girl voice.

"It's kinda new. I didn't want to jump the gun."

"I can't believe it. You guys are perfect for each other. I don't know why I didn't think of it before."

"Probably because I was already engaged." Duh!

"Oh, right. So, when are you two going out next?" Her voice danced in a sing-song kind of way.

"Saturday," I said, and she screeched again.

Saturday would be our third official date. We met for coffee on Wednesday and planned a movie over the weekend. Things were going well, but moving slowly. Too slowly. He hadn't even kissed me except for on my hand and cheek. Usually by the third date things really heat up. At least that's what many of my friends experienced. At this rate I'd be lucky if I got a single goodnight kiss.

That weekend, James and I met at the movie theater to watch a new action drama. I tried to amp up the flirting by giving him a sultry "kiss me" gaze before the movie started, but that didn't work. I inched closer to him, leaving my hand lonely and cold on my lap, easy for him to grab. Nothing. Maybe he was purposefully ignoring my signals. About half way through the movie, I decided to give up and sulk as I ate my popcorn and Goobers.

James dropped me off at my apartment the same as our previous dates. He wished me goodnight just like before and asked if I wanted to go out again just like before, and I, of course, said yes just like before. What's the definition of insanity? I started to wonder if he was a fictitious boyfriend or a boy who was a friend. I shut myself in my apartment and threw my hands in the air. Am I ugly? Does my breath stink? Why hasn't he kissed me?

The next afternoon, he took me on another "date" to the San Francisco Conservatory, which was a museum of flowers that I rarely visited. I admired the architecture of the building as we walked inside. To me, it looked somewhat like the White House and the Taj Mahal made a building baby.

"Do you like flowers?" he asked and I looked at him strangely. Who would say no to a question like that?

"James, everyone likes flowers." He smiled and shook his head.

"That's not true. I dated a girl who despised getting flowers. I gave her a nice bouquet once and she tossed them right in the trash."

"That's kind of a strong reaction." He agreed, then I added, "Maybe they were ugly flowers."

He laughed and said that he thought her distaste for flowers stemmed from a traumatizing incident with a rose bush.

"Would that be considered Post Traumatic Thorn Syndrome?" I asked.

He smiled. "You're the shrink. You tell me."

We walked through the conservatory, admiring the beautiful greenery and ornate flowers. James leaned in and asked, "What's your favorite kind of flower?"

"Guess," I said. He let out a thoughtful hmm sound and tapped his finger on his chin.

"Tulips," he said. I shook my head.

"Lilies?" He tried again. Still no.

"Roses?" I shook my head again and gave him a tight-lipped smile as if I were holding the name of my favorite flower hostage inside my mouth. He gave up on guessing and we went easily onto another topic. It was about an hour into the tour when I realized he was walking a safe distance from me. Close enough as friends, but too far for lovers. Romantic relationships don't exist without a little romance, especially in the beginning. And while I was getting plenty of romantic dates from James, I wasn't getting any of the passion or obvious tension. It wasn't nearly this difficult with Anderson or Chad. Neither could keep their hands off me.

James was giving me his opinion on the healthcare system in America when I finally got fed up. I was a modern woman and if I wanted something I had to go get it my-self. It was time to go for it and lay one on him. What was the worst that could happen? What did I have to lose? I walked in front of him and planted my feet. He almost ran into me, which was the closest we had been, probably ever.

"Hey!" I said, surprising even myself.

He was startled then puzzled. Perhaps it wasn't the best way to prompt a kiss. I stared at him unable to make a move. He opened his mouth to speak, but before he could speak I said, "Why haven't you kissed me yet?"

"What?" He blushed.

"This is our fourth date and you haven't so much as held my hand. I don't understand what we're doing." My frustration was on the table and so was my crazy.

"I thought we were having a good time," he said like it was no big deal. That's when I realized I was in the friend zone. He wasn't into me at all. We were hanging out like a couple of middle school kids. Despite the fact that I was in control of the situation, all of the rejection was starting to get to me.

I dropped my head and mumbled to myself, "I'm so stupid." I turned and walked away. He followed me and called out, "Marin." I stopped at the display of Birds of Paradise flowers.

"What's this all about?" he asked. I turned to him and looked up, but not directly at him.

"I thought you liked me," I said with defeat.

"I do like you."

"No, I mean like, like me."

"I do."

"Then why aren't you moving things forward? We're not in high school. By now we should be, ya know, getting to know each other better," I said, trying to be obvious with the innuendo.

"Marin, dating hasn't changed since high school. You just asked me if I like, liked you." He gave me a cute smirk, and I felt kind of silly.

"Truthfully," he said, "I wanted to take it slow for you. Rachel told me about your engagement ending, and I didn't want to rush into 'getting to know each other better' yet."

"What did she tell you?" I wasn't keen on him knowing all the awful details, and I hoped that Rachel had been vague.

"Only that you guys broke it off not that long ago. I figured if you wanted to talk about it you would."

"Yeah," I said and realized I might be forced to have that conversation with someone in the future.

"Plus, you kind of seem like you're not there yet, like you're not really in it. Do you know what I mean?"

I had to hand it to him. He was trying to be a gentleman and consider my feelings because I had just gotten my heart broken. He was pretty intuitive picking up on my emotional distance. Yep, playing with James wasn't some old lady's card game. I had to put my best poker face forward.

"Yeah, I see what you mean," I said.

"It's not that I don't want to kiss you, because I do," he said, and I smiled. "Do you want me to kiss you now or later?" he asked and sarcastically moved around me like he was trying to figure out if he should make a move or not.

"No." I laughed. "You have to surprise me."

"Okay, I'll make it a surprise." He took my hand and held it tightly in his.

"Orchids," I said. "My favorite flowers are orchids."

"Good to know," he said with a smile.

We continued on our walk through the conservatory enjoying each other's company. I felt a little self-conscious after my confrontation about the kiss, but I played it cool. Not that he would let me forget it, because he kept pretending to initiate kisses. What he didn't know was two could play the pretend game.

Like the gentleman that he was, he walked me to my door once again.

"I'm not going to kiss you now, because it would be too predictable." He was very matter-of-fact. I blushed and covered my face with my hands. He was definitely not letting me live it down.

"Goodnight," I said and closed myself in my apartment. I was only inside for a minute when there was a knock at the door. It was James. He stood there staring at me like he had something to confess.

"I forgot something," he said.

"What?" I asked, wondering what he could've possibly forgotten. Then he grabbed me tightly around my waist. His thumb rubbed gently against my cheek.

"This." And then he kissed me. His lips were soft, his mouth was warm, and his smell was intoxicating. My skin tingled with excitement. As first kisses go, it was pretty damn good. I was rendered speechless, surprised for sure. He released me from his arms and smiled.

"Goodnight, Marin," he said and walked away. I let out a delayed, "Goodnight" after him.

I closed the door and let out a deep exhale, the kind of exhale that's triggered by a strong mint. My head was cloudy from the rush of dopamine and norepinephrine. I took a deep breath and came to my senses. I thought to myself, *WhooHooo!* Now we're getting somewhere. I did a victory dance around my apartment and relished in the prospect of a beautiful, fictitious relationship.

9

Catch Me If You Can

THREE WEEKS AND NINE DATES LATER, James and I were still seeing each other. I played it cool during every interaction, hoping we would soon take the next steps—commitment and sex. In the meantime, I enjoyed his company, but kept my eyes peeled for any suspicious activity. So far, he proved to be a decent guy.

We met after work one evening for a quick bite to eat and a run in the park. Running had become a frequent activity of ours since he was helping me train for the marathon. The sun set as we walked briskly, cooling ourselves from the run. James slowed and I followed.

"Hey," James called to a man who was stretching by a bench.

"James," the man said and shook James' hand.

"It's been a long time. How've you been?" James asked.

"Great. Stephanie just had a baby."

"Wow, congratulations." James gave the man a friendly pat on the arm.

"Thanks."

"Marin, this is Josh. We went to college together. Josh, this is my girlfriend, Marin." I offered my hand to Josh.

"Nice to meet you, Marin," Josh said.

"Likewise."

"Well, it was good running into you. Send our best to the family." James ended our little stop and chat.

"Will do," Josh said as he waved goodbye.

James immediately began talking about how long it had been since he had seen Josh and how they met in economics class their first year. I tried to pay attention, but kept thinking about my introduction.

"I don't know if you noticed, but you introduced me as your girlfriend back there," I slowed our walk to a complete stop.

"Yeah, that's what you are, right?" he said as if we'd been dating for years.

"Well, we never really talked about being exclusive," I said.

James shrugged. "I guess I thought it was one of those unspoken things. I mean I'm not seeing anyone else, and . . . wait." He paused. "Are you seeing other people?"

"No," I said with a giggle.

"Good, then let's just see each other." He smiled.

I smiled too, accepting his exclusive offer. He kissed my forehead, took my hand. He went on while I silently congratulated myself. It was official. James was my *boy-friend*.

James made dinner plans for us on Friday night, which worked well since it was time to get the show on the road. It was the night we were finally going to have sex. That evening I took a long luxurious bath, making sure to shave everything. Yes, everything. The date was casual so I slipped on a light floral summer dress and cute sandals.

He arrived just as I was packing an extra pair of panties and a travel toothbrush. If things went well, I would be out all night.

"These are for you." He greeted me with a kiss and surprised me with a dozen long stemmed orchids sitting delicately in a simple vase. My favorite flowers and only the second time I had received them as a gift, and the first time I had received them as a romantic gift.

"Thank you," I said.

He kissed my cheek and told me how beautiful I looked. His blue eyes sparkled at mine, and I was caught for a moment. Then I dropped my eyes, using them to trace the frame of his body. He escorted me outside and I inhaled his delicious smelling cologne.

"Where's the cab?" I asked.

"Right here," he said leading me to a dark blue SUV.

"Is this yours?"

"Yeah, I just bought it. What do you think?" he asked. I gave it a once over.

"I like it."

He opened the door, and when I sat inside, I caught a whiff of that overwhelming new car smell.

"We'll save a ton on cab fare," he said.

"I'll save a ton on cab fare, you'll spend a fortune on gas," I said. He smirked before shutting the door. I examined all the knobs and features on his dashboard as he started the engine, then I noticed he was staring at me. When I turned toward him, his eyes came up quickly from staring at my legs that were exposed beyond my short summer dress.

"You ready to go?" he asked.

I gave him a sultry look and pursed my lips. "Yep, just waiting on you." Before I knew it, we were flying down the road.

Later at the restaurant, we were enjoying our food and having a conversation about movies. When he asked my favorite genre, I told him that I loved any movie with Leonardo DiCaprio.

"Do you have a crush on him?"

"A crush? Please. Haven't you seen his last two films?"

He took a second, then said, "Point taken."

"Besides, I'm more of a Hugh Jackman kind of girl," I said with a wink.

"Oh, I see," he smiled with a hint of sarcasm.

"Who do you like?" I asked. When he answered I nearly spit out my food. The actress was famous for her wild past and humanitarian, child-adopting present.

"No, I mean talent wise," I said with a slight chuckle.

"She's talented," he said, widening his eyes incredulously.

"You can't be serious?"

"I am serious. Did you see the movie with her and that

Latin guy, I can't think of his name? He does voiceovers in those animated movies now," he said in a way to prove his point.

"I know what movie you're referring to, but no."

He threw his hands up in disbelief.

"What's it about?" I asked.

"This Spanish guy sends for a wife and he falls in love with her." I nodded to show I was listening. "But she's really trying to put one over on him and take his money and run."

"That's original," I frowned.

"You have to see it."

That's his best defense?

"So, what happens?" I asked.

"You'll have to watch the movie." He teased.

"What? I'll never watch it. You can tell me," I said.

"No way. I have it at home. We can watch it together sometime." James concluded then shoved his fork in his mouth. I stared at him for a moment. A movie at his house was the perfect way to achieve the task at hand, the task being sex, of course. I could see the doors of opportunity opening and my plan falling right into place.

"Let's watch it tonight at your place," I said.

He stared at me if I caught him off guard, as if he knew what I had in store for him. "Yeah, that's a good idea."

Yes! I was in. Inside, I could hear myself laughing like a villain. It was show time.

After dinner, we drove to his apartment, a place I'd visited a couple of times before. This would be my first time seeing it at night. It was a bi-floor loft with a huge window that looked out onto the front street. His place was simple and uncomplicated like him.

As usual, we were greeted by his Great Dane, which he had dubbed Marvin. James got Marvin when he was only a pup, but now the dog was as tall as me if he stood on his hind legs. In fact, I was convinced he wasn't a dog at all. Rather, he was a small horse. Dogs have always liked me. My guess is they could sense my loving nature. But Marvin wasn't like other dogs. Every time I got near him he grumbled at me then walked away. James said he was usually warm with strangers and thought that Marvin might have an aversion to my perfume. I think it was James' way of rationalizing the fact that his dog didn't like me.

"Would you like something to drink?" he asked.

"Wine, please."

"Comin' right up," he said and walked to the kitchen.

"Can I use your restroom?" I asked.

"Of course."

I headed up to the bathroom in his upstairs bedroom and locked myself in. The last time I was in his apartment I looked through the bathroom cabinets for anything suspicious like the lady bic I found in Anderson's bathroom. He was clean last time, and by the looks of it, he was clean again. I freshened my breath, lipstick, and perfume, then headed back downstairs. When I returned to the living room two glasses of wine sat on the table, the lights were low, and the movie was ready to go. He rested his arm along the back of the couch. I settled next to him and snuggled up in his arms. The moment I was comfortable, Marvin dug his nose in between us to create some distance, as if he were James' chaperone.

"Go lay down," James commanded and gently pushed him away. Marvin planted himself in front of us and stared. James repeated the nudge and command to no avail. Instead, Marvin grumbled and exhaled a sharp breath out of his nose like a bull.

"Marvin, why are you acting like this?" James said as he stood up. He gave me an apologetic look. "He usually listens really well. I don't know what's gotten into him."

James took Marvin by the collar and ushered him to the kitchen. Marvin dragged his paws on the floor, and it only took a minute for James to get him to lie down. He returned to the couch, and I cuddled in his arms just as before.

We sipped our wine and watched the beautiful actress use seduction like a spell. About halfway through the movie, I realized how ironic it was. We were in similar situations, pretending to be into someone when we really had an ulterior motive. My cheeks started to flush as I wondered if James mentioned the movie because he secretly knew what I was up to. He smiled warmly when I looked at him for reassurance, so I shook off the ridiculous thought. No way he knew my true intentions. I snuggled deeper into him and began tickling his knee with my fingers. The movie progressed to a fever pitch, giving us the perfect push. A very steamy sex scene began, the kind that inspires either arousal or embarrassment.

I began softly running my fingers on his neck. In one

swift, very sexy, move I straddled him. Our faces were only inches apart. He said nothing while my fingers ran sensually through his soft hair. He looked deep into my eyes and kissed me gently, yet fervently. My body pressed into his and he held me tightly. His kisses moved down my neck, and I threw my head back pushing my chest out. A shiver shot through my body as his hands ran up my thighs and under my dress until he reached my lower back. He caressed my skin as we kissed, the movie still blaring in the background.

I sat back to unbutton his shirt, then slid it off. His chest rose and fell as he breathed the sensual air. I traced a line down his chest to his belt and unfastened his pants. He kissed me again and pulled my dress up and over my head. He unlatched my bra and it popped right off like a broken rubber band. I stood and whispered, "Let's go upstairs." He followed close, yet far enough away for him to get a good look at what I had going on.

James came up behind me kissing my neck and touching every inch of my body. I reached around and pushed his pants to the ground. I crawled onto the bed. He grabbed my hips and kissed me along my back until he reached my shoulders. He held his body up with his strong arms while I flipped onto my back.

"Are you sure you're ready for this?" he asked. His blue eyes gleamed at my hazel ones. I rubbed my hands down his back, slipped my fingers into his boxers, and began to pull them down.

"Yes," I said. And I was. He sucked on my neck and slipped off my panties, careful to take his time. I helped slide him inside me, which sent a tingling sensation all over my body. He moved his hips at an easy pace as we kissed passionately. There I was again, completely free, uninhibited, and in control. The soft light from downstairs reflected off his defined body. I found pleasure in the sight and the sensation. His gaze caught mine and for a second I was fixed. Feelings of vulnerability began to unravel, causing me to close my eyes and turn my head. He leaned in to kiss me, then pulled away, softly kissing my chest. He continued down inch-by-inch until he reached my stomach, then lightly ran his tongue below my belly button. I threw my head back enjoying his attention to detail until he resumed his previous position.

I was feeling close, but didn't want it to stop. He pulled my legs back and cupped his hands around my ass. It sent me over the edge and before I knew it I was having those tingling flashes of pleasure streaming through my whole body. James immediately followed.

"Oh, wow." He breathed and rolled on his back.

"I know," I said, also trying to catch my breath.

"Did you uh . . . ya know?" he asked.

"Yeah," I said. "When it's good, it's good."

"That was great."

I woke up in one of James' undershirts and a pair of his boxers. Not since my early days with Chad had I looked so cute in a morning after outfit. It was just after seven and James was missing from the bed. The bathroom door was slightly open. The sound of rushing water resounded from it. *Kinda early for a Saturday.* I got out of bed to check my face in his bedroom mirror and wiped the smudged mascara from underneath my eyes. When I heard the shower shut off, I hopped back into bed, pretending to be sleeping.

James came out a few moments later wearing nothing but a towel. Water dripped from his thick, dirty-blonde mane down his beautifully sculpted chest.

"Hey," I said in a groggy voice. He turned around quickly as if I caught him sneaking out.

"Good morning." He smiled showing off his pretty white teeth.

"I didn't know you were such an early riser."

"Not usually this early, but this is my Saturday to volunteer at the children's hospital."

"You volunteer at the hospital?" *Was this guy for real?*

"Yeah, just once a month." He dried and dressed.

"I guess I better get ready to leave too," I said, pushing the covers off.

"No stay, sleep in, it's still really early. There's coffee and croissants if you're hungry," he said, pulling a shirt over his head.

"Are you sure?"

"Yeah, I'll be gone most of the day, but I'll call you later."

I cozied myself under the covers. He kissed me good-bye and grabbed his bag to leave. I rolled over and watched him walk down the stairs, which was easily seen from his loft bedroom. After a minute, the sound of the front door closing resonated in the loft, and I sprung out of bed. My heart raced as I made my way toward the stairs. Marvin, who had been sleeping on the floor, followed. I held the railing as I walked briskly down when Marvin wedged his large horse-dog body between the rail and me, nearly knocking me off balance. He probably did it on purpose. He hates me.

Ignoring the near fall, I hurried to look out the living room window. James was walking to his car. Once he took off, I looked back at Marvin who sat behind me, staring me down like I was his enemy. I gave him a snide glare. He wasn't going to deter me.

After I checked to make sure the door was locked, I relished. I was alone in James' most sacred haven; his apartment. Then I looked at Marvin. Well, mostly alone. At first I was overwhelmed and unsure where to start. How do you clean? From top to bottom. I headed upstairs. The bathroom had already been searched, so I went through every dresser drawer, under the bed, and in all the closets for any clues of an ex-girlfriend or a slew of lovers. It was clean. Downstairs his hall closets and living room nooks and crannies were well organized. Still nothing. His answering machine had one message from his dentist and his kitchen wasn't much help either. That's when I saw it, the place a man keeps his real secrets. His laptop.

I made my way over to grab it, but Marvin beat me to it and placed his paws on top of it. My knowledge on the behavior of Great Danes was shallow, but this one was smart as hell and a pain in my ass. My eyes searched his. Did he have a human soul somewhere in his oversized dog body? I tried to grab the computer out from under his paws, but he guarded it like it was his special bone.

"Come on, Marvin," I said, then looked toward the window.

"Marvin, what's that?" I said and pointed in that direction. Marvin's ears perked up and he looked at the window. While he was momentarily distracted, I swiped the laptop.

"Got it!" I said, and he barked at me. "Oh, stop," I told him. Marvin disappeared upstairs leaving me to investigate the computer at my leisure. No password. Good. First, I looked through his Internet history, which was mostly news sites and a few cooking sites. I looked in his picture files and finally stumbled upon his porn stash. It was a fair amount, so I decided to take a look to see what he was into.

Naughty Office featured a blonde woman dressed like an assistant. "I cancelled all your other appointments this afternoon," she said shutting the door behind her. After that it was pretty much her and the "boss" getting it on all over the office. There was quite a bit of spanking, but probably not enough to be considered fetish porn.

"James, you naughty boy."

I riffled through a few more movies. All were similar in nature, boy on girl action, nothing out of the ordinary. So far my search had been a bust. I put everything back in its place, grabbed a croissant, and headed home. The cab ride was nauseating due to an overwhelming odor of urine. I couldn't wait to take a shower, because the pee stink seemed to permeate my clothes. After I was showered and dressed, I realized that the pee smell wasn't from the cab, but was from my purse.

"Dammit, Marvin! This is Kate Spade." I shouted. The purse was immediately escorted to the dry cleaners. Later, I met Telly for lunch to get her input and expertise on my search at James'.

"Oh, my God, Marin!" Telly said after I told her that James and I finally slept together. I smiled shyly as I stirred my iced tea. "So how was it?"

"It was actually really great," I said. "There's something about having sex without all those emotions that makes me feel uninhibited, almost powerful."

"I've been trying to tell you," she said.

"This isn't just about good sex," I said to change the subject.

"Oh, right. Any new developments?"

"He left me alone in his apartment this morning, so I did some snooping."

"What'd you find?" Her eyes widened in anticipation of a great delivery.

"Nothing."

"Nothing?" She couldn't believe it either.

"Well, I did find some porn on his computer," I whispered.

"Oooh, what kind?" I leaned in closer trying to be discreet. "That's the thing. It was just regular guy on girl porn."

"So what's wrong with that?" She looked confused.

"A man's private porn stash exposes his deepest sexual desires. They make porn for every kind of masturbating bastard on this planet. Foot fetishes, racial specific, mature, chicks with dicks, masochistic sex—"

"Two girls and a cup," she said.

I grimaced. "That's gross, Telly." She snickered and I continued in a more serious tone. "It's true. Men are deeply disturbed. But this guy isn't deviant at all."

"No. I'm not convinced. There has to be something," she said.

"But where do I look?"

"You've got to get into his phone. Check his text messages and contact list. A guy's computer is like his bat cave, but men are stupid when it comes to protecting their phones."

I nodded, thinking of how I could possibly get his phone long enough to look through it all.

"That reminds me," I said. "Have you heard of Ashley Madison?"

"Marin, I'm a divorce attorney, of course I've heard of it," she said with a mouth full of food. Ashley Madison was an ambiguously named site I had stumbled on during my recent research. Its sole purpose was to help adulterers hook up. Seriously.

"You know they have more than twenty million members?"

"That's a lot," she said.

"It's not a lot, it's too much. That's twenty million marriages affected. What's wrong with our society when we tolerate and encourage this kind of philandering?"

"Marin, this is America, land of the free. We're inundated with unlimited choices and we're always gonna keep our options open. It's the American way."

"I get that. But, if that's the case then men should

communicate openly about their choice to stay free so they don't hurt the other person."

"How many of those twenty million are women?" she asked for the sake of throwing my argument.

"You know as well as I that women don't cheat for the same reasons as men. It's not just about the sex."

"I've cheated for sex," Telly said, disproving my point.

"Were you in a loving, committed relationship?"

She looked up in thought. "No."

"Then it doesn't count. Besides you don't count. You are basically a man with a vagina."

"Cheers to that," Telly said, raising her iced tea glass to mine.

After James' shift at the hospital, he called and invited me to dinner at his apartment. I arrived promptly at six. He greeted me with a welcoming kiss and told me how much he missed me before rushing back to the kitchen where he was preparing Thai curry. I followed him and the spicy aroma to the kitchen.

"Do you need any help?" I asked.

"Nope, I'm all set. Dinner should be ready in about fifteen minutes." He threw peppers into the pot. It certainly was new to have someone cook for me. Chad didn't know how to make anything other than protein shakes and eggs. The table displayed a romantic setting of candles, wine, and cloth napkins.

"You did all this for me?" I smiled.

"Yeah, I wanted to do something nice for you." I gave him an appreciative kiss. He stirred the curry, and I stood closely behind him, observing his culinary skills. My eyes wandered about the kitchen, and I noticed his phone sitting on the opposite counter, out of plain sight.

"I'll be right back, I'm just going to use the bathroom," I said, inching away from him.

"Okay," he said, still fixated on his hot pan. I crept over to the other counter and quickly confiscated the phone before disappearing upstairs. My pulse was rapid and I broke a cold sweat. I sat on the edge of the tub and began to look through his text messages. Some friendly messages from David, guys he played soccer with, and some work related texts. Then I found it. Jackpot.

I can't wait to see you Friday. Miss you.

It was from someone named Amanda, and it was sent earlier that day. *Who's Amanda?* I took a deep breath, washed my hands, and returned to the kitchen. James was still facing the range, so I was able to safely put his phone back. I exhaled, thankful I had gone unnoticed. The find was relieving, but I could use the information to my advantage. That's when I pulled out an oldie, but goody.

"I forgot to tell you I'm going to a mental health conference this weekend in San Diego. I leave Friday."

"Oh, yeah, that sounds fun," he said.

"Uh huh," I murmured, awaiting his next comment. He took a moment to speak.

"I've got a pretty busy weekend coming up, so that works out." His back still turned away from me. Easy for him to lie when he wasn't looking at my face, huh? I bet it did work out well for him. He just didn't know it worked out well for me too.

That week brought me an interesting visit with a couple, The Gartons. Carmen Garton began seeing me about a year prior to deal with some father issues. After working with her for a while, we decided it would be good to bring her husband Seth in the mix to help him understand some of her insecurities and work on their relationship as well. Carmen was unusually suspicious of his whereabouts and often thought he was out using drugs and soliciting prostitutes.

"So did you both do your self-reflection exercise?" I asked.

"Yeah, I have mine here," Seth said and handed me a manila folder.

"Carmen?" She gave no indication that she was prepared with her exercises.

"I think we should talk about something else," she said, and I inched forward to listen. "I want to talk about why Seth took five-hundred dollars in cash out of our account on the same day that he claimed to be working late."

"Seriously, Carmen?" Seth rolled his eyes.

"Carmen, what's this about?" I asked.

"I know that he's sneaking off, getting high and blown by hookers." She turned to Seth. "You disgust me."

She was perfectly serious and the scenario wasn't unfamiliar. We were starting to make some progress, but any evidence she stumbled on always regressed her back to square one. Seth shook his head then stood.

"You know what? I'm done." He turned to me. "We're here for two seconds and she starts in with this bullshit. I can't take it anymore. It's not worth it." And with that he stormed out. Just another eventful day at Dr. Johns' office.

"See, I'm right," Carmen said, staring after him and then turning to me. "He could at least try to explain himself, but he has no real excuse."

"Are you absolutely sure about that?" I asked.

"Pretty sure, but I'll be able to prove it soon."

"What do you mean?"

"I hired a private investigator."

"Really?" *A private investigator?*

"Yeah, I found him in the yellow pages, in the Castro."

And that was exactly what I needed for the weekend, a private investigator to keep an eye on James while I was "at a conference." It was perfect.

"Do you have his number?"

10

The PI

I TWIDDLED THE BUSINESS CARD between my fingers. *Ed Rogers, Private Investigator.* Life really does change in an instant. Not long ago I was blissfully engaged and unaware. My life was assimilating to that long established path of marriage, babies, and happily ever after with someone I thought I knew. Instead, I'd found myself in a fake relationship, ready to hire someone to follow him undercover like some kind of criminal. Then again, what men do, what James was about to do, was a crime.

In truth, I was excited to close this chapter in my life. With any luck, the PI would be able to confirm my suspicions and this whole thing would be over. What will Holly say when she finds out I not only went through with my plan, but that her brother-in-law's best friend was the one who proved it right? The mere thought of that proposed victory tasted justifiably sweet. I picked up the phone and set up an appointment for Thursday.

"Did I just hear you make an appointment to meet a PI?" Andy asked as he swooped into my office. *Nosey much?*

"Didn't your mother ever tell you it's rude to eavesdrop?"

"So, it was a PI." He seemed proud that he solved the case. I stared at him, silently willing him to leave. "What are you up to, Marin?" he asked.

"You caught me. I hired a PI to stalk you."

"Nice try. I gotta go. You can tell me the real story later." He glanced at his watch and left my office. I shut the door behind him and dialed Telly.

"Ello, Bay-bee," she said in a bad French accent.

"You feel like getting out of town this weekend?" I asked.

"That depends. Where am I going?"

"How about we spend a couple of days at the wine country B&B and spa?"

"Oooh, sounds good. And to what do I owe this pleasure?" she asked in an even worse English accent.

"Short version? You were right about the cell phone. James thinks I'm out of town this weekend, but really I'm hiring a PI to be my eyes and ears."

"Okay, wow. Well, the answer to your first question is yes, and you can tell me the rest on the way."

"I'll book the rooms, you drive."

How exciting. Not only would I catch James cheating, but I'd also get to relax and enjoy it with Telly at the spa.

Ah, life has a funny way of working itself out sometimes.

Thursday afternoon arrived with anticipation for my meeting with the private investigator. The only knowledge I had about PIs was from movies, and I wouldn't exactly call that knowledge. That day I wore a black suit with a pencil skirt and pumps. If I had worn a fashionable 1940s hat, I could have easily been reminiscent of a bewildered woman wandering into the office of a private detective. Up on the fourth floor, a single door plaque marked his suite. Thankfully, the occasion made me feel theatrical, because I'd have to put on a convincing show for Mr. Rogers. As far as he was concerned, I was just an innocent victim of yet another philanderer. I gathered my thoughts at the door, reviewing my plan. After a deep breath, I swung open the unpredictably lightweight door and nearly took out the bookshelf that stood on the other side of it. I winced at the crashing noise, and for a second I thought I broke the door in half.

"Ms. Johns?" a voice called.

My eyes opened, the door was still intact. In front of me stood an older gentleman with an unkempt mustache and a wrinkled, collared shirt. I regained my composure and glided over to him. "Mr. Rogers, pleasure to meet you."

We shook hands and he motioned me to take a seat. His small office was packed with a messy desk, bookshelves, filing cabinets, and the smell of stale coffee. He was clearly a one-man operation.

"Would you like some coffee?" he asked, pulling out a carafe of dense black coffee.

"No, thank you." I smiled. He poured himself a cup and sat down.

"So . . ." He examined me. "You think your boyfriend's having an affair?"

My eyebrows lifted. "Unfortunately, yes."

"What makes you so sure?" he asked with an untrusting stare.

"Well, before it was just a gut feeling. You know, a woman's intuition." He raised an eyebrow at me. "Then I saw a text message on his phone from another woman saying she couldn't wait to see him this weekend and she missed him."

His face relaxed. "Well, that is disturbing."

"If I don't have hard evidence he'll only deny it. I'd spy on him myself, but I'm afraid I wouldn't be very good at it."

"And so you came to me," he said.

"Exactly."

"Well, I've had plenty of cases like yours. If there is anything to find, I'll find it. I just need to get some information, then we're in business."

"Great."

That night I packed my things for the weekend away. Dressed in my pajamas, I settled on the couch with a hot cup of tea and a new episode of my favorite doctor drama. It was about eight-thirty when there was a knock at my door. The unexpected visit startled me enough to spill some of the hot tea on my hand. *Ouch!* I rose slowly from the couch. *This better be good.*

It was James.

"Hey, what are you doing here?" I said as James came in for a big hug.

"I wanted to say goodbye before you left for the weekend."

"Oh, how sweet," I said.

"I guess you're all packed up."

"Yeah, I am," I said. *You sneaky son-of-a-bitch.* Coming over to make sure I was leaving for the weekend. Hmm, two can play that game. He only stayed for a few minutes, claiming he'd had a long day working and would see me when I got back.

Telly and I left in the afternoon for Napa, which was only about an hour away. With traffic, we'd be lucky if we made it there in two. After escaping the city, we headed up I-80. I slipped my shades on, took my shoes off, and kicked back for the ride. Telly and I updated each other on the latest news. She told me that Zack Morris finally made a move and things were getting pretty hot between the two of them. I told her all about the mysterious text and my trip to the PI's office. Forty-five minutes later the conversation ran dry, and I flipped through the radio for something appropriate or at least decent.

"Wait," Telly said before I could turn the station again. A classic eighties rock piano intro seeped through the speakers. Telly and I knew the song well. She turned it up so loud that it vibrated my chest. We rolled down the windows and sang the verse. I rocked the air guitar while Telly kept the beat on the dashboard drums.

We finally took the exit for Napa and it wasn't long before we were at the White House Inn and Spa, a white

colonial surrounded by beautiful, lush, and green land-
scaping. The foyer was equally as stunning with a wooden
staircase, intricate molding, and soft, warm lighting. My
spacious room was painted in cool beige and furnished
with dark woods. A king bed near the window was
dressed in fluffy white sheets, which swallowed me. Then
I remembered James and the reason I was swallowed up
in fluffy sheets in wine country. I sent him a quick text.

*Made it to San Diego. Having dinner with some colleagues. I'll
call you when I can.*

He quickly replied.

Ok, have a great time!

Telly met me in the foyer around seven o'clock for
dinner. We headed to Zuzu, a local tapas restaurant we
were unfamiliar with, but which came highly recommended. Zuzu had a quaint European feel, and we were seated
up on the balcony. The waiter rushed out Telly's merlot
and my pinot grigio. Everything was going fabulously.
Fabulous food, fabulous ambiance, fabulous company. I
couldn't have asked for a better girl's outing until Telly's
face turned a shade of pale.

"What's wrong?" I asked. She didn't move, only stared
behind me.

"It's Will," she said finally. I whipped my head in his
direction, wide eyed and gaping. It was Will all right. Telly's longtime on again, off again boyfriend. They met in
college when she was a freshman with newfound freedom
and he was a junior in love. When I met Telly, she and
Will were on the outs of their latest relationship. I only
met him a couple of times, but Telly told me about every

fight, every break up, and every incredible make-up sex session.

He spotted us and stood. His approach made me nervous, but was probably nothing compared to Telly, who had regained her composure and smiled like she hadn't missed a beat of our fabulous time. Will was tall with wavy, brown hair and a sexy five o'clock shadow. He wore a tailored blue suit, light grey shirt that was unbuttoned at the top, and a very expensive watch.

"Well, if it isn't Chantell Torres," he said standing over us. Telly stood to greet him and he kissed her cheek.

"Hi, Will."

"You look gorgeous," he said. Telly looked away, blushing a little. "What brings you to Napa?"

"Marin and I decided to get away from the city for the weekend." He took his eyes off of Telly just long enough to acknowledge my presence.

"Of course, Marin. How are you?" he asked and shook my hand.

"Very well, thank you."

He nodded cordially, then reverted his undivided attention back to Telly. "So, where are you staying?" He inched closer to Telly. *Sniff, sniff.* Smells like trouble.

"We're at the White House Inn," she said.

"You're kidding." He beamed. "I'm staying there too."

Well, well, look at that. Telly was having herself a little reunion, and I'd be going to bed alone while my pretend boyfriend cheated on me. My getaway fell sour.

"Is that right?" Telly responded without an ounce of excitement or interest. "Maybe I'll see you around."

"Yeah, I'm having dinner with some prospects, but if you want to have a drink later I'd love to catch up."

"Sure, I'll let you know." She brushed him off like a pro, but he handed her his business card.

"It was great running into you, Telly," he said, stars apparent in his eyes. She gave a tight smile and he walked back to his table, gazing at Telly before he sat down. Telly downed her merlot like it was a shot of tequila.

"I'm gonna need another one of these," she said, catching her breath from the long gulp.

"Are you okay?" I asked.

"I'm fine," she said with an increased tone. I didn't know if she was trying to prove it to me or to herself. Probably both.

"Are you gonna meet him later?" I asked. She shrugged and looked away.

We spent the rest of the evening engaging in our usual Telly-Marin banter. She managed to steal a few glances at Will. The first time I brought it to her attention she seemed annoyed, so I ignored it the rest of the night. We headed back to the Inn and to our respective rooms, both of us tired from the workweek and tipsy from the wine.

The silence of wine country allowed for a restful sleep. The next morning, I wandered out to the pool to meet Telly for breakfast. She hid behind the Chronicle, sipping her coffee, and eating eggs and bacon. Her wine country chic ensemble included white shorts, a navy blue top, and her signature dark shades. I was more on the side of sleepy-chic with my heather gray yoga pants and white zip up hoodie. We ate our breakfast, enjoying the view of the tranquil pool, full-bloom gardens, and the cool gentle breeze.

"So, what are we doing today?" Telly asked.

"We have a massage and facial at eleven, lunch, then tonight we're going to a wine tasting party."

"Oh, nice," she said and let out a big yawn.

"Late night?" I asked.

"No, not really." Hmm . . .

"You seem a little tired, thought maybe you met up with Will." Her silence was incriminating "Did you hook up with Will last night?" I asked in a whisper. She blushed.

"Okay, fine, I met him out here for one drink. Big deal," she said like I caught her taking one cookie from the cookie jar. But, Telly's not one for moderation.

"Is that all?" I said.

"Yeah. We talked and he kissed me goodnight." She buried her head deeper into her newspaper.

"Aw, that's sweet, Telly. Now what?" I asked.

"What do you mean?"

"Are you going to see him again?"

"I don't know. Maybe if I run into him in the city."

"So that's it, huh?"

"That's it."

"Good for you. Get in and get out."

"Any word from your PI?" she asked, strategically changing the subject.

"Not yet. I don't know if that's a good sign or a bad sign."

"Well, let's forget about the guys for today and enjoy ourselves, okay?"

"Okay," I said and leaned back in my chair, gazing quietly over the garden.

There was something about getting a body massage and skin pampering that made life feel easy breezy. I forgot about Chad, about James, and about all the troubles of my recent life. For a short time, I could just let go. Telly and I were fully refreshed when we arrived at a nearby vineyard for a wine tasting.

It was held at a Victorian cottage with a wraparound deck adorned in twinkle lights and candles. There was an impressive spread of Mediterranean foods and, of course, lots and lots of wine. Each sip of wine was more unique and intoxicating than the last. I was feeling a little tipsy, so I went to the hors d'oeuvre table to fill my stomach. Then, I felt a vibration in my purse. It was the private investigator.

"Hi, Mr. Rogers. How's everything?" I asked.

"Well that depends."

"What do you mean?" I asked.

"How do you feel about tall blondes spending the night at your boyfriend's house?" I felt my heart drop deep into the pit of my stomach. *That son-of-a-bitch is actually cheating on me.*

"Do you have proof?" I asked.

"Pictures. I'll email them to you along with the report. I'm so sorry, Ms. Marin. You were right."

"Thank you." I put down the phone, grabbed the closest glass of wine, and downed it. Telly was talking with a salt-and-pepper gentleman when she spotted me and excused herself immediately.

"Are you okay?" she asked.

"I just got a call from the PI."

"And?" I didn't have to say anything my silence was answer enough.

"Unfucking believable," she said. "Come on, we're going back to the city to shove it in his tiny little dick hole." She tugged my arm to leave, but I planted my feet.

"No, no. We're here. We're having a good time. We leave in the morning. There's no reason to spoil the night."

"Are you sure?" she asked.

"Absolutely."

"Are you sure you're okay?"

"Yes," I said, forcing a smile. "Besides we knew this was gonna happen. It happens to everyone."

As much as I wanted to believe what I was saying and relish in being right, I couldn't. Instead, I felt singled out. The harsh truth was settling in once again. When it came to my own cheating boyfriends, real or fake, I was still on a learning curve. I snagged another glass of wine.

Telly and I made our way through the crowd, mixing and mingling with nearly everyone. We were laughing and joking, flirting with cute guys, and of course indulging in some of the best wine I'd ever tasted. The more wine I had, the more relaxed I felt, and the more I forgot about what I would have to deal with when I got home.

The next morning I woke up to a knock at my door and a roaring sensation of being knocked over the head with three bottles of wine. I stumbled to the door, praying the knocking would stop.

"Who is it?" I called, trying to rub the ache out of my head.

"It's Telly." I let her in and returned to the bed as soon as my feet could carry me back.

"I feel like shit," I groaned and covered my eyes.

"I thought you might. It's ten o'clock."

"What?" I shot up and looked at the clock. It was almost time to check out and head back to the city. "Did I miss breakfast?"

"Pretty much. I brought you some toast and Excedrin." I leaned back on my pillow and began nibbling on the toast.

"No coffee?" I said. She revealed a Venti-size coffee cup.

"You're my best," I said and took the cup from her.

"What are you going to do when you see James?" she asked. I shook my head.

"I'm not sure. Part of me wants to tell him the truth, but I think I have to keep playing the trusting girlfriend."

"You are going to break up with him, right?"

"Yeah, but I'm hoping to inspire some serious guilt."

"Did the PI get pictures or video?"

"Yeah."

"Good, if you don't have proof they will turn the story around on you like that." And she snapped her fingers.

"That reminds me, he sent a report." I went over to my laptop and logged onto my email. There it was. The subject read, *Johns Report 1-1*. I clicked it open to see the file and used the password Li214 to open the attachment. The report accounted for both Friday and Saturday. According to the PI's description, James and an unidentified blonde woman arrived at his house by a dark blue SUV around six in the evening. They left the house together by foot at seven-thirty, not returning until after nine. Neither was seen leaving the house again until ten the next morning.

I scrolled down and saw about ten pictures of the two of them coming and going. Some of the pictures showed them walking arm-in-arm. One of them looked like he was kissing the side of her face. None of the pictures showed them kissing mouth to mouth, but the fact that she didn't leave his house all night was a sure sign they'd spent the night together. The evidence was clear. I uploaded the photos to a one-hour print shop and packed my things to go home.

I was so angry with James, angry that he was such a good liar, so deceptive that it made me sick. The need for retaliation surfaced, even if it was just a kick in his balls. He certainly deserved it. At the same time, I felt relieved. My mission had been accomplished, and I could finally move on from the trouble that had plagued me since the night I came home from Las Vegas. Then, I was sad. My operation was exciting and dangerous. It gave me a sense of passion that I hadn't felt in so long. Now, it was over.

The drive home was quiet. The pounding from my headache subsided and was replaced by the pounding of my thoughts. Telly dropped me off at my apartment after we picked up the prints. Aside from the news of the report, it had been a really great weekend away with my best friend. A peak into the new life I was going to lead.

I flipped through the pictures, contemplating confronting him immediately or later. My guess was the woman might still be at his apartment, and I was ready to catch him in the act. My pulse quickened as I went up the stairs to his building. Someone was leaving the building, which allowed me to walk right in without having to buzz him from outside. Even better, I could really surprise him now. Bastard. Every step I took fueled my rage more and more until finally I made it. I banged my fist against the door hard and loud. Marvin barked like a ferocious beast on the other side. James answered.

"Marin!" he said surprised. I pushed past him into the apartment and looked around. No sight of anyone.

"You're back early," he said.

"I have to talk to you," I said. James shut the door.

"Everything okay?" he asked. I looked up the stairs and there I saw a leggy blonde in shorts and a tank top. My jaw dropped. As dumb blondes go, she took the cake. I mean what kinda girl on the side walks downstairs when the girlfriend comes home. She smiled, which infuriated me. I glared at James, but he started leading me toward her.

"Marin, this is my sister, Amanda. She's visiting from New York," James said.

I turned to him, then to her.

She beamed and stuck out her hand. "Marin, it's so nice to finally meet you. James' told me so much about you," she said.

I gaped, breathless, as I shook her hand. *Amanda? His sister? Huh?* It was not what I expected when I stomped over. I was too quiet for too long, so I conjured a bright smile.

"James' sister, Amanda! Wow, what an unexpected surprise."

"I wasn't sure if it was too early to introduce you to my family. So when you said you had a conference in San Diego this weekend, I took that as a sign to keep it quiet," James said. It made sense, the text, the embracing walk, the unmentioned visit. It all added up.

"Well, I'm sorry to have barged in on your visit," I said feeling stupid, but also excited to continue my feat.

"No, I'm glad you came by," James said.

"How long are you in town?" I asked Amanda.

"I leave in the morning," she replied.

"Oh that's too bad, now that we've only just met."

"Why don't you have dinner with us tonight?" she said.

"No, I don't want to intrude."

"You won't be. It'll be fun," James said. I looked at Amanda who, for some reason, wouldn't stop smiling.

"Okay, sure. What time?"

11

Family Ties

I MET JAMES AND AMANDA AT BACCO, an Italian restaurant that Amanda was fond of. We shared a nice bottle of wine and Amanda told me all about her life in Albany. She was a patent attorney who lived with her husband Evan and their four-year-old daughter, Addison.

"So, what was James like growing up?" I asked.

"Well, for a long time he was the baby," she said, as the oldest by four years, "and he followed me and Andrea around all the time. If we were playing hide and seek, he wanted to play hide and seek. If we were playing dolls, he wanted to play with dolls too." James' cheeks were freshly flushed.

"Dolls huh?" I turned to James. He cleared his throat robustly.

"I was really little."

"He was adorable and so polite too. He was a football star in high school, but was friends with everyone. Now look at him, a successful physical therapist living in San Francisco with a beautiful girlfriend," Amanda said.

I smiled at James who was still blushing.

"But," she said, looking at James. "You'll always be my little brother." She leaned over and gently rubbed his cheek.

My phone buzzed. It was Telly for the second time in ten minutes. I ignored her call again.

"How come Andrea didn't come visit too?" I asked.

"She's stationed in Australia," James said.

"Stationed?"

"She's an officer in the military. She's up for orders pretty soon. Hopefully back to the states," Amanda said.

"Oh, wow," I said.

James and I had a lot of conversations, but never talked much about family. Maybe that was my fault. I usually avoided the subject of family so I didn't have to talk about my own.

"I talked to her last week on Skype," James mentioned to Amanda.

"Oh, yeah, I talked to her earlier in the week too."

"It's nice to see you're all so close," I said with an adoring smile, but feeling a little jealous that I didn't have the same fuzzy feelings about my family. I loved them all very much, but close was not a word I would use to describe our relationship.

"Do you have any brothers or sisters, Marin?" Amanda asked.

"An older brother," I said and took a sip of my wine.

"Does he live close?"

"Yeah, about forty-five minutes."

"That's nice. You must see each other all the time."

"Not too much, holidays mostly. He's very busy." I smiled, hoping she would drop the topic, but nope.

"Oh, what does he do?"

"Cancer research."

"Fascinating. You must be so proud of him," she leaned in and batted her eyelashes.

"Couldn't be prouder." *Not!* I forced a smile. Telly called again. It was a welcome interruption and I excused myself to the ladies room and huddled in a stall.

"What's up, Telly?" I whispered.

"Why are you whispering?"

"I'm in the bathroom at Bacco. I'm having dinner with James and his sister."

"What the fuck! Didn't you confront him about the other woman?" she asked.

"His sister is the other woman."

"Eww, gross. Incest?" she said.

"No, Tell. His sister is the girl in the pictures. She's visiting from New York. That's why they were so close and she stayed at his apartment."

"Holy shit! Are you serious? That means he didn't cheat on you."

"Nope."

"Well, I guess it's still game on." Yeah, but hanging out with James' wasn't a game I wanted to play.

"So what's up? Why did you call a dozen times?" I stepped out of the stall.

"Oh, uh . . . you got a second?" Her tone changed

from aggressive to passive.

"Yeah."

"So, yeah . . . I kinda slept with Will the other night," Telly said.

"I knew it. You're such a liar," I said.

"I know. I'm sorry, but listen. He's calling me to go out again. I don't know what to do," she whined. In every other area in her life she was levelheaded and in control, but when it came to matters of the heart, her sense was somehow missing.

"No, Telly. How many times have you done this to yourself?"

"I don't know. Four or five?" she said as if to downplay their number of breakups. Before I could say another word, Amanda walked in.

"I gotta go, Telly. I'll call you later," I said.

"No, wait! Marin, you need to—"

I ended the call and looked up at Amanda. "Hey."

"Hey," she said and walked to the sink. "I came in to check on you. You've been gone for a while." She ran her hands under the running faucet.

"Yeah, my friend's having a little crisis." I held up my phone and shrugged.

"I'm sure it's nothing you can't handle." She smiled.

I joined her at the sink. "I hope so."

"From what James tells me you're a good friend and good girlfriend too."

"He said that?" I asked keeping my head down. I couldn't look her in the face.

"He really likes you, you know? It's kind of a big deal.

He's not the type who's eager to give his heart away." That makes two of us. "James is a really good guy, and I've seen him get hurt before. Be careful with him, okay?"

"Okay." I smiled with a shrug as if I had no intention of being reckless with him. Why did she feel the need to tell me that? Was it a courtesy to me or to James? Could she see through my façade? Or was she just being a protective big sister? Whatever the case, she made me uneasy.

Later when James dropped me off at my apartment, I told Amanda it was nice to meet her, and I hoped we could meet again sometime soon. I was being polite, of course. The late hour and unexpected events of the day were exhausting, and I couldn't wait to be alone in my apartment.

I called Telly on the way to work to find out what she did about the infamous Will.

"I went out with him last night," Telly said, as if it was no big deal.

"What?" I stopped in my tracks. It was one thing for her to have a little reunion fling in Napa, but it was quite another to start seeing him on the home front.

"Telly, why did you do that?"

"You hung up on me remember? I needed you to talk me out of it." For a lawyer it was a terrible defense.

"You're really gonna have to start listening to your own good conscience."

"Too late now."

"What happened?"

"We kinda had sex," she said.

"What?" I stopped in my tracks again. At the rate I

was going, I'd never make it to work.

"I know, I know," Telly whined.

"You know I'm all for you having these flings, but if you told me any ounce of truth about you and Will, then this is a very dangerous venture."

"I know. What's wrong with me? Why can't I tell him no?"

"Because you haven't learned your lesson yet."

Telly let out a frustrated grunt.

"Do you want to learn it all over again?" I asked.

"No," she said.

"Well then, you can't see him anymore. Say you won't see him again." Silence hung on the line. "Telly?"

"Okay. I won't see him anymore."

"Good, problem solved." I approached my office building and quickly realized there was a huge crowd standing outside. My vision expanded revealing several police cars and a fire truck.

"Telly, hold on a sec." I took the phone away from my ear. "What's going on?" I asked a woman standing in the crowd.

She turned to me and said, "A fire broke out on the fourth floor."

"Oh, my God! Was anyone hurt?" I asked.

"A couple people were taken to the hospital. I think they're okay. Probably smoke inhalation." I could hear Telly trying to get my attention by yelling through the phone, and I put it back up to my ear.

"There was a fire in my building," I said.

"How bad?" she asked.

"I can't tell. Doesn't seem too bad."

"Any cute firemen?"

I looked around, spying a small group of San Francisco's finest. "Yep." I smirked.

"I'll be right there." Telly hung up without an ounce of sarcasm. Before I could get her back Katie appeared at my side, worry covered her face.

"Are you okay?" I asked.

"Yeah. I arrived just as the fire truck did." We stared up at the building, looking for some indication of the condition of our office.

"So now what?" I asked.

"We go home. They shut the building down for today. It could be the whole week."

"Oh, no," I said. "What about our appointments?"

"You better start calling your patients. I'll call you when we can go back to work." Katie seemed annoyed at the situation. On the outside I sympathized with her, but on the inside I was excited and relieved to get an extra day to myself. My relaxing weekend away turned out to be somewhat stressful. I peered over the crowd, wondering if everyone else was secretly thrilled about getting to close up shop for the day. Then, I spotted a familiar face. Telly was schmoozing a group of firemen. I made my way to her, noting the increasing waves of laughter with each step. She was obviously laying on her lucky charms and they thought she was delicious.

"Marin!" She waved me over. "This is my best friend, Marin. Marin, this is Jake, Doug, and Sebastian." She pointed to one smitten fireman after the other. They gawked at her as she handed each of them her business card. "If you need a divorce attorney, I'm your girl!"

They turned back to stare at Telly every few steps as they returned to their truck.

"How did you get here so fast?" I asked.

"I was on my way to the office only a couple of blocks away."

"When you said you'd be right there, I thought you were kidding," I said. Telly stared at the suited-up firemen still loading into the truck.

"Sweetie, San Francisco firemen are no joke."

"You feel like playing hooky?" I smiled and did a playful dance.

"Wish I could. Hey, maybe I can start a fire in my office?"

I let out a small chuckle and told her to catch up with me later. Not knowing what to do with a whole day to myself, I decided to treat it like a Saturday. I cancelled my appointments, picked up groceries for the week, then went for a long invigorating jog around the park. The US Half Marathon was still months away, but with my recovering knee I needed all the preparation I could get. Before I knew it, it was three in the afternoon and I had nothing left to do. I settled on my couch with the paper and a glass of iced tea. I had just gotten comfortable when I heard it, *Drip, Drip, Drip.*

The sound of a leaky faucet.

Thinking I probably didn't shut the water off all the way, I went over to the kitchen to investigate. The faucet was all the way off, which meant it was a leak that needed to be fixed. No problem, right? Wrong. Not only did I not know anything about fixing faucets, but my landlord always took his sweet time getting to repairs. I once spent two weeks without a working stove, causing me to gain five pounds from all the take out I was forced to eat.

No way I was going to let the sound of dripping water disrupt my sleep and run up my water bill. Holly was handy and so was Chad, but both were completely unavailable to me. Then I remembered . . . I have a boyfriend. I picked up the phone to call my beau. Since I had yet to catch him in the sack with someone else, I figured I might as well take advantage of the situation.

"Hey, you. What's going on?" He sounded happy to hear from me.

"I need your help with something."

"Sure, what is it?" he asked eagerly.

"My kitchen faucet is leaking. Do you think you could help me fix it?"

"Yeah, no problem. I'll come over after work and bring dinner too."

"What a relief. Thank you so much." I couldn't hate the fact that he was so accommodating.

I turned on some music to disguise the dripping sound, then read until James came over, which he did promptly at five-thirty. When I answered the door he held a bag of takeout in one hand and a tool bag in the other. He wore jeans and a grey t-shirt that hugged his swelling biceps.

"Dinner and a wrench. You're my hero." I smiled and gave him a little kiss as he walked in.

"I prefer the title Awesome Boyfriend," he said as he set the food on the breakfast bar.

"I suppose that works too."

He walked over to the sink and I followed. "What seems to be the problem?"

"I'm not sure. It's dripping constantly," I said as I unloaded the food. He examined the faucet and quickly came to a diagnosis.

"It just needs a washer."

"Let's eat first," I said.

"I'll take care of this first. It'll only take a few minutes," he said. I didn't know much about sinks, but I would be impressed if he could fix it that fast. He turned off the water and then took apart the faucet.

"So, Amanda really likes you." His voice was muffled from under the sink.

"Oh, yeah? I really like her too." I set the table, having a flashback of the conversation with Amanda in the bathroom.

"So when am I going to meet your brother?"

I shuddered at the suggestion. "You want to meet Michael?" I asked, hoping I misunderstood.

"Well, yeah." Who was this guy? Usually women are begging their boyfriends to meet their family and here he was offering himself on a silver platter.

"He's really busy, you know, trying to cure cancer. But I'll see if we can get together with him."

"That sounds good." He turned the faucet on and began washing his hands.

"You're finished?" I said in disbelief.

"Yeah, check it out. I told you it would only be a few minutes."

I examined the faucet. No leak. Impressive. I looked up into his striking blue eyes and said, "Thank you."

"You're welcome," he said, and then he kissed me.

We talked over dinner, and I told him all about the fire in my building and the "conference" in San Diego. He told me about the weekend with his sister. I was half listening and half surveying my apartment for things that needed fixing. If James was going to continue to be "faithful," then I might as well get some use out of him, which I did later in my bed. He didn't stay the night since we both had to be up early for work. At least that's what I thought.

Not long after waking, I got a call from Katie. The building wasn't yet ready to return to. It would've been nice to sleep in a little that morning since I didn't have to be at the office, but once I'm awake, I'm up. Repeating my same Saturday routine, I was done by ten. I rested on my couch with a cup of coffee that tasted like a little piece of heaven and contemplated going to the library, a museum, or Crate and Barrel. Then, my thoughts drifted to the conversation I had with James about meeting my brother.

There wasn't much point in James meeting Michael. After all, I knew eventually the "relationship" would end and my brother would see it as another one of my failed relationships. It'd be another reason to get crap from him and my parents.

Truth be told, I hadn't seen Michael since Christmas and the only correspondence I'd had with him was a brief call when I told him that the wedding was off. It wasn't the greatest of talks, but one thing about Michael, he was incredibly honest. I decided to rent a car and make the drive to Berkeley to surprise my cancer-curing brother.

"I'm looking for Dr. Johns," I asked the medical assistant behind the reception area.

"And you are?" she asked with her lips pursed and eyebrow raised.

"Dr. Marin Johns," said an unmistakable voice behind me. I turned and sure enough it was Michael. He was only a couple years older, but the years had been good to him. With his job, two kids, and a wife, I was amazed that he managed to keep his dark wavy hair combed let alone perfect. But that was Michael for you, the brains and the beauty. He towered over me for as long as I could remember and his almond shaped brown eyes stared down at me, looking surprised.

"Hey, big brother. How are you?" We engaged in an awkward hug.

"I've got two sick kids at home, a series of paper cuts on my left hand, and I have the medical board up my ass about budgets. What brings you all the way up here?" he asked with little patience. *Nice to see you too.*

"Just wanted to visit. I haven't seen you in months," I said.

"That's it? You came all the way here just to visit?"

He gave me the same look I'd seen a million times, a look that diminished me. It was so easy for him to make me feel like his ridiculous little sister, with her silly counseling job, in her tiny apartment, and husband-less existence.

"Yeah." I cowered.

"That's too bad, because I'm really busy. You want to visit? Come up on Fourth of July weekend." And just like that, he started to walk away. The nerve of him. If I thought it would do any good, I would have called up our mother to tell on him right then. I followed with a little more stomp in my step.

"What? Michael, I drove all this way and you can't even spend five minutes with me? You didn't even ask me how I was since, I don't know, the last time we talked I told you my wedding was off." My voice started doing that high-pitched, neurotic, nagging thing I hate. Surely, he hated it too.

"What do you want me to say? Chad was a douche, and I never use that word. You're better off," he said.

I stopped in the middle of the hallway and felt my cheeks get hot, and a tear surfaced.

"Wow, you really don't give a shit about me, do you?" I said in a much more severe, low voice. He paused about five feet ahead of me and dropped his head. His eyes rolled when he turned to me.

"Don't be ridiculous, Marin. You want to talk, then come here."

He grabbed my arm and ushered me into a lab room entryway. He handed me some sterile medical clothing where we dressed and washed our hands before entering a lab. The first thing I noticed was a wall of caged mice or rats. I really didn't know the difference. Michael's younger lab assistant sat at a large workstation in the middle of the room mixing chemicals with droppers and tubes.

"So this is where you work?" I said looking around and squinting at the bright lights.

"Most of the time." He looked over some of the rat cages and wrote a couple of notes.

"Is there a place we can talk alone?" I asked him, quietly hoping that his intensely working assistant couldn't hear me.

"Hey, Chase," Michael called out to the assistant whose trance was broken by the sound of my brother's voice. "Take a lunch." Chase put down what he was doing and left the lab.

"Is that better?" he asked. I sighed and sat down at the workstation, watching Michael work. Maybe it wasn't the best idea to disrupt his day. If he were a plumber or architect it would be different, but he was trying to save lives. I didn't really long for quality time with Michael. I had a question to ask. With all the information I was getting and all that I was experiencing, I knew if I could trust anyone to give me a straight, unbiased, brutally honest opinion it would be Michael. If I came out and asked him point blank he'd be offended, so I opted for a little embellishment.

"I'm writing an article about modern marriages, and I wanted to ask you a couple of questions." He looked reluctant. "In the name of research," I added. He didn't consider my line of work science, but I was hoping he would approve since current research meant a great deal to him.

"Okay," he said.

"First question, have you ever been unfaithful to Jennifer?" I asked. His head whipped in my direction.

"What?" He scoffed. I guess he wasn't expecting that.

"Come on, Michael. It's a simple question." I stood firm, but he looked annoyed.

"No," he said and turned to the caged rats.

"Bullshit!"

"Excuse me?" Michael looked back at me with a twisted expression.

"I think you're lying." I crossed my arms and darted my eyes. He just rolled his.

"Did Jennifer put you up to this?" he asked.

"No, does she have a reason to?"

"I don't have time for this. You have to go." He began steering me out of the lab, but I planted my feet.

"I knew it. You're brave enough to step out on your wife, but too cowardly to admit it."

"Where's this coming from?" he asked.

"Just forget it. I should've known I couldn't count on you for an honest fucking answer," I said and hit the exit button at the lab door. Hurrying down the hall with a ball of anger welling up inside me, I was almost as heated as the moment I caught Chad. Then it all came back to me. The disappointment from knowing that there were no honest men. As soon as I got to the elevator, that anger turned into despair, and then came the tears.

12

In The Mood For A Melody

MY TEARS FELL ALL THE WAY HOME from Berkeley. I felt the pain from my broken heart all over again. So much had changed, and I was starting not to recognize myself. Who did I think I was barging in on my brother's busy afternoon and asking him such a personal question? That wasn't me. It wasn't like me to pretend to be someone's girlfriend and play games to prove a point either. I was ashamed, an emotion I wasn't counting on to surface for my actions. Sure, I had my reasons, but even if they were good reasons did that make them right? Was my deception so different than Chad's was or James' would be? Was I really better or more honest than either of them?

I wished I still lived in my perfect little world, wearing my rose colored glasses. Then again, it was naivety that led me to such a dark place, and I wondered if the world would ever be right again. Would I ever find someone to love and respect, who could love and respect me back the same?

If cheating had always plagued relationships, then why weren't more wives and girlfriends calling men out on it? Women share the most personal details of their lives with each other, but it's rare to hear of an affair, and when you do it's a big deal. If they're not talking about it, they're in denial. If all men were unfaithful, and I had such a problem with infidelity then I'd have to settle for being alone. I wasn't about to subject myself to a life of looking the other way. I couldn't. Call me righteous, crazy, or morally sound, but I couldn't pretend that everything was perfect when it wasn't. Even if it meant giving up a husband, a family, and a house in the suburbs. I'd have to forge on and live with the outcome of my findings.

All the downtime made me think unnecessarily, and I gladly welcomed the distractions that work provided when we returned to the office the next day. Through the course of the day, I felt more and more unsettled about what had happened with Michael.

I called his cell. After about five rings, it was clear he wasn't going to pick up. Yep, voicemail.

"Michael, it's me. I'm sorry about the way things ended with us yesterday. It wasn't my intention to upset you. I just needed your insight on a subject, and I thought I could count on your honesty." This was awkward, trying to be tactful and not sound as guilty as I felt. *Keep it simple, Marin.* "Call me back if you want to talk."

I took a deep breath and instantly felt better. It was short lived. A few minutes later, my phone rang. I jumped and my heart skipped a beat at the thought of Michael calling me back to talk about things. Instead, it was Rachel.

"Marin! Oh, my God. I feel like I haven't talked to you in so long!" Rachel screamed with excitement.

"Well, I'm sure you've been busy, being a new wife and all."

"Yeah, things have been a little crazy. But now that school's out, I have a whole summer to fill."

"What's going on?" I asked, but really wanted to say, *what do you want?*

"I feel like I've waited a fair amount of time. It's been almost two months, and I want to go on a double date with you and James." *Uh Oh.*

"What did you have in mind?"

"Friday night, MicX," she said like it was the hottest thing.

"Is that a restaurant?"

"It's a dueling piano bar. I went a few weeks ago with my girlfriends and had a blast."

"Sounds good. Would you mind if we made it a triple date and brought Telly?" I figured with another couple we'd be less likely to have deep couple on couple chats where the whole conversation was in "wes."

"Yeah, bring her. We'll meet you there at eight."

What did I agree to? A night out with my real friends and my fake boyfriend. It was easy to play the role with James, but a lot harder to pretend with everyone else. Call back. Cancel. No, there was no escaping it. At least Telly would know the truth, and I'd be free to look over to her for reassurance any time throughout the night. That was if I could convince her to go.

With a good hour to kill before my next appointment, I went to the kitchen to make myself a cup of tea. On my way, I noticed Andy reorganizing his bookshelf. I popped my head in.

"What are you up to?" I said. He turned to me briefly, then back at his bookshelf.

"Just trying to de-clutter. You need something?" he asked with his back turned.

"No, just wasting time."

He whipped his chair around to face me. "Oh, yeah?" he said and motioned me to sit. "Something on your mind?"

"My mind's always going. Just like yours."

He smirked.

I took my seat across from him. "Actually, there's something I want to get your opinion on."

"Okay."

"Will all men cheat?"

He stared right at me without blinking an eye. "Why are you asking?" He leaned back in his chair with his hands steepled in front of him. He looked suspicious of me.

"Come on Andy, I'm not asking you as a therapist. I'm asking you as a man." I could tell he was trying to get inside my head, as he always was.

"And as a man, I want to know why you're asking." This surprised me, because Andy usually took any question or comment and used it as an excuse to talk for ten minutes. Instead, he was responding to my question with a question. Clearly this cheating-man truth thing really was for a privileged few to know.

"It seems the longer I work with couples, the more I discover how frequent infidelity is among men." It wasn't a false statement entirely, just a bit exaggerated.

"Well the answer to your question is yes," he said.

"I knew it," I said in a victorious whisper. He shrugged. "Why is it such a secret?"

"It's no secret. I mean, yes, the specific occasions are often kept secret, but the fact itself is widely known. Don't you already know this stuff?"

"Yes, but statistics say about sixty percent of men cheat, not one hundred percent. I've always subscribed to the dads and cads theory, sixty percent are cads, forty percent are dads."

"You want to know the real difference between dads and cads?" he asked.

I nodded.

"Dads don't get the right opportunity to cheat, and so they're faithful by default. They're no better or more special than the cads. Because dads and cads are all men and men are biologically inclined to spread their seed. You can't blame 'em, Mother Nature designed it that way."

"We're not wild animals, we were born with a sense of morality. Why can't they choose to be faithful in the face of opportunity?" I wasn't trying to debate him because I knew what he said was true. And for the first time in our four years as colleagues, I actually agreed with him. He took a moment as if mentally putting himself in a situation to choose fidelity over infidelity. I saw his dark eyes light up.

"Because they don't want to. Haven't you ever looked temptation in the face, known it was wrong, said *fuck it,* and did it anyway?"

I tried to look back at the various temptations in my life—one too many drinks, one too many cookies, one too few condoms. I made careless mistakes in the past, but I couldn't think about any vows or major promises broken either.

"It's not the same thing," I said.

He walked over to me. "Yes, it is." He put his hand on my shoulder and led me out of his office. "It's called being human. We all have good and bad in us, so you better get used to the idea. We work in therapy for God's sake."

Once I was safely outside of his office, I opened my mouth to get in another point.

"I have an appointment," he said. And he closed the door. Figures, the one time I actually wanted to continue a conversation with Andy, he shut me out.

A couple of phone calls and a couple of days later, James and I met Rachel and David at the dueling piano bar. The music was so loud that I could hear the bass of the pianos pounding through my entire body. They were playing a classic 70s rock piano song. The dim lit bar was huge, the stage front and center. Two guys sitting at two baby grand pianos played in unison and sang loudly into their mics. The audience sang as loudly and drunkenly back. Rachel found an empty table toward the back of the bar. Telly was nowhere to be found. Fashionably late as usual.

David and James were at the bar, getting our drinks, when Rachel leaned over to me and shouted in my ear, "How are things with you and James?"

I put my face close to her ear and shouted, "Fine."

"I've never seen him with a girl before. He must think you are really something." She smiled big like a beauty pageant contestant.

"That's nice of you to say."

She shot up out of her chair. "Telly!" she called and waved her arms wildly. Telly was with Will. I was quite puzzled considering the last time we spoke she agreed to stop seeing him. But was I really surprised? No. Telly introduced Will to Rachel, and Will and I greeted each other with slight familiarity. He joined the guys at the bar and a beaming Telly sat next to me.

"This place is really cool. Why haven't we come here before?" Telly asked.

I was straight faced. "What?" she frowned.

"You know what. What is he doing here?" I kept my stern look, as if I had some kind of authority.

She gave me an unsure shrug. "I like spending time with him." My stare persisted. "It's not serious. We're just having fun."

If it were any other guy I might have chosen to believe her, but this guy had a special hold over her. One I had only heard of, but would now get to experience first hand.

"It's all fun and games until someone gets hurt," I said

raising a single eyebrow.

"Relax, Marin. It's fine."

"What are you guys talking about?" Rachel asked, trying to lean in between us.

Telly and I smiled. "Nothing."

The guys returned to the table with beers, wine, and cocktails. I was thankful we were on a group date that didn't require much talk. Instead, we sipped our drinks and listened as they played one familiar song after the other. The more we drank, the more we sang along, and within an hour we were all shout-singing and playing air piano, which I never knew existed until then.

James leaned in. "I can't believe how much fun this is!"

"I know." And I actually meant it. With the mask of booze and loud music it was easy to play the part. I took a big gulp of my margarita and heard an intro to a classic song that filled me with excitement. Telly and I turned to each other with huge grins.

"I love this song," James said.

"Me too!" I shouted.

"You wanna dance?"

"Yeah."

James grabbed my hand, and we rushed over to the bar where there was just enough room for us to snag a spot. We swayed to the music, singing to each other. I didn't know if it was the song or the drinks, but in that moment with James, I was able to let all of the stress, the cheating, the lying, and the pretending go. I felt free as a bird as he spun me around on the dance floor. In the blur of the song and the dance, I saw Telly, Will, David, and Rachel out on the dance floor with us.

For the first time in a long time, I was truly enjoying myself. I slowly looked at the faces of those I shared the moment with and noticed there was one important face missing. Holly. We hadn't spoken in so long, and I was starting to forget what it was like having her around all the time. I missed her and felt guilty that I hadn't thought of her much since she'd been gone. Back at our table, I sat beside Rachel.

"Have you heard from Holly?" I asked.

"Not since that email she sent everyone a few weeks ago."

"I wish she was here now," I said, feeling a little tear surfacing.

"Me too." Rachel pouted her lip trying to sympathize with me. I forced a smile and she returned it.

"I need another drink," I shouted. James kissed my face and headed to the bar.

Within another hour, I had consumed three more drinks. I was lit to say the least. David and Rachel were near the bar, dancing to the piano version of a 90s hip-hop song, Telly was in the ladies room, and James was getting another beer for himself. It was good 'ole Will and me. Throughout the night, I tried to ignore his presence or at least my preconceived notions about his presence. But I was drunk and feeling ballsy.

"What do you think you're doing?" I shouted at him over the music.

"What?" He cupped his ear.

"What do you think you're doing? With Telly?" I shouted louder. He twisted his expression.

"What do you mean?"

"I mean, I know all about your history together, how you've mistreated her in the past. Probably cheated on her a few times. I'm not gonna sit back and watch you hurt her again."

"It's not my intention to hurt her."

"Save it, Will. You might be fooling her, but you're not fooling me." I sat back in my chair, arms crossed. Will leaned over, but I wouldn't look at his face.

"I know we don't know each other very well, but believe it or not, I care a lot about her." I rolled my eyes.

"How can she ever trust you?" I yelled, then Telly appeared to my right.

"What's going on?" she asked, looking really concerned.

"Nothing," Will said as he sat back in his seat.

"Not nothing!" I shouted and stood up. Everyone returned to our table just in time for the show.

"He's a liar, Telly. Can't you see that?" I blurted out while a diminishing sober voice inside of me screamed *shut up, SHUT UP!* "They're all liars, every single one of them." Not only had I lost my inhibition, but I had lost control. There I was making a scene in front of everyone and I couldn't stop it.

"Why can't you tell her the truth?" I said to Will. He glanced around at everyone with a disbelieving expression as if to say I was being ridiculous.

"Marin, what's going on?" James asked.

Telly grabbed hold of me, and pulled me away from the table, toward the bathroom. She ordered me to sit on the counter while she put cool, wet paper towels on my neck and blotted my forehead with them.

"Shit, Marin. I know you don't like Will, but you have to pull yourself together," she said.

My stomach churned, and I hopped off the counter and ran into the stall. There was no time to shut the door before I started yakking into the toilet. Telly came in after me and held my hair away from my face.

"Oh, God." She grimaced.

When I was finished, Telly helped me back to the sink where I washed my hands and splashed cold water on my face. My head felt a little clearer, but my heart filled with regret. Why had I said those things to Will in front of everyone? When did the night turn sour?

"I'm sorry Tell. I don't know what I was thinking."

"You weren't."

"I can't go back out there. I'm so embarrassed."

She gave me an undeserved, reassuring smile, "You don't have to. I'll take you home."

Telly snuck me out of the bar and left me with the valet while she went in to tell everyone that I had too much to drink and needed to rest. She told Will I was sorry about what I'd said and told James I'd call him later. We took a cab back to my apartment. She helped me inside and into bed. It was the most maternal Telly had ever been, and I appreciated her so much more. When I was settled in my sheets, she lay next to me.

"How could I be so stupid? I almost blew my cover

182

back there." I hid my face with my hands.

"Yeah, you did."

"I'm beginning to think I'm not cut out for this."

"Sure you are. It's just a matter of whether you still want to keep going."

"Yeah." I buried my cheek into my pillow and gave a long sigh. I thought of Will and why his presence pissed me off so much.

"Why are you seeing Will again?" I asked, staring into Telly's brown eyes, hoping for a real answer.

She shrugged. "He makes me feel good." I raised an eyebrow. "I know you think I'm making a mistake, but I've learned that he is the way he is. And now I'm enjoying him for that. I have no expectations from whatever it is that we're doing. No matter how many times we push each other away, we always come back for more."

"So, you're saying you're some kind of emotional masochist?"

She laughed. "No, I'm saying that's Will and me." She rolled on her back and gazed up at the ceiling. "It sounds crazy, but I think we're the love of each other's lives."

Will, the love of Telly's life? It seemed hard to believe, but she had a point. The two of them were like magnets. All they needed was a little push before they were stuck together again. I guess it was a pattern she was used to and perhaps even expected. Maybe in her mind two things were certain with Will; they would always break up and always get back together. I thought about Chad and couldn't imagine being back with him again.

"You know what I think?" I asked.

Telly perked up. "What?"

"Chad really wasn't the love of my life. Don't get me wrong. I loved him very much, but I think it's good that we didn't get married. Like a blessing in disguise."

Telly looked at me very seriously and tapped her index finger on her mouth.

"I think that's what you psychologists call closure." The corners of my mouth turned up while she tried to keep a straight face, but it only took a moment before we ended the night with a good laugh.

13

Bombs Bursting In Air

AN EARLY MORNING PHONE CALL woke me from a deep drunken sleep. I felt a slight twinge in the middle of my forehead. When I opened my eyes, the morning light set that twinge on fire. That wasn't the worst of it. That early morning call was my mother.

"Hello?" I answered in a fog.

"Marin, it's Ma. Are you sick?" she asked.

"No, I'm still sleeping."

"Sleeping? Marin, you're not getting any younger. You shouldn't waste your time sleeping in. I've already had breakfast, read the paper, and done the gardening this morning."

"That's great," I said with a yawn.

"I heard you have a new boyfriend," she said. My eyes shot open. How did she know? "Why didn't you tell me?"

"Who told you?" I tried to think fast. I didn't say anything to Michael when I saw him. Did she hire a PI to follow me around? Nope, it was . . .

"Mrs. Jensen," she said. Figures. Rachel must've told her mom about James and her mom, Mrs. Jensen, told my mom. "Mrs. Jensen says he's David's friend from college and that he's a nice young man."

"Well, it's very new. I'm not quite ready to introduce him or anything."

"Why not? I think it's wonderful and so soon after your break up. I guess you're not a complete time waster." Of course, she only cared about marrying me off. "I want you and that new boyfriend to come spend the Fourth of July with us at your brother's." The fourth was two days away, and I wasn't too keen on spending my extra day off with my brother again. Surely, he wasn't either.

"I don't know, Mom. Did Michael say it was okay?"

"Of course, why wouldn't he?" She wasn't patient enough for my attempted answer and continued. "I don't want any excuses. I haven't seen you in months. I want to know you're all right. The barbeque starts at one. I'll see you there."

"But—"

"No buts, just be there." She hung up before I could argue.

My head pained as I sat up. I wished that the call had never happened and that I was blissfully still asleep. I needed to get out of taking James to visit my family, but how? Could I just skip it? No, if I did I would soon regret it. It was just an afternoon after all. How bad could it be?

After an Independence Day brunch, James and I packed some wine and cheesecake in a cooler and headed up to my brother's house. He seemed a little anxious, but more than willing to spend the holiday with my family. It was a quality that most looked for in a mate. A quality I didn't care for, especially in this case.

"Is there anything I should know before I meet everyone? Any pointers?" James asked.

"Let's see," I said, trying to think. "My dad's name is Robert, but address him as Dr. Johns first. If he really likes you he'll ask you to call him Robert. He doesn't say much, but bring up golf or the history channel and you'll get him talking. My mom is Mei Li, she's from Beijing and still has a heavy accent, so listen carefully. She's sharp as a tack but takes very kindly to flattery." James nodded attentively as he drove.

"Michael is quiet like my dad. He's always in his head. His wife Jennifer is very friendly. She stays home with the kids and paints portraits on the side occasionally. She's very talented."

"Okay, Dr. Johns senior and junior are quiet, Mei Li likes flattery, and Jennifer's a painter. Got it," he said.

"Don't forget the kids," I said.

"Oh, right, and they are?"

"Miles and Jillian. They're great kids. Miles is five and he's very active, loves sports. Jillian is seven. She's a little genius. A talented pianist too."

"Really? At seven?" He sounded impressed.

"Yep." I smiled, excited to see the kids again. They were the only two members of the family that I adored.

"Do you think they'll like me?" James asked with worry.

The truth was I wasn't sure if they would like him. They were never crazy about Chad or any boyfriend for that matter. It didn't matter if they liked him or not, but I wanted the day to go smoothly. So I lied. "Of course, they'll love you."

It was about one o'clock when we pulled up the long driveway of my brother's traditional Victorian home that sat beautifully on a half acre lot. Like a photograph, the picturesque setting remained unchanged and steadfast in its perfection. I envied it. Not that I didn't love my apartment back in the city, but Michael had created what looked like a perfect life. Perfect house, perfect wife, perfect children, perfect job, all the beautiful perfections I would dream about, but never achieve.

"Are you ready?" I asked. James grabbed the wine and cheesecake.

"I think so." He smiled nervously, and I felt the same.

I rang the doorbell.

Miles and Jillian burst through the entrance. "Aunt Marin!" they screamed. Miles wrapped his arms around my waist, and I held him tight. He looked up and smiled.

"Where have you been, Aunt Marin? We missed you."

Staring into his little brown eyes, I had forgotten how much I loved those two.

"I missed you too." Jillian waited patiently for her greeting.

"Come here, Jillie." She gave me my second biggest hug of the day.

"I learned a new song on the piano, Aunt Marin. Can I play it for you?" she said in her soft sweet voice.

"Of course, I can't wait."

"Who's this?" Miles demanded bluntly, standing in front of James with his hands on his hips. James let out a little laugh and knelt so he was eye level with Miles.

"I'm James. I'm a friend of your Aunt Marin." James stuck out his hand and Miles shook it.

"I'm Miles."

We walked into the oversized foyer and headed back toward the kitchen where Jennifer was preparing a vegetable tray.

"Marin!" She ran over and greeted me with yet another big hug. "It's been too long. How are you?"

"I'm well. How are you?"

"Great, keeping busy with the kids, you know." She looked to James.

"Jennifer this is James, James this is my sister-in-law." The two shook hands.

"You have a lovely home," James said. Jennifer thanked him and sent me an obvious wink of approval.

"Where is everyone?" I asked.

"They're out back. Why don't you all go out? I'm right behind you."

The kids led us to the deck, which backed up to a large backyard with lots of trees, a perfect place for two children to explore.

"There she is!" my mom shouted as she walked up steadily to greet me. We embraced and she pulled me away to give me a once over to see if I had gotten too fat

189

or too skinny.

"You look pretty good considering," she said.

"Mom!"

My dad approached looking a little older than I remembered. "How are you, Marin?" he asked with a smile.

"Good." I sounded apprehensive. "I want you all to meet James."

By this time my brother made his way over. They all gave James a once and twice over, but they didn't seem to have the weary reaction that I'd expected. Instead, they greeted James politely. Michael offered James a cold beer, which he kindly accepted. The five of us sat at the patio table watching the kids play in the yard.

"So, James, how did you meet Marin?" my dad asked, prompting the conversation.

"Funny story actually." He grinned and positioned his body to tell a long tale.

"Oh, no," I said and buried my face in my hands.

"Wait. I want to hear the story," Jennifer said as she appeared with the veggie tray and other snacks. She sat next to Michael eager to listen.

"So, I was walking home from an appointment in the city when all of the sudden I hear this awkward yelp."

"It was not a yelp," I said, annoyed.

"Oh, yes. It was a yelp." James chuckled. "I see this woman face down on the ground with her purse spilled all over the sidewalk."

"It was Marin?" my dad asked. James nodded.

"Did you forget Marin's a klutz, Dad?" Michael's comment made my cheeks flush.

"That's true," my mom said.

"I ran over to see if she was okay, and she was except for a small scrape on her knee. So, I helped her over to a bench. I carry a first aid kit when I work, so I was able to patch up her knee right there."

I watched James tell the story with enthusiasm and purpose as if he had rehearsed it. He really seemed to enjoy it.

"She looked so embarrassed, but through the flushed cheeks I saw a familiar face. I realized that she was at David and Rachel's wedding. She recognized me too, and we've been together ever since." James relaxed in his chair and gazed at me as if his eyes wanted to say something.

Jennifer and my mom *ahhed* at the story, commenting on how cute it was and that finally my clumsiness resulted in something good. I pretended to enjoy the story as much, but I really wanted to roll my eyes and gag. James rubbed his fingers over my bad knee.

"Your knee's been much better," he said quietly referring to my long-term injury.

"Yeah," I said. "I just hope I'll be ready for the race in November."

"You will." James assured me with a smile.

"What race?" my mom asked.

"The US Half Marathon for St. Judes, Mom," Michael answered.

"How'd you remember that?" I asked Michael.

"You've run that race for years." I raised my eyebrows in suspicion. He continued, "What? You think I don't pay attention to your interests."

I threw my hands up to surrender.

We continued the friendly conversation for another twenty minutes before Michael and my dad started the grill. So far, the afternoon was going well. No condescending looks or comments. My best guess, they wanted to take it easy since I had just been jilted or they didn't want to be rude to James. That would be a first.

Miles ran up to Michael with his bat and baseball. "Dad, can you play ball with me?"

"In a little bit, Miles. I have to get the food started so we can eat soon." Miles put his head down and went back to the middle of the yard.

"Hey, Miles," James called. Miles looked up.

"I can play with you until your Dad's finished." Miles' face lit up.

"Yeah!"

I smiled at him, appreciating his kindness to my nephew. James tossed the ball to Miles who tried to hit it with his bat.

"Look at him, he's a natural dad. He's a keeper," Jennifer said. "You did good."

"I like him too," my mom said.

"Seriously?" I asked. She looked at me as if liking James was the most natural thing in the world.

"Yes, Marin. Why is that so hard to believe?"

"You've never liked any of my boyfriends. You hardly liked Chad, you were just glad someone finally wanted to marry me."

"Well, it's true you haven't always had the best taste in

men, but all that matters is that you're happy. Right?"

"Right," I repeated slowly, skeptical. My mom never exhibited this nurturing attitude before. Something was up. "What's with you? Are you dying or something?"

"No. Why would you ask me something like that?"

"Because you've never said all you want is for me to be happy."

"Don't be ridiculous, Marin. You are my child, of course I want you to be happy." She seemed offended that I would suggest such a thing, but I wasn't buying it.

"Is this because I just called off my wedding? You're trying to be nice, right?" I said. Yeah, that makes sense.

"Oh, Marin. Get over yourself," she said, then walked back into the house. Jennifer and I exchanged astounded looks.

Jillian ran up from the yard and asked if I was ready to hear her song. I followed her into the house and into the family room where she had a beautiful baby grand piano to practice on. She settled on the piano bench and twiddled her fingers. She stroked the keys and immediately I recognized the song. "Canon" by Pachelbel. The same song I was going to walk down the aisle to. The song my mom walked to. I had dreamed about the song at my wedding since I was a little girl. Jillian played it so well that I became overwhelmed with pride and a bit of sorrow. When she finished I clapped as hard as I could and praised her wonderful playing.

"Why are you crying?" she asked, and I wiped my wet cheeks.

"I'm so proud of you." I brushed her cheek and gave

it a little pinch. "Why don't you go back outside and play? I'll be there in a minute."

Jillian ran for the backyard, and I stayed in the family room. I scanned the assortment of family photographs that Michael and Jennifer collected over the years, from their wedding, to baby pictures of the kids, to pictures of the family at Disneyland. They truly had a picture perfect life, and I mourned over a life I could never have, a life I always wanted. I thought about the argument I had with my brother and how defensive he was when I asked if he had been faithful to Jennifer. It was clear that he probably had an affair, maybe two. All the late hours he worked. I imagined him with a sexy lab assistant or distinguished chairwoman of the board at the research center. Did Jennifer know? What would she think if she found out her picture perfect life wasn't so picture perfect? I wiped the running mascara from under my eyes and headed outside. I heard a burst of laughter as soon as I opened the door. It was my dad, Michael, and James enjoying themselves by the grill.

"What's so funny?" I asked.

My dad turned to me. "James was telling us about an incident he had with some quicksand on the golf course."

"I didn't know you played golf," I said.

"I've been known to hit a few balls around the course," he said, miming a golf swing.

"Next time, don't go after the ball," my dad continued with James.

"You got that right, Dr. Johns."

"Call me Robert."

Then I saw my dad give James a friendly pat on the back. It was a rare gesture, especially since they'd just met. My dad liked James. I felt my stomach churn, thinking about the disappointment my family would feel when James and I split, even if his infidelity was the cause. They still didn't know that's what really happened with Chad.

The hours of the afternoon passed like minutes. We spent them eating hot dogs and salad, playing badminton in the yard, and talking over iced tea and beer. Despite the awkwardness of faking it with James in front of my family, it was a great afternoon. I couldn't remember the last time I had such an easy time with everyone.

While the sun set, Michael and I sat together drinking our beers with little words. My parents retreated inside to cool off, Jennifer stored the left over food in the kitchen, and James played with Jillian and Miles in the yard.

"I'm glad you came today," Michael said with a slight smile. I shot him a look of doubt. "Seriously," he said.

"Me too. I actually had a nice time."

"Yeah, I think everyone had a nice time." We watched the sky turn pink, then purple, and finally midnight blue.

"I haven't, Marin," Michael said. I looked at him, confused by his unprovoked comment. "The question you asked me in the lab. That's the truth."

I gazed into his eyes looking for a trace of guilt or dishonesty, but I didn't see any.

"Really?" I asked.

"Really. I came close before, but I didn't do it." He gave an assuring smile, and I couldn't help but believe him.

"Didn't do what?" Jennifer asked as she approached from the backdoor. She put her arm around Michael's shoulder and he looked slightly panicked.

"Sky diving," I said. Jennifer threw her head back in a good laugh. It was a believable save. Michael was a dare devil in the lab, not so much in an airplane.

"Everyone ready for fireworks?" my dad shouted with his arms full of an assortment of Fourth of July paraphernalia. The kids howled in delight. James and I watched from the deck as the kids held sparklers and my dad illuminated the backyard with colorful explosions, red, green, purple, blue, and yellow. No matter how old I get, fireworks are always enthralling.

James stood behind me as I leaned on the deck rail. He wrapped his arms around my waist and whispered in my ear, "This was a really fun day. Thank you for bringing me."

I didn't know if it was the relaxed last eight hours with my family, the fireworks, or the little buzz I got from the few beers I drank, but in that moment my heart leaped. Something about being there with him, with them, felt right. I called off the guards of my own fight, at least for the night.

14

Working Late

FOURTH OF JULY WEEKEND was eye opening. Between my brother's affirmation, my family's positive reaction to James, and their new
compassion toward me, I felt different, hopeful. Maybe
there were good guys out there. If decent men existed,
then James would definitely be one of them. Over the
next few weeks, I felt myself relax. I maintained my
guard, but I wasn't so obsessed about catching him cheating. I spent more time enjoying his company, his laughter,
his handyman skills, and his skills in bed. Yes, things were
good.

That was until one afternoon in August when I had a
sudden jolt back into reality, and my summer romance
came to an end. James and I were taking our usual condi-
tioning jog around the park. Out of nowhere, I heard a
woman yell for James. We turned around to see a stunning woman in her running gear, which included skintight

pants and matching Nikes. She could have easily been shooting a magazine ad with all the make up she had on. James ran ahead to greet her.

"Hey, Shanna. How are you?" he said.

"Great. You?" she said in a sensual tone, breathing heavily. Heart rate up or not, it was uncomfortably seductive.

"Great!" James stared at her a moment too long and I cleared my throat. "Oh, uh this is Marin," he said. No "girlfriend" this time, huh? "Shanna's a patient of mine."

"Hi," I said. She looked me up and down as if she were giving me a mental veto.

"Well, got to go. See you Friday." She waved bye to James and ran in the opposite direction.

"Bye," James waved and turned to watch her jog away. Her perky little ass bounced with each stride, and I swear I felt my own droop with resentment. I scoffed and crossed my arms. Was I really jealous? It was the first time I had seen James act slightly suspicious. Something was up. I could feel it and not like last time when the other woman turned out to be his sister. No, there was definitely something to discover, and I was going to find it.

Later at James', I perused his appointment book while he was in the shower. Shanna Costa was entered for four o'clock on Friday. A late day appointment, huh? I put the book away and opened the bathroom door, steam covering my face.

"Hey, you wanna go to dinner on Friday?" I asked over the sound of running water.

"Wish I could babe, but I have a late appointment," he said.

"How late?"

"Um, like eight."

"Eight? That's a little late for work, don't you think?"

"Yeah, but sometimes I have to work around my patient's schedule. Let's have dinner on Saturday."

I agreed and didn't say another word about it. There was no eight o'clock appointment in his book. I double-checked. Shanna's four o'clock appointment was the last one. Now why would he want to give himself an extra four hours? *Because he's sleeping with her!* I knew he was too good to be true.

When I got home later that night, I called in for back up.

"Do you have a black outfit?" I asked Telly after she answered my call.

"For what occasion?" she asked.

"Spying." It felt almost as exciting as it sounded.

"I'm listening."

I told her the whole story, and she agreed to accompany me on a special spying expedition. There was only one Shanna Costa listed in San Fran, so it was easy to find her address. I only hoped it was the right one.

Telly pulled up to my apartment on Friday afternoon. When I opened the door, I saw she was dressed in head to toe black with sunglasses and a black beret. I was also wearing black, but opted for a ball cap with my hair tied in a ponytail.

"What's with the beret?" I asked.

Telly whipped her head in my direction and in a phony French accent said, "It goes with le spying out-feet."

I raised my brow. "We should get le going." Within seconds, we sped off.

If James, in fact, had a four o'clock appointment with Shanna then it would be ending by five, which is exactly when we pulled up to Mayberry Street with its series of beautiful Victorian style townhomes on a steep hill. The kind of picturesque neighborhood revered on San Francisco postcards. Hmm, there was no sign of James' SUV.

"Shit, he's not here."

"Do you think we missed him?"

"I don't know." I glanced at the house. Shanna was carrying a bag of groceries inside. Alone. "That's her," I whispered and ducked down in my seat.

"Why are you whispering?" Telly said, trying to pull me upright. I surveyed the street again, thinking I missed his SUV, but it was nowhere to be found.

"Well, at least we know it's her house," Telly said.

"Yeah."

"If they had a four o'clock appointment she wouldn't have just come back from the store," she said.

"True." I was trying to get a handle on the discrepancy.

"Unless," she started slowly, "she just got back from their appointment at his office."

"Maybe, but he primarily does house calls." I checked my watch again. It was only five after.

"Didn't he say her appointment was at eight?" Telly asked.

"Yeah."

"Let's get something to eat, then come back later. Besides the sun will be down and we'll be able to go up to the house without being noticed." I stared at Shanna's house, hoping that if I looked long enough James would suddenly appear like one of those magic eye pictures. Reluctantly, I agreed with Telly and we left for dinner.

We returned to Shanna's neighborhood by eight with two large, or rather, Venti lattes from Starbucks. Telly drove up the street to look for James' SUV. This time it was parked right in front. She pulled forward and parked about half a block away. I retrieved a pair of binoculars from my purse and studied the outside of the house. The first floor lights were on, but the second floor lights appeared to be off.

"So, what do you wanna do?" Telly asked, waiting for an assignment.

"Nothing yet."

"You don't wanna go up to the house and get a better look?"

"No, I think we should stay here and see if anything happens."

"Like what? Watch James leave? That won't prove anything."

"It will if they leave together." The truth was I really didn't have a plan. I figured when I arrived I would know what to do. My hope was that Shanna and James would emerge from the house with their hands all over each other. Then, I would have undeniable evidence, but who knew how long that would be. I was prepared to stay all night.

"Okay, you're the boss," Telly said as she sipped her latte. I sighed and relaxed in my seat.

"So, how's Will?" I asked, trying to pass the time.

"Good. We've actually been spending a lot of time together."

"It's not serious though, right?"

"I don't know. I don't want to put a label on it. It is what it is."

"Which is?" I drew out the question.

"Like I told you before. We're having fun and enjoying each other's company. Nothing more, nothing less." She gave me a stern look as if to tell me to stop with the questions.

"Okay. That's cool."

"Can we talk about something else?" Telly asked.

"Sure." I kept my eyes steadily on the house. Telly scooted around in her seat and curled her knees to her chest. "You know what this reminds me of?" she asked.

"What?"

"The night we spied on my landlord. Do you remember?"

"Yes!" I snapped my fingers, recalling that evening.

Telly and I went out to a gay bar one night, and it happened to be the same night as their weekly drag show. We were having a blast—cocktails, sexy chiseled gay men, and drag queens galore. Telly recognized one of the drag queens introduced as Fuchsia Turner. She was convinced that he was her landlord, but didn't want to approach him in case he was private about it. 'I'm not going to shit where I sleep,' I believe were her exact words.

The following night, after dinner and cocktails at her house, we took the opportunity to spy on her landlord who lived in the same building as Telly. He left his apartment around eight-thirty. We followed him by car keeping a safe distance until we finally ended up at the same gay bar. He entered through the back of the building with a duffle bag. To me it was enough evidence to convict, but Telly needed more. "Reasonable doubt," she said. *Lawyers.*

We waited until we saw another guy enter the back of the building and stopped him before he made it inside. Telly asked if he knew Charlie Jones, her landlord's name. He said he did and that he would be performing tonight as a she. He asked if we wanted to go backstage, but we refused.

To this day, I don't know why Telly was curious enough to follow her landlord to prove he was a part-time drag queen. I only wanted to support her, which is exactly what she was doing by dressing like le spy, sitting in a dark car, and watching an unknown house.

After about forty-five minutes, I became restless. "Do you wanna go up to the house?" I asked.

"Yes. Let's go." We climbed out of the car trying not to make any noises that might trigger a nosy neighbor or barking dog. We made our way to the fenceless yard, walking like ninjas in the night, and found a deck attached the back of the house. It was completely dark except for the light coming through the windows. Telly kept a look out while I made my way up the deck. The windows were too high for me to see into. I climbed the back stairs, leaning over to the window, but it was still too far away.

"Can you see anything?" Telly whispered.

"No, it's too far."

"Try that lattice."

To my left was a vine-covered lattice attached to the house much closer to the window. I walked down the steps and gave the lattice a good pull to see if it would hold. Seemed sturdy enough. Putting one foot in front of the other, I climbed up about three feet to see the window. I peaked in through the kitchen, which had a view of the living room. Trying to keep my head low, I saw James rise up as if he was getting off of the ground or getting off of Shanna. He appeared to be dressed, but I couldn't see much more. I climbed another foot higher and saw Shanna lying on the floor fully clothed. He was doing some kind of floor work with her. I waited to see if he or she would make any sexual advances, but I waited too long. There was a snap and the vines rustled.

Uh oh . . .

The lattice detached from the house. My body slammed against the deck.

"Oh, shit!" Telly whispered. She ran over and pushed the lattice off of me. "Are you okay?"

I winced in pain but mostly shock. "Yeah, I'm okay." Telly helped me to my feet.

"We have to go. Now," she said.

We rushed out of there as fast as we could and sped off in the opposite direction of the house in case they heard us, which I was pretty sure they did. On the way back to my apartment, I told Telly everything I saw, which was nothing of note.

"Well, it was a good try," she said.

"Yeah," I sighed. My hand was burning and I noticed that I had a pretty gnarly scrape that needed attention. I hissed at the sight of it. Telly grimaced, and I wasn't sure if she was more concerned with my scraped hand or getting blood on her upholstery.

"Spying is fun and all, but next time let's leave it up to the professionals."

I thanked her and told her I would call her later. Safe inside my apartment, I tossed my hat somewhere in the living room and went to the bathroom to shower and clean my hand. I imagined washing the events of the night away as I washed my hair. Looking back, it wasn't the best situation to be in. I wondered how long I would have to keep it up.

Exhausted, I settled in my pajamas and made a cup of hot tea. My body was a little sore from the fall, and I knew it would be worse in the morning. At almost ten, there was a knock at my door and I had no idea who it could be. I peered into the peephole to find James and opened the door. He scooped me into his arms and gave a relieved sigh as if he hadn't seen me in months.

"Are you okay?" I asked, his hold as tight as possible.

"Yeah. I'm glad to see you."

"What happened?" I asked, wondering if it was guilt he was feeling.

"I was in the middle of my appointment when we

heard this loud bang coming from the back. I went to investigate and saw that her lattice was broken. I think I got a glimpse of someone running away."

"Oh, my God," I said, genuinely looking stunned, but for a different reason.

"We called the police and answered a few questions, but they said there wasn't much to go on."

I continued to gape at him. "Someone tried to break in?" I asked.

"Looks that way."

"I wonder who it was." My nerves were in overdrive, but I calmed myself down by remembering that I wasn't in any criminal database.

"Who knows? It shook me up a little, and I wanted to check on you to make sure you were okay." He hugged me tightly again.

"Yeah, I'm fine." He pulled back and took my hands, then looked a little closer at my left one.

"What happened?" he asked.

"I, uh, tripped when I was running earlier. Just a scrape. You know me, I'm a klutz." I smiled innocently and he returned it.

"I can't stay. I have the children's hospital in the morning." He kissed me and told me that we would catch up the next day after he got off work.

That night, I lay in bed staring at the ceiling, then at my scraped hand. That had been a close one. Too close. Who knew this venture would be so dangerous? I guess in this game you have to get your hands dirty sometimes . . . and scraped.

15

The Man Test

THE SHANNA INCIDENT CONVINCED me to take a break from my spying gig. Though I waited patiently for the opportune moment, nothing presented itself. I researched other methods only to discover one dead end after another. Three weeks passed and I was running out of options, forcing me to weigh in on the only two I had left—wait it out or give it up.

One afternoon, I wandered out of my office for a break after completing a session with a violently arguing couple when I ran into a sobbing woman in the hall. She was in her late forties, perhaps an executive in her tailored suit and bobbed haircut. She was alone, and as a therapist I felt compelled to stop.

"Are you alright?" I asked. She glanced at me from behind her tissue.

"Yeah, I'll be okay." She waved me on as if I shouldn't bother with her silly tears, but there was something all too familiar about her cry.

"Is there something I can do? Would you like me to call someone?" She blew her nose into the tissue.

"No, really I'll be . . ." Then she lunged at me, letting out a resounding cry. I caught her in my arms while she sobbed on my shoulder, and I tried to comfort her as best as I could. Minutes later, she calmed down and pulled herself together.

"I'm so embarrassed. I don't even know you," she said sniffling.

"Don't be. I'm a therapist. I see a lot of crying," I said with a sympathetic smile. "What happened?"

"I'm getting a divorce." She struggled to restrain new tears.

"I'm so sorry."

"Yeah," she inhaled her sadness. "He had an affair." *Surprise, surprise.* "And the worst part is I have a complete written account of what happened."

"Really?" *Go on . . .*

"It's so detailed. I keep reading it over and over again. The things he did with her are unbelievable. I can't believe I was married to someone like that for sixteen years."

"How is it that you have a detailed account of this affair?"

"Man Test," she said with a straight face.

"Man Test? What's that?"

"It's a service that sends a woman to seduce your husband. If he falls for it, you get a complete report the next day." My jaw dropped. *What a brilliant idea!* How did I not know about this? The wheels in my head were spinning so fast I could no longer focus on her or her situation. "That bastard," she whispered under her breath.

"What's your name?" I asked.

"Connie."

I handed her my business card. "I'm Marin. I work in this building. If you need someone to talk to, please give me a call."

"Thank you." She accepted the card.

"Hang on, I have another one," I said pulling out Telly's card. "If you need a divorce attorney, this one is great."

"I really appreciate this. Thank you, Marin."

"You're welcome." She took the cards and turned to walk away.

"Connie," I called after her. "You wouldn't happen to have a business card for that Man Test service would you?" As luck would have it, she did.

I sauntered into a restaurant that evening where I met Telly for dinner. We hadn't seen much of each other over the past few weeks since she was shacking up more frequently with Will, a man I still couldn't warm up to.

"What's going on with you?" she asked as I wiggled into my seat.

"The most amazing thing happened to me today." I beamed.

"Did you win the lottery?"

"Nope."

"Did you get a great deal on shoes?"

"Nope." I shook with anticipation.

"Did you catch James cheating?" A laugh squeezed through my lips.

"No, but I will!" I screeched with the same sorority girl enthusiasm as Rachel. Telly waited for me to finish. I pulled out the business card and gave her a run down on Man Test.

"So, it's like escorts with ulterior motives," she said.

"Exactly."

"Why didn't I think of this? With all my client's cheating spouses, probably wouldn't be admissible in court though. Are you sure it's legit?"

"Who cares? It is brilliant! They're very discrete and work only on a referral basis. They don't want the word to get out or else every husband and boyfriend will think they're being set up and won't be themselves and go for it. Which, now that I think about it, could actually be a good thing."

"Probably not too good for business." She looked the card over a few times. "So, what are you going to do?"

"Set it up, of course."

"When?" she asked sipping her drink.

"As soon as possible. I look at it like this, I could play this game with James for who knows how long or I could send in the bait and watch him catch it like a stupid fish. I'm tired. I want this to be over so I can move on with my life."

"Do you think he'll go for it?" A dumb question in my opinion.

"Of course he'll go for it. Cheating is all about opportunity. When a man encounters a discreet, mess-free opportunity to have sex with a woman he won't say no. It's in their DNA. There are always opportunities, especially for eligible guys like James. This is the ultimate test, finding out if he can resist opportunity."

"So, you're pretty much setting him up to fail?" she asked as if there could be another result.

"Yeah, that's basically my take on romantic relationships now," I said like a cynical champ.

"Doesn't that belief make you less effective at your job?"

"I think it makes me more effective." She shrugged. "Do you want to set one up for Will?"

"What? No," she said.

"Oh, I get it, you're in the bubble."

"Bubble, what bubble?"

"Telly, I haven't seen you in weeks. Your life is work and Will, work and Will. You're trapped in this bubble where it's all about you two."

"Call it what you want, but if I'm in a bubble so are you," she said. I rolled my eyes scoffing. "Oh, come on. I know you like James."

"Sure I like him, but I don't have any real feelings for him that would put us in some kind of a bubble."

"Well, he's definitely in your bubble. The way he looks at you. I almost feel bad for the guy."

"Now you know how I feel about everyone you date."

She smirked. "Oh, is this what it's like?"

"Yep," I smiled.

She shrugged. "I'm just not a relationship person."

"Neither am I." I raised my glass and she toasted me in agreement.

The next day I scheduled the Man Test. I was relieved to know that in only two weeks the truth would be out, and I could finally stop pretending. It was the equivalent of quitting a crappy job. Since it was coming to an end, the next couple of weeks would be easy.

That same night, James made a surprise visit to my apartment. When I asked what his visit was for, he handed me a sleeping bag and waltzed in.

"What's this?" I said, baffled. "Are we having a slumber party?" He took a beer from the refrigerator.

"Better! We're going camping." He threw out his hands as if it was the greatest news to have ever come knocking on my door. "Do you mind if I have this?" James pointed to the beer. I nodded, still in shock. *Camping!* No way, I was a city girl, a city girl who didn't sleep on the ground.

"Sorry James, I don't camp." I handed the sleeping bag back to him.

"What? Why not?"

"Because, I don't like bugs or roughing it." I pleaded my case, which really wasn't up for discussion.

"So you've been camping before? That's how you know you don't like it." His attitude stunk of arrogance. I crossed my arms and reluctantly told him that I had never been camping. Once he got over the shock that a thirty-one-year-old had never slept in the woods, he began to explain how great it is. The fishing, the campfires, the scary stories, and let's not forget the camp coffee.

"David and I always go camping for Labor Day weekend. This time we want you and Rachel to come." He gave me a sappy face, but I wasn't falling for it.

"Wait, did you say Labor Day weekend?"

"Yeah, it's a tradition." He continued to look hopeful. Labor Day weekend fell after the Man Test weekend. By then we would be broken up. In that moment I didn't see the harm in saying, "Okay, I'll go."

"Seriously?"

"Yeah, I can see it means a lot to you."

He grabbed me tightly and lifted me from the ground. I couldn't help but laugh. His excitement was infectious. Besides, I had my own reasons to be excited.

The night of the Man Test arrived on the twenty-eighth of August. It was a Saturday night and James was going out with David and some other friends for a night on the town. He'd be drinking, of course, so his defenses would be down. The conditions were perfect to be ravaged by a beautiful woman.

I remembered going to the Man Test office a couple weeks prior. They don't take appointments by phone. For whatever reason it was important for them to meet me and for me to meet the woman. Monica, the woman assigned to my case, had perfectly bronzed skin, long dark hair, and blue eyes that could pierce a man's soul. Her voluptuous hips were paired with a tiny waist and full, perky breasts. She was a temptress all right, and as far as I could tell it was a foolproof system.

The case manager, Jane, explained the entire process.

She told me Monica would locate James and approach him like any lady lusting after a man. Monica would talk to him casually so that he'd feel comfortable, and then crank up the intensity. Eventually, she would flat out ask if he wanted to go "home" with her, giving him all the reasons that he should. That was the test. His only options were to say no and get out of the situation or say yes and go for it.

In either case, Monica would document the entire night in a report, quoting things he said, explaining every detail of their intimate encounter, presenting every truth typed in black and white. When I asked Jane how many men passed the Man Test she said very few.

"There are faithful men, but we don't usually get wives and girlfriends that are curious. Our clients are already suspicious. We have a saying around here—where there's smoke, there's fire."

It was difficult to imagine any guy passing the Man Test, not James, Chad, Will, or even my brother despite his admitted fidelity. I lay on my bed thinking about how the night would play out. It was a quarter after eight and with any luck James and Monica had already met. I pictured James playing it cool at first, but he wouldn't be able to resist her when she stared into his eyes with her crystal blue ones, cleavage showing, nipples hard, her hand on his crotch, telling him that no one would ever know. All because he's a man, a reckless, lying, cheating man.

The next morning felt like Christmas. The day after the Man Test, the day I got my package hand delivered, disclosing all the dirty details of James' casual encounter. The day wide open with nothing to do but sit tight until the courier delivered the news. I relished the lazy Sunday and avoided the one call I got from James. I previously told him I had a lot to do and wouldn't have a chance to see him. Hour after hour, I waited. By two o'clock there was no news, and I was a little frustrated. I figured the later the message, the better the news. If there was a lot to tell then the report would be lengthy. Long reports take time to write. The thought of this made me giddy. Then, my palms became clammy as I let it sink in.

Even though I was okay with me being emotionally devoid in our relationship, it made me a queasy to think that James would do something so hurtful after being so loving and faithful. The way he looked at me, the things he said, his seeming sincerity. Was it really all for show? Were we both trying to put one over on each other?

Finally around five, there was a knock at my door. I opened it quickly to find a woman in a trench coat and sunglasses. Seriously . . . a trench coat and sunglasses. She was straight-faced.

"Marin Johns?" she asked.

"Yes."

"This is for you." She shoved the package in my hand. By her lack of warmth, I had a feeling the news was as expected.

"Have a good day, Miss," she said and took off like a secret spy in the night.

I closed the door without taking my eyes off the brown envelope. My heart raced and my hands trembled.

There it was, the moment of truth. I tore open the envelope and pulled out the thin report.

Dear Ms. Johns,
We are happy to report that James Young has passed the Man Test. This is an extremely positive indication that James is faithful even in the most tempting situation. Congratulations, we wish you and James all the best.

Sincerely,
Jane McGee

What? This couldn't be right.
"He passed?"
I started to read the report and skipped down to the end where they explained how he denied Monica. I became furious, irrational, barely understanding the words I was reading. I wanted to faint, yell, and cry all at the same time. I ripped the report in half and let out a frustrated scream.
"Are you fucking kidding me?" I stomped into my bedroom and slammed my hands against the wall. "Unfucking believable!" Through the rage, I managed to put on my shorts and running shoes. There was only one way to get out this kind of anger.
My run lasted a good hour that night, and I only stopped because my knee wouldn't allow me to keep going. The words of the report resounded in my head. Why was this guy not taking the bait? I cursed James, cursed Chad, Man Test, and the last five months I had spent

consumed with thoughts and research of infidelity. It wasn't fair. Why couldn't I get the one thing I wanted? Just this one little thing to set me free. Didn't I deserve a break?

After a hot shower, I felt a little more relaxed. The report was torn and scattered on my living room floor. I wanted to read the encounter with an objective eye, so I pieced it back together with some tape. With a deep breath, I began reading.

It started almost as I imagined. Monica trapped him while he was getting a drink at the bar. Their conversation started casually, and then began to heat up. According to the report, James was very polite, but didn't seem to respond to her advances. She spent the night talking on and off with James, and by the end of the night she laid down the law. He refused her by saying, "I'm sorry. You're a beautiful girl and if I were single I would take you home in a second. But I'm not." And he walked away.

I went over the report in my head again and again and gathered that he was interested, but declined because of me. How was it that of all the men in San Francisco, I had literally found the only ideal faithful one? James wasn't a cheater, not that I would put it past him forever, but he was loyal. What was even more impressive was the fact that our relationship was still new. We hadn't committed to each other with I-love-yous or moving in together. In truth, we were at a point where we had the freedom to walk away easily if he wanted. That's when I realized that this was my karma. I took advantage of someone and this was the universe's way of throwing it back in my face.

Well-played Universe. You really had me going.

16

Gone Fishin'

JAMES DIDN'T BUY ANY OF MY EXCUSES to not go camping, so at seven on Saturday, I got a knock at my door.

"Good Morning!" Rachel said, beaming when I answered the door. Her chipper attitude was more annoying than usual since I hadn't yet had my coffee. She strolled behind me as I went back to the bedroom to grab my things for the trip.

"You about ready to go?" she asked. Her eyes pried around my room.

"Just about," I said, putting my toothbrush into my bag. I looked at my unmade bed, thinking how cozy it would be on that cool September morning. Ah, to be sleeping in. My eyes drooped at the thought.

"What's this?" she asked with a youthful curiosity. It was my Man Test package. She held the business card in her hand, studying it for clues of its real purpose. The last thing I wanted was Rachel bringing it up in front of the guys, both were waiting safely outside. Just a guess, but that kind of thing could put a damper on the weekend.

I explained that it was a service that helped wives and girlfriends determine if their mate was a cheater. She asked what I was doing with such a service and if I had used it on James.

"After what happened with Chad, I had to know if I was dealing with another, ya know, cheater," I said, playing the victim.

"Of course," she said. "Did he pass?"

"Yes, he passed," I said clenching my jaw and forcing a pleasant smile. She smiled a ray of hope. "Please don't say anything to anyone. I don't want James to think I don't trust him." Rachel pretended to zip her lips, a promise to keep it between us.

"Do you mind if I take this card?" she asked.

I hesitated. Since she was practically my own little sister, I wanted to shield her from the ugly realities of relationships. Then again, she was a grown woman. Why shouldn't she have the opportunity to know the truth about David if she really wanted?

"Sure," I said. "But Rachel." Her gaze shifted from the card to my eyes. "Be careful when you go looking for trouble, you just might find it."

"Oh, it's not for me," she brushed off my words of wisdom. "It's for a friend."

"Right." Sure it was. I hear "my friend" in therapy a lot. It's a protective mechanism of sorts. "Be sure to tell your *friend* the same."

"Marin?" James called from the living room. I grabbed the Man Test package from Rachel and stuffed it in a drawer. We made our way out to the living room with my two overnight bags in tow. James greeted me with a smile and a large cup of hot coffee. My mouth watered as I held it to my lips.

"What's the hold up ladies? It's time to hit the road," James said. Rachel and I looked at each other with a hint of secrecy.

"Just girl talk," Rachel said. James picked up one of my bags. Rachel gave me a little wink and I returned it.

"Well, you can save it for the campfire," he said.

"We're only going for a couple days. Do you really need two bags?" he said as we left my apartment.

"Yes," I said. "Rachel, how many bags did you bring?"

"Two."

I smiled at James, batting my eyelashes. "See." James rolled his eyes and loaded my bags into his car.

"See you at the lake!" Rachel waved and hopped into the other truck with David.

When I got in the car, I saw that Marvin had taken up the entire back seat.

"He's coming too?" I asked. "Of course, Marvin always goes camping with us."

"Great," I mumbled as I turned to face the front, hoping Marvin and I could ignore each other during the trip. He stuck his head between the front seats and grunted like a bull. I scowled and took an indulgent sip of my hot coffee. It was going to be a long weekend.

Two hours later, we arrived at the campground. San

Fran may have been two hundred miles away, but it felt like a thousand. We hiked about ten minutes until we found our campsite. David and Rachel assembled their tent while I attempted to help James with ours. After a while, I let James finish without me since my lack of experience and ability to take simple direction seemed to be holding us back. The only tent I ever helped pitch was morning wood, which is exactly what I told James. He laughed and told me he had no problem with that.

I felt a call of nature coming after my large coffee and the twenty-ounce bottle of water I had on the way.

"Where's the bathroom?" I asked.

"Wherever it's private," David said, approaching with a roll of toilet paper. I accepted the toilet paper with caution.

"Come on, I'll show you where I always go. It's completely hidden." Rachel pulled me into the woods.

The two of us staggered into the woods to this so called hidden forest toilet. All of the sudden, I didn't need to go anymore. She led me to a part of the woods only a minute's walk from the campsite. Thick trees enclosed it, but plenty of light peeked through the branches. After five minutes of awkward squatting, I finally had a release. It wasn't the proudest moment of my life, but as far as peeing outside goes, it wasn't so bad.

When we returned to the campsite, everything was set up. James motioned for me to come inside the tent. It was roomier than I imagined, complete with my two bags and full-sized air mattress.

"See, it's not so bad?" James said. With a smile I

agreed, thankful I didn't have to sleep on the ground. I grabbed a magazine from one of my bags with the idea of reading while the guys gathered wood for the campfire. Before I could get comfortable in one of the fold out chairs David called out, "Ready to go to the lake?" Marvin barked and James gathered his things.

"What's at the lake?" I asked.

"Dinner," James said.

I carried my backpack with some trail mix, my iPod, and magazine to enjoy while everyone else fished. We trekked down a pathway, which finally revealed the lakefront. It was breathtaking. The water was calm and reflected the trees and hills that surrounded it like a crystal clear mirror. There was definitely something serene about looking over that beautiful body of water.

"You ready to do some fishin'?" James handed me a fishing rod. I sneered and handed it back.

"Sorry, I don't know how to fish."

"That's okay." He returned the rod to me. "I'll teach you."

"I don't think I'll catch anything," I said, holding it toward him.

"Well, you'll never know until you try." He smiled encouragingly and waved me over to follow him. I took the fishing rod, and he positioned himself behind me.

"All you have to do is pull back." His hands covered mine while he guided the rod over my shoulder. "Now, in a swift motion, cast the rod forward." James used his rapid glide and helped me cast the fishing line into the lake. It didn't seem so hard.

"Now what?" I asked.

"Now, we wait."

He kissed my cheek and picked up his fishing rod. Rachel and David already had their lines in the water, and I watched James cast his.

It wasn't long before David felt a little tug on his line and began to reel it in. Nothing. He recast his line.

"What happens if something catches?" I asked James.

"Don't worry, I'll help you reel it in."

I sighed nervously.

"Relax, this is supposed to be relaxing," he said.

Relax? I didn't feel very relaxed holding a fishing pole and keeping a slight watch on Marvin who wandered nearby. My shoulders were tense and my neck was stiff. I gazed over the water and let its beauty calm my restlessness. It wasn't long before I could hear nothing but birds chirping, water swaying, and my breath. It became as centering as a yoga class or running by the bay. David, James, Rachel, and the dog were all so quiet, and I imagined they were having a similar experience.

I looked over at James and thought about his fidelity, his commitment to us. Suddenly he looked handsomer than usual. The wind blew his soft hair and he squinted in the sunlight, making him look sweet and rugged all at the same time. His choice not to sleep with the Man Test girl was a mystery to me. Somehow, I'd have to get him to tell me about it without implicating my position in the whole ordeal. Only by his explanation would I be truly satisfied. I stared at him, hoping that if I stared long enough I could read his mind to see what he really thought, how he really felt. Then, there was a tug on my fishing rod.

"Uh oh," I said.

"You got something, Marin?" James called. There was another tug so strong it almost pulled the rod from my grip.

"I think so," I said. He got behind me like before, telling me to reel it in. I used my strength to turn the reel while he helped me steady the rod. Even with my lack of experience, I could tell there was a big fish on the other end of the line. I reeled the line faster and faster and soon I saw it coming out of the water, a fish. The closer it got, the bigger it appeared. We reeled it all the way in and James released it from the hook.

"Oh, my God!" I shouted. James examined the fish, then placed it in the cooler.

"Nice catch!" David yelled, still firmly holding his fishing rod.

"See. You can fish," James said.

I beamed and felt a sense of exhilaration. Not only did I catch the first fish of the day, but it was a nice catch too. "I wanna catch another one," I said.

He helped me bait my hook and cast the line back into the water.

"Go, Marin!" Rachel shouted. I waved at her, grinning. Who knew fishing could be so fun?

By the time we were done, I caught another three fish. The rest of them only caught one each, which meant I had beaten them by a mile. I wasn't feeling smug about my success, just excited.

Heading back to the campsite, Rachel and I carried the

fishing rods, while David and James followed farther behind with the cooler full of freshly caught fish, Marvin by their side. We were almost to the site when Rachel unexpectedly fell to her knees.

"Rachel!" I called and dropped to the ground to see if she was okay. Her breathing was shallow and her face was a pale green.

"Are you alright?" I asked. She grimaced and turned the other way to get sick. I pulled her hair back as she heaved and vomited on the ground.

"David!" I shouted, looking out for the guys. "Come quick!"

They ran toward us, Marvin barking along the way. When they arrived a moment later, Rachel had stopped throwing up and let out a little cry.

"What happened?" David asked as he dropped to the ground to Rachel's aid.

"I don't know. She fainted and got sick."

James retrieved water from his bag and poured it on her wrist and splashed it on her forehead.

"She might be overheated," he said as he helped her take a sip.

"Are you okay?" David asked.

"I'll be alright."

"Can you stand up?" James asked.

She tried to rise, but it was obviously difficult. David picked her up and carried her back. James and I followed, making two trips for all the supplies. During that time, David and Rachel decided it was best to pack up their stuff and head back to the city. We agreed and wanted to return with them.

"No, you guys should stay. Enjoy the rest of the weekend," Rachel said holding her tummy. After we helped David load his truck, I kissed Rachel on the forehead and wished her better as she climbed in. We waved goodbye as they drove off, and then headed back into the woods. With each step toward the site I grew more anxious about the two of us out in the woods with nothing to do but spend time with one another, quiet time at that.

We gathered firewood, and I watched James as he filleted the fish we kept, using special care with each one. He prepared the fish over a gas grill and we recalled the afternoon over our romantic camp dinner. To my surprise, the fish was delicious, even better than some of the fish I'd had at specialty seafood restaurants. James said it was because I caught it, to which I blushed.

Night fell and the only light beaming was the fire. It was more peaceful then any night I had ever experienced. Clusters of bright stars sparkled the night sky, and I tried to remember the last time I had seen so many at once. I don't think I ever had, especially since the lights of San Francisco drowned them out so much. The temperature dropped quite a bit, but I bundled myself in a warm sweater and cozy blanket. James appeared from the tent carrying a bag of marshmallows.

"Ready for dessert?" he asked, revealing chocolate and graham crackers.

"S'mores?" I asked.

"Yep. It's not camping if you don't have s'mores, right?"

I shrugged, reminding him that I really didn't know what camping should and shouldn't have. We warmed the treats over the fire and indulged in their delightfulness. There was something about gooey, melted marshmallows and chocolate that made me feel like a little girl again. I think James felt the same because we sat innocently, laughing at each other's "yum" sounds.

"So now what?" I asked as we cleaned up after our s'moresfest. It was only eight and I wasn't tuckered out enough to go to sleep.

"David and I usually sit by the fire and drink beer until we can't keep our eyes open. But, I brought something special for us." He disappeared into the tent and reappeared with a nice bottle of cabernet.

"Oooh," I sang. *I could use a bottle of wine.*

"Would you like a glass?"

I nodded and he poured the wine carefully into two plastic wine glasses then sat across from me near the fire while Marvin lay by his side. We stared at each other from across the flames and slowly sipped our wine. The robust liquid felt warm as it ran down my throat. A perfect way to keep warm in the cold outdoors.

"What do you think about camping so far?" he asked.

"I like it. I'm a little surprised that I like it, but it's been fun."

"Good." He smiled.

"I want to ask you something," I said as I sat up and leaned forward.

"Okay."

"I've been hesitant to bring this up, but I want to

know how you feel about us?"

It was a little trivial asking this, but I wanted to gauge his thinking. Why did he turned down Monica? He shrugged. "I feel good. I care about you a lot and I like being with you. I think we've both been taking our time expressing those feelings. You have your reasons and I have mine," he said. "But I'm not going anywhere. I think we have something, and I want to see where this goes."

"What are your reasons?" I asked, puzzled. He sighed loudly and brushed his hand over his face. His body language screamed that he was uncomfortable.

"I'm divorced," he said.

Divorced?

I was shocked. It was the first I'd heard the D-word come out of his mouth. Apparently, he was capable of keeping secrets.

"I'm sorry I didn't tell you before." He kept his head down and focused on his glass of wine.

"Why didn't you?" I asked.

"It was a long time ago. I was young and stupid. It's not something I'm proud of."

I sat for a minute absorbing the information. James was in his early thirties. It wasn't uncommon for a man his age to have some baggage. I certainly had mine. Part of me felt troubled by his omission, but then I remembered all I was hiding and tried not to think too harshly on it. After all, he had passed the Man Test.

Instead, I began to feel something else. Relief. James seemed so annoyingly perfect, but he had a failed marriage. It was his flaw, the big X on his permanent record.

"What happened?" I asked.

"She broke my heart. She told me it was a mistake, that we shouldn't have gotten married so young. But it was a lie." His heart slowly poured out. I began to feel like I was less of a fake girlfriend and more of his real therapist.

"What do you mean?" I asked.

"She just wanted to be with someone else; a guy we went to college with. I had no idea she was unhappy. She never acted any differently, never gave me any signals, and then one day . . . she was gone."

"I'm sorry, James." By his side now, I put my arm over his shoulder and lightly rubbed his back. It was evidently a painful memory.

He cleared his throat. "After that I dated casually. Very casually. Then I realized that no one was going to fill the hole she left. So I focused on my career. I went on a few dates, but I was still heartbroken. It's not like I still loved her, but it was hard for me to trust anyone else, you know? And then I met you." He looked at me honestly, his blue eyes breaking down my wall. It was too much, and I had to look away fearing my deceit would be revealed.

"Even before I knew about—" James cut himself short.

"What? Before you knew what?" I asked. His eyes looked away from me.

"Before I knew about your breakup with Chad." This admission was more alarming than the last.

"What do you know about my break-up with Chad?" I

asked, a hint of irritation in my voice.

"I know he betrayed you the same way Vanessa betrayed me."

My pulse increased at thought of my exposure. "You knew all this time? Why didn't you say anything?" I wanted to know why James didn't cheat, but I wasn't prepared for the heart to heart. To think that he knew about Chad this whole time. He never said a word. I walked a few feet away, feeling his eyes burn my back with the stare of pity, and why wouldn't he?

"Because I know how humiliating it was for me. I didn't want anyone to know either. Plus, you avoided conversation about your last relationship, and I wanted to respect your privacy."

He knew the pain I knew. The same pain that drove me to date him in the first place.

"I'm sorry," he called and walked over to me. I kept my back turned and felt a wave a tears prickling my eyes. Why had I felt so emotionally overwhelmed? Was it his honest revelation? The fact that he knew I had been jilted by a cheater? Or was it that he too had been left by someone as bad, if not worse than Chad? James faced me and grabbed my shoulders tightly. He lifted my chin so I could look up onto his face. My eyes were wet with fresh tears.

"I'm sorry I brought it up. I didn't mean to upset you," he said softly.

"I didn't want you to know about any of that," I said sniffling and trying to look away, but his face followed mine with persistence.

"Trust me, I get it. I want to tell you something else," he said. I looked at his face and kept his intense gaze.

"I will never hurt you that way, ever." His words were genuine enough to inspire more tears. "Marin, I promise, I could never be like that."

I believed him. And for the first time since Chad walked out of my apartment, I felt that I might be able to trust another man. Maybe that man was James. And suddenly, it was like a huge weight had been lifted from my shoulders. Not the weight of knowing I couldn't trust men, it was the freedom of knowing that I could possibly love again. He wiped my tears from my cheeks, and I lifted myself on my toes to kiss him. His arms wrapped tighter around me and I kissed him harder.

For the first time in our entire "relationship" our affection felt honest and real. He lifted me like I was weightless, and I wrapped my legs around his waist as he carried me into the tent. He kissed me again and laid me down. He said nothing, just kept kissing, kissing my lips, my face, my neck. He took off his shirt, then slipped off mine, gently kissing my shoulders and chest. Slowly we undressed, one piece of clothing at a time until it was just us, as we were made. I straddled him so we were face to face. He stared into my eyes, then gently moved the hair from my face revealing my vulnerable expression. It frightened me, the honesty of it, but I held his gaze anyway. Facing it. Facing us.

There was a connection, something real, something true, something beautiful. My heart leaped and my stomach fluttered. The smell of his skin intoxicated me like a dangerous drug as he breathed softly on my neck making my whole body tingle. I could see the silhouette of the campfire ablaze, like the fire I felt burn inside of me. Falling deeper and deeper with each passing second of an act I can only describe as making love. We made love continuously into the late hours of the night until I fell asleep wrapped in his arms.

The next morning I woke up next to James, and in the morning light everything seemed a little brighter. My memory flashed back and I relished in the night we spent together. I was changed. The only question, what would I do with my newest revelation?

James and I spent the morning drinking campfire coffee and the afternoon hiking in the woods with Marvin. Even though we were having a great time, dark clouds rolled in and we decided to head back to the city early. After an hour's drive, we passed all traces of rain. We talked while the radio played quietly in the background and Marvin snoozed in the back seat. He actually looked sweet when he was sleeping.

Fresh air breezed through the car. As the sun set, the sky turn beautiful shades of pink, purple, and gold. Then, a familiar song played on the radio, the one from the piano bar. James smiled and turned up the volume. We sang loudly, lyric by lyric, dancing in the car, and waving to the other road patrons to sing along. Like Telly, he played dashboard drums, while I rocked the air guitar. A perfect end to our trip in the woods.

James took me home, but I wasn't ready to end our time together. I asked him to stay over and he easily agreed. Then, I explained to Marvin that if he wanted to stay in the house he would have to be good and not pee on anything. He seemed more relaxed around me and behaved himself the rest of the night while James and I made love once again.

Sleep didn't come as easily as it did in the woods. I lay in the dark next to a sound sleeping James. He looked so lovely, peaceful, and certain. The things keeping me awake wouldn't cross his right mind. My thoughts raced over everything that happened in those last six months—where I started, where I ended up, and everything in between. By two in the morning, I had exhausted every story ending in my head. I made several clear conclusions. First, James was in essence a faithful man. It was a reassuring thought that gave me hope that love and fidelity were still possible. My second conclusion complicated things and made me uneasy. I genuinely had feelings for him, which tore me up about my final conclusion. I had to end it.

Relationships should be built on trust and honesty. Not in good conscience could I continue my "relationship" with him, even if my feelings turned real. The guilt would eat me alive, and if he ever discovered the truth . . . well, I didn't know if he would ever forgive me. Yes, I needed to make a clean break and start over once again. It was the honorable thing to do. Not that I had acted honorably the past few months, but there was no reason for me not to right my wrongs. If I had my own therapist, which wasn't a bad idea at this point, I think he would call this growth.

17

Welcome Back Holly

JAMES WAS MISSING FROM MY BED when the scent of french toast and bacon drew me to the kitchen. He was making breakfast and listening to his iPod.

"Good Morning," he said. I wiped the sleep out of my eyes, smiling a drowsy smile, and sat at the breakfast bar. He poured me a fresh cup of coffee and kissed my forehead.

"How'd you sleep?" he asked.

"Not bad," I said, even though it was a restless night. "How about you?"

"Like a baby," he said, serving up a delightful plate.

We enjoyed breakfast together and spent the morning reading the paper, taking turns with each section. Then in the early afternoon, I helped him gather his things and walked him to the door where we said our goodbyes. I told him over and over how much I enjoyed the weekend, then watched him walk out of the building. That's when I felt it for the first time, I was actually sad to see him go. It might be the last time he would be at my apartment. I ran after him.

"James." He turned around. I stopped only inches from him, gazing again in his sweet blue eyes. I brushed my hands on his cheek. "You're a good man."

His eyes lit up. "You're good too, Marin."

I grabbed him and kissed him like it was the last time, because I was sure it would be. When we came up for air he smirked. "We should say bye more often." I let out a little laugh and waved him goodbye.

Back inside the apartment, I felt a surge of butterflies. Even though it would end soon, I allowed myself to feel the new, pleasant sensation. Then, there was a knock at the door. My heart jumped. No doubt it was James returning for another goodbye kiss. I opened the door.

"Holly?"

I almost didn't recognize her. She was thinner than I had ever seen. Her skin had a beautiful dark hue and her brown hair was wild with natural curls. We stared at each other, almost like strangers. Then, she smiled.

"Is it really you?" I asked.

She nodded and I embraced her in the biggest hug I could muster, pulling back to get another look at her, and then hugging her again. We giggled like little girls. I invited her inside and she followed with several pieces of luggage.

"What are you doing back so early?" I asked.

She leaned into the couch as if she hadn't rested in days. "We finished the initiative early, so I came home."

"Why didn't you tell me?"

"I wanted to surprise you. Plus, I didn't really know until a couple of days ago."

She spent the next forty-five minutes telling me the details of her expedition in Thailand. She told me about her team that worked the initiative, the people of the country, the amazing food, fascinating culture, and extremely cheap Thai massages. She brought me several souvenirs; beautiful woven Thai pants that were cut like capris, Buddhist beads, and a stone carved elephant pendant. I thanked her for the thoughtful gifts and continued to beam at her. So much of my time had been occupied with my endeavor with James that I hadn't realized how much I truly missed Holly.

"So I need a big favor," she said.

"Anything," I said.

"My apartment's being sublet until next month, and I need a place to stay. Would you mind if I stayed here?"

"Of course not," I said, excited by the opportunity to make up our lost time. She let out a sigh of relief.

"Good, I wasn't sure if you would mind since you have a new boyfriend and everything." My heart skipped a beat, and I paused to make sure I heard her right. What did she know about my boyfriend? James' name hadn't come up once since she walked through my door.

"Don't play dumb." She smiled. "I know you're dating James Young." My puzzled gaze turned horrified.

"How do you know that?" I asked.

"Rachel told me. She sent an email about a month ago updating me on everything that's been going on. That was one of the BIG updates." She threw up her hands for emphasis on the word big. "So, is it real or is he your experiment boyfriend?"

My eyes hit the floor weighed down by a mix of shame and sadness. It was more than enough to answer her question.

"Oh no, Marin, you didn't. With James?" She was clearly disappointed. I put my head down, not knowing what to say or how to defend myself.

"What happened?" she asked.

"Nothing. He hasn't fallen for any of my traps and he won't. James is, for all intents and purposes, a faithful man. I'm going to end it." It hurt more to say aloud.

"Why?" Holly asked, which surprised me. I figured she would want me to let him go as soon as possible.

"Because real relationships should be built on honesty and trust. Ours has neither."

"But what if you came clean and started fresh?"

I just shook my head. "I think that would be worse. He has his own trust issues. The only valid choice I have is to make a clean break."

"When?"

"As soon as I can figure out how." The idea of having to break things off with James made me dizzy. What would I say? What reasons would I give him? Holly sighed and patted my shoulder.

"Well, at least wait until after Saturday," she said.

"Why?"

"Rachel's throwing me a welcome home party and you're all coming." I moaned in my grief. Saturday was almost a week away. I needed to wipe my hands of the whole thing immediately.

Over the next week, I avoided James using made up, reasonable reasons. It had been successful until Friday night when he made a surprise visit. I was drinking margaritas and playing penny poker with the girls.

"Hey, Marin," he said with a big goofy smile on his face as I invited him in. He looked at Holly and Telly, and I could tell he suddenly felt intrusive, which he was.

"Oh, sorry. I didn't realize you had company."

"It's okay. We're having a girl's night."

Telly waved. "Hi, James!" He returned her greeting. Holly greeted him with a hug.

"It's good to see you, James."

"Wow, Holly, I almost didn't recognize you. How are you?"

"I'm doing great," she said smiling, then she looked at me for a second. Her face was all smiles, but her eyes were saying *I can't believe you did this with my brother-in-law's best friend.* It was the first time I had seen James since our weekend getaway. Being so close to James and Holly at the same time unnerved me, like I was about to get caught doing something bad.

"I'm gonna head out. I don't want to interrupt . . . " He lifted his head to get a better look at the table. "Penny cards or anything."

"Are you sure you don't want to stay? We could turn this into strip poker," Telly said with a playful smirk.

He seemed to consider it for a moment. "It's okay. I'll see you guys tomorrow." The girls wished him goodbye, and I walked James to his car. The moment we were totally alone, he grabbed me and kissed me like he hadn't seen me in years.

"I missed you so much," he whispered.

"I've missed you too." Which was true. Evidently, I wasn't the only one to feel the shift in our relationship. James appeared to have turned his own page. Unfortunately, we were not on the same page, not even in the same book really. I thought about our time together a lot over the course of the week and secretly wished we were a normal couple, but knew I would not be able to take back what I had done. There would be no clean slate, no do-overs. It wouldn't be long before I would be faced with breaking his heart, so I tried not to indulge his affection too much. Instead, I sent him home with an innocent goodbye kiss.

The next evening, James and I arrived promptly at Rachel and David's townhouse. Holly was already eating spinach dip and crostinis and enjoying a glass of wine. We joined them in the living room, and Holly regaled us with stories from Thailand. Everyone listened quietly, engaged in the details and fascinated by her experience. I had already heard the story but was still enthralled. In the middle of her tale, James grabbed my hand tightly and kissed it. He gave me a warm, loving smile that melted my heart like a campfire marshmallow. I tried to return it but could feel the space between us become greater. And in that moment, I longed for it to be real between us. My nose tingled and I knew a tear was close behind. So I got up for another glass of wine to avoid an onslaught of tears. A moment later, there was a knock at the door.

"I'll get it!" I called out to the living room. On the other side of the door, I found a gloomy looking Telly holding two bottles of wine.

"Hey," I said.

"This is for the party." She handed me one bottle. "And this is for me." She raised the other.

"What happened?" I asked as she walked passed me into the kitchen to open her personal bottle of spirits.

"I broke up with Will."

"Oh, my God. Why?"

Telly poured herself a glass and downed it. "I'm not a relationship person, and it started to feel too much like a commitment."

"But I thought you said he was the love of your life?" Since day one, I had been hoping for Telly and Will to separate. I should have been thrilled, but instead it baffled me.

"He is, but we don't do well when we're in a relationship. That's why we always break up. I wanted to end it before it got too hard."

"Are you okay?"

"Yeah, I'm fine." She sighed. "It's Holly's night so let's not talk about it anymore."

Telly wasn't being thoughtful to Holly. It was her best excuse to avoid talking about her feelings, especially when they had been hurt. I agreed to keep quiet and she plastered a pleasant smile on her face.

Everyone greeted her warmly, and I watched as she downed glass after glass of wine. Her voice became louder and louder, and she became a little too flirtatious with David.

"Dinner should be just about ready," Rachel announced as she checked her watch and went into the kitchen. We made our way to their dining room, elegantly set with tiered place settings of wedding china and silverware. She even created place cards for each of us. Telly snatched Will's place card and tore it to pieces.

"Everything okay, Telly?" Holly asked.

Telly looked up urgently. "Yeah, everything's fine."

Rachel brought out a beautifully roasted chicken, greens, fresh bread, salad, and a few other deliciously scented sides. The elaborate spread looked tasty, but with all the stress of planning to break up with James, I wasn't hungry. The new wife and cook beamed at the success of her beautiful dinner party as we enjoyed the feast.

The doorbell rang. Rachel's eyes widened and her face lost its color.

"Who's that?" David asked with a full mouth of food.

"Not sure," Rachel said and cautiously stood up to leave the room. The group continued to converse in her absence. Minutes later, she returned face red and wet with tears.

David rose to his feet. "What's wrong?"

This alarmed the whole group. We had no idea what could have happened. Then, I noticed the brown envelope in Rachel's hand with a small pile of papers and prayed that it wasn't a Man Test failure report.

"You son of a bitch!" Rachel yelled at David. "This is what's wrong." She pushed the papers and photographs against David's chest. He glanced down at them and lifted his face to reveal a horrified expression.

"You slept with that girl, and you didn't even know her."

"It didn't mean anything," David said.

"Kind of like our marriage. How could you do this? We've only been married for five months."

"Rachel, I'm sorry," David said and rushed over to her. She shoved him away.

"Don't touch me!" she yelled. "I can't even look at you right now." Rachel crossed her arms over her stomach and left the house. David started to follow her, but I pulled him back.

"David," I said, "let her have her space, okay?"

He reluctantly stopped. "I can't just do nothing."

"Listen," I said firmly. His eyes followed Rachel. "You have to trust me on this. I deal with this a lot. Just give her some space."

David sat down with his head in his hands. Holly ran outside after her. I followed. There was no sign of her.

Holly turned to me with the fiercest anger I had ever seen from her. "No, Marin," she yelled.

I stopped short. "I can help."

"You've done enough," Holly said. "I don't know how, but I know you had something to do with this. What did you do, Marin? Is this one of the tricks you pulled on James? Did you set David up and send Rachel the results?"

"No, of course not," I said, but felt a surge of heat from the guilt. It was my fault. I told Rachel about the

Man Test service, but I never thought she would really use it.

Holly shook her head. "Just because you're miserable and heartbroken doesn't mean you have the right to bring everyone else down with you. You really messed up this time."

I felt compelled to give her some perspective. "You think this is my fault? No matter what led up to it, David cheated. I didn't make him do that. I tried to tell you. Men are liars and cheaters. I'm sorry that it happened to Rachel and you need someone to blame, but this isn't my fault."

Holly looked stunned. "Don't act so righteous. Maybe you didn't cheat on James, but you've certainly deceived him. What you did is just as bad, worse even. You took advantage of some poor guy, setting him up to prove a point. God, Marin! James is a great guy. He's the perfect guy, and even though I asked you not to, you went ahead and played your little game. And what did it get you? Nothing. You couldn't catch James cheating because he wasn't cheating. You had a good thing and you ruined it, and you potentially ruined my sister's marriage. So no Marin, you're not coming with me. You're done."

My head swam with her harsh words. Holly had never been so angry, especially not toward me. Maybe I couldn't expose James, but David exposed himself, which proved that I was right. I couldn't help but reaffirm my belief about all men being liars and cheaters. And why wouldn't I? After all, I worked with it, had been a victim of it, and here it was again rearing its ugly, but honest, head. Even though it was a painful truth, it was a truth, and that made me feel justified.

"You and Chad aren't as different as I thought," Holly said. Her words sent a cold shiver up my spine. She rushed away to find Rachel.

"Marin," James said.

Shit . . .

I turned around. Surely, he'd heard everything.

"Is that true? Was this whole thing a set up?" he asked. Part of me felt guilty, but the other part wanted to stick it to him for what David did.

"Yes. It's true," I said. His eyes widened with shock.

"Why?" he asked. "Why would you do that?"

"Because you're all the same. All that stuff about fidelity and trust, it's all bullshit." I could feel my body quiver from a surge of adrenaline.

"What are you talking about?"

"Maybe you're not cheating on me now, but what happens when we're together for ten years, twenty years?" It was a valid point that I hadn't considered much before with James' recurring fidelity.

"I don't know. You seem to have all the answers." He paused and glared at me. Neither of us not wanted to back down though we secretly wanted it not to be true. "You believe what you want, but you don't get to play the victim. You're the one being deceitful. You're the liar," James said matter-of-factly. He slammed the car door and sped off.

I covered my face with my hands and hunched down sick—sick with anger, sick with guilt, sick with sadness and uncertainty. Tears started, but I forced them back. I refused to fall apart on the sidewalk in front of the house of a cheater and his heartbroken wife.

Telly ran to my side.

"Are you okay?" she asked. I didn't know how to answer her, so I didn't. "Marin?" she said with a nudge. Slowly, I unburied my head from my hands and looked upon her worried face.

"Are you okay?" she asked again.

"Can you just take me home?" I sighed. She nodded and helped me up. What an awful mess I've made.

18

Everyone Hates Marin

I PACED AROUND MY APARTMENT all night waiting for Holly to come home or at least return my calls. By six in the morning, I gave up and went to sleep. When I awoke around eleven, she still had not come back. My body ached with fatigue, but my mind raced. I poured myself a cup of chamomile tea before returning to bed. Every thought tightened the knots in my stomach. It took everything I had not to leave my apartment and search for Holly and Rachel. Both were incredibly hurt for all kinds of reasons, some my fault, some not. I knew it was better to keep my distance. Let them be. Still, it left me with unsettled feelings that made my skin itchy. Feelings of restlessness, righteousness, guilt, sadness, and relief filled me simultaneously.

I had to be patient, and since I had the whole day to be patient, it was time to do a little reflecting, analyzing, and psychoanalyzing. I was a therapist after all. It was the array of mixed emotions that attributed to my annoying unsettled feeling. I made the attempt to divide and conquer. My guilt and sadness only ran as deep as my friendships with Holly and Rachel, which were pretty significant. Terrible, what happened to Rachel. I had no idea she enlisted the Man Test service. In all fairness, I warned her not to go looking for trouble unless she was prepared to deal with her findings. She knew perfectly well what she was getting into. Though her little heart was shattered, she'd eventually be able to put back the pieces, like I had, and move forward.

I didn't think she blamed me for what happened, but Holly definitely did. In her mind I subliminally put Rachel into a dangerous situation in which there was no way out. She would probably say it was the "law of attraction" or something. I put the idea of a cheating man into Rachel's subconscious and in turn her husband cheated on her. Of course, I thought that was absolutely insane. Otherwise, why didn't I attract a cheating man? Counting Anderson I guess I did, but none of that mattered anymore.

Holly was angry, angry with me for following my instincts on something critical. Okay, so what? We disagreed, but the fact that she was displeased with me was too much. It was her discontentment that left me the most unsettled, restless, sad, and guilty. How could I make her understand? I had to wonder, was she partly upset because she knew I was right? This brought me to my strongest feeling—righteousness.

Maybe what I did wasn't exactly up to moral code, but the results spoke for themselves. Given the right opportunity, men are extremely likely to cheat. It was horrible that Rachel had to learn the hard way, especially after making a life long commitment. David was just one example. There are so many men who do the same thing, make the same shitty decision.

I had to admit that it irritated me that James hadn't stepped out of the confines of our "relationship," but he was probably just somewhat sensitive to infidelity given that he too had been on the other end. Like I'd told him, what were the chances that he'd remain faithful after ten, twenty, or thirty years? My prediction? Unlikely. Not that I would ever get the chance to know for sure anyway. James and I were over, which brought me to my last emotion—relief. I hadn't pictured our breakup going quite like it had, but somehow I was freed. James knew the truth and so did I. Wasn't that the point? The reason I'd done it all? Wasn't that what I wanted?

Later, Telly and a bottle of vodka came to keep me company.

"Do you wanna talk about it?" she asked, handing me a fresh martini.

"No. Do you wanna talk about Will?"

"No." We sat quietly, sipping from our pretty martini glasses, neither of us caring to share our feelings on the most recent events of our lives.

"Do you think Holly will ever forgive me?" I asked.

"Yeah. It's not your fault David fucked up," Telly said.

"I know, but she thinks it is," I said, tears filling my eyes.

"Hey," Telly said, halting the tear. "You can't beat yourself up over this. Holly is upset because you were right, and it hurt her little sister. You went with your gut on this and proved the truth. You shouldn't feel bad about that."

Her words were encouraging, and I was thankful that she always had my back on the most controversial of issues, maintaining her honesty but never judging.

"Yeah, I guess you're right. Then again, Rachel and David might be done. I'm not sure if the end justified the means."

"That's for you to decide. All I know is you've been obsessed with catching a cheater and by proxy you did. Isn't that what you wanted?"

There it was, the same question that plagued my whole day. It *was* what I wanted, I just wasn't sure if I still did.

The next day I returned to work as normal. Holly was still missing. Who knew if I would ever hear from her again? The notion killed me. I found myself marching into Katie's office, looking into her sweet green eyes, and thinking she was too smart to put herself in a position like mine.

"I need your help. It's personal," I told her. She asked me to sit and tell her what was wrong. I divulged everything, all the details about James, my tricks, Rachel and David, Holly, and even Anderson. When I finished, her face was riddled with utter disbelief.

"Shit, you really did it this time," she said. I bit my lip and awaited the rest of her advice, but she just stared me.

"So?" she asked.

"So, that's it. What do I do now?" I asked. Hello?

"Oh, God, I don't even know where to begin. You're going to need a lot of therapy. You probably should've already been in therapy. You have four major problems: One, your friendship with Holly; Two, Rachel and David; Three, James; and Four, yourself and your feelings about this whole thing."

"I just want everything to go back to normal," I whined.

"I'm afraid it's too late for that. The damage is done, and now you have to pick up the pieces. You have a lot of work to do. I'm going to refer you to someone else." She began typing away on her computer.

"No, please. I don't like therapists." She shot me an offended glare. "I mean I don't like other therapists."

"I know. Doctors make the worst patients, but it's okay. I'm handing you over to one of our own."

"Who?" I asked.

"Andy," she said.

I sighed. As much as I'd started to warm up to Andy over my recent views of cynicism, he wasn't really what I would call a good therapist.

"Did you call me?" Andy entered the room. *Just in time.*

"Yes, Andy," Katie said, "I put Marin on your calendar for two o'clock today. She needs some guidance."

"Great." Andy looked at me like an animal about to devour his prey. "I've always wanted to psychoanalyze you." He smirked, then left the room.

I turned back to Katie. "I think I'd rather see someone else."

"Come on, Andy's a great therapist. His methods are a little unconventional, but they work. I think it's exactly what you need."

At two o'clock, I opted to "forget" my appointment. By two-o-five, Andy was in my office.

"Hey, time's running out. What's taking so long?" Andy said.

"Sorry about that. I'm swamped," I said appearing to be extremely busy in order to put him off. He sat down and cleared his throat.

"Bullshit." He called me out, which should've been no surprise, but it startled me. "Katie brought me up to speed on your case, and I have to say Marin, I'm impressed."

"Excuse me?"

"I had no idea you could be so ruthless. That Chad really messed with your head."

"Fuck you, Andy." He became infuriating all over again.

"See what I mean?" he said calmly, not fazed by my crude tone or insult. *Damn jaded prick.*

"I can't talk to you about this!" I stood up, ready to throw something at his head.

"Good," he said and motioned for me to take a seat. "Let me do the talking."

I sat down fuming and he rose to a lecture stance. "First, you have to know what you did was about as immature and manipulative as a teenage prank." I crossed my arms. "But I've seen worse from someone suffering traumatic stress."

"Like Lorena Bobbit?" I said.

"Let me do the talking, please," he said with a smug expression. "So let's start at the beginning. You catch your fiancé cheating, which caused you to call off your wedding and sink into a depression. Instead of seeking professional help to deal with your loss, you have a stroke of genius and decide to fool some poor guy so you could rid yourself of any responsibility in your own relationship failure. Because after all, if every guy does it then it didn't just happen to you, it happens to everyone."

I couldn't tell if his assessment made me feel better or worse.

"Now that your friend's husband's been caught red-handed," he said continuing on without taking a breath. "You probably feel pretty justified. It satisfied your mission, right?" He paused just long enough for me to shrug. "The problem is your boyfriend, Jimmy—"

"James," I said.

"Whatever." He rolled his eyes. "He was faithful. And I think deep down you knew that. I also think you hoped he would be faithful. The fact of the matter is you're no different than any other woman out there. You pretend to be the essence of a modern woman with your career and self-sufficient attitude, but you really just want to fall in love, get married, and have a baby or two." Andy was annoyingly presumptuous, but deep down I wasn't sure I totally disagreed.

"Your pretend relationship with Jim—"

"James!" I yelled.

"Who cares? The point is that it was a way for you to

take a look inside and protect yourself from getting hurt if it wasn't right. You built up a wall." He crouched down, leaning his elbows on my desk and held his hands up so I couldn't see his face. Then he brought them down. "You're the only one inside the wall and everything else is on the other side. No one can get in, but you can't get out either. Do you see what I mean?"

"Where are you going with this?" Hopefully out of my office.

"It's simple. You get your heart broken, and instead of accepting it for what it was, you turned it on the entire male species. It gives you no accountability in what happened, and if you think about it, it doesn't hold Chad accountable either. You accepted the idea that ALL men cheat as truth so you wouldn't have to deal with your own feelings about what happened."

"No, I—"

He shushed me. "The bottom line is you're not going to be able to make things right again until you realize that your generalization about men and fidelity is fallible."

"Wait," I interrupted and he finally let me. "I thought you agreed. You said all men would cheat."

He cocked his head back with a sour look. "Please. Nothing fits perfectly. You have to make exceptions."

I was quiet.

"You need to accept that what happened between you and Chad was just between you and Chad. Maybe it was your fault. Maybe it wasn't. Either way, you can't make everyone suffer for your unresolved issues."

"Are you done?" I asked.

"Yeah, that pretty much covers it." He stood with his hands on his hips and smiled as if he'd accomplished something great.

"How is it that you're so arrogant?" I said staring at his self-satisfied face, which was also annoyingly kind of handsome. He was right, and I found myself in the position of being obtuse. In fact, most of the time he was right, which drove me crazy. He made everything sound so obvious, but until he spelled it out for me the answer hadn't been so clear. It still wasn't, and I wasn't quite ready to admit defeat. But I had the feeling I'd soon have to.

"I'm right, aren't I?"

Yes, I thought, but instead said, "Let me think about it."

"Fine." He turned to leave. "Same time next week?"

"Definitely not!" I yelled out, but I was sure he ignored me.

Over the next couple of days Andy's words rang in my head like a bad tequila hangover. Holly and Rachel made no contact with me, and of course, I hadn't heard anything from or about James. I couldn't quiet my mind. I couldn't sleep. I could barely eat, and I hadn't heard a word of what my patients were saying during our sessions. My life had become a total mess, a mess I created. More and more, I began to realize the whole thing was my fault, and there were fewer and fewer reasons to justify my actions. How could I have let myself make such a huge, irreversible mistake?

Andy said I couldn't make things right until I realized

that not all men are unfaithful. I couldn't let it go, haunted by the fact that I'd been so badly duped. How could I escape the idea that the men in my life were always trying to put one over on me? Then again, as far as I knew James and Michael had been faithful. While David, Chad, and Anderson were not. If I had been performing a real study and those men were my sample, then statistically sixty percent of men are unfaithful, which is exactly what the published studies had concluded. Maybe it was true. Maybe forty percent of men were faithful. It still wasn't enough. Who was to say Michael and James wouldn't make a bad choice eventually? There was a lifetime of opportunity and temptation.

I needed convincing, one more answer to push me to one side or the other. The next day, I left work early and drove down to San Jose to see my dad on the golf course where my mom told me he would be. By the time I got there, he was on the ninth hole.

"Dad," I yelled. With the bright sun overhead, he squinted when he looked my way.

"Marin, what are you doing here? Is everything okay?" He approached concerned and since he was my daddy, I started to cry.

"No, Dad," I sobbed. "I need your help. I really messed up."

"What happened?" he asked. My tears went from a light mist to a humiliating down pour. It was the first time I had cried since the night everything went to shit. He rubbed my back while his golf buddies stared. I willed myself to stop, but I couldn't control it.

"I don't even know where to start," I said through my tears. He called to his friends that he had to leave, then took me inside the clubhouse for a drink.

Finally, my tears ceased and he asked me again what was going on. I told him everything, the truth about Chad, the book *Unspoken*, the scheme I came up with, how I fooled James, how David fooled Rachel, and how I had made a fool of everyone, me being the biggest fool of all. He listened carefully and even though I knew he was appalled at most of the things I told him, he was kind enough to keep it hidden.

"I need to ask you something, and I need you to answer honestly." I stared into his hazel eyes that mirrored my own and started to tear up again. "Please, Dad, please tell me the truth. I will never say a word or bring this up ever again." He took a deep breath and agreed.

"Have you ever been unfaithful to Mom?"

I had done it, asked one of the most intimate and personal questions ever asked, especially of your own father. He and my mom had been married for almost forty years. The two of them were madly in love. It was the kind of love that inspired me to fall in love, get married, and be a couples therapist. On the other hand, he surely had plenty of opportunities and temptations. He was a good-looking, successful doctor and my mother wasn't always easy to deal with. His answer could easily have been 'yes.'

He gave me a thoughtful look and took my hand.

"No," he said. "I can honestly say I've never been unfaithful to your mother." I gasped as if my lungs had been restored with fresh air and shed a tear of relief.

"But the book says men will lie to their grave about indiscretions." It was a little snide of me to say, but this was too important to take at face value.

"Have I ever lied to you?" He asked, and I tried to think back. I couldn't remember him ever lying about something important. Even when I questioned him about Santa at only six, he told me the truth.

"No." I said, and so I believed him.

When I returned home, I was emotionally drained, but my mind was racing. There was only one remedy that could help clear my head—a run. The air had cooled since the early afternoon and it was slightly overcast. My temperature stayed even while I ran, which helped maintain my stamina. It was perfect and allowed plenty of time to sort my thoughts about how I could fix things with Rachel and David, Holly, and particularly James.

My guilt worsened over those last few days. I felt compelled to reach out and explain myself to him even though he probably never wanted to see or speak to me again. Why did I care so much about James when Holly and Rachel meant so much more? I thought about how we first met and how kind he was to such a clumsy girl. I thought about the fireworks on the Fourth of July and how much my family liked him. I thought about our camping trip, and how I felt when I realized he wasn't a bad guy. He was actually a good guy, a really good guy, and I had messed it all up. I was a fool. Not just because I was careless with him, but because I had been blind to him. Did I really give him up on the notion that he might cheat on me one day? It was no way to live, and it was definitely no way to love.

There, running underneath the clouds in the park, I felt it, a shift in my thinking, the realization that Andy was talking about. I tossed the ideas about infidelity out of my head and onto the pavement, leaving room for all the beliefs I held before. For the first time, I accepted my feelings for James. Real feelings. Strong feelings. Feelings I wanted to feel, beliefs I wanted to believe for a man I wanted to love. I wanted happily ever after, and I wanted it with him.

Then, like an act of God, raindrops fell from the sky. I looked up at the clouds. The rain covered my face and cooled me from the run. It was like a fresh shower to wash away all the horrible things from the past six months and break new ground for the future. Walking home in the downpour left me exhilarated by the release of my once heavy burden. I recalled the affirmation from the meditation book Holly gave me, the one I so proudly threw away, and thought it over and over until I got home. It was my found-again truth—I am a strong woman and I deserve love.

19

Make It Right

MY SOAKED SNEAKERS SLOSHED as I walked into my building. All I wanted was to take a warm shower and head to bed so I could start fresh in the morning. Instead, I walked inside and found Holly on the couch. I stood still, waiting for her face to show some indication of what she was thinking, feeling, doing, but it didn't.

"Hey," I said.

"Hi." She was distant, like she didn't want to be in my apartment.

"You're back."

"Yeah," she said quietly and stood.

"How's Rachel?"

"Not great, but she'll be okay."

I nodded and glanced at the floor, watching the water drip off of me, leaving a puddle at my feet. Tears began to surface as I felt a sudden urge to bare my soul. I looked into the eyes of my best friend, wondering if our friendship would ever be the same. The urge became uncontrollable and my tears burst free, startling Holly.

"Holly, I'm so sorry. I made a huge mistake. I know that now. If I could go back I would undo everything, but I can't. I don't know if you can ever forgive me, but please know I am so, so sorry." I sobbed my pitiful apology and continued to cry for the moments she stood there staring at me. Then, she put her arms around me.

"I know, Marin. It's okay," she said in her sweet, loving voice. Her sympathy didn't absolve my crimes, but did increase my guilt.

"No, it's not. I strained our friendship. I ruined Rachel and David's marriage, and . . . and . . . I lost James. I was so stubborn that I couldn't see the truth right in front of me. How can I ever fix this?"

She gave a familiar long face, one I had seen many times over the years when I had any sadness in my life. A look that meant she understood and even felt my pain.

"I don't know," she said.

After a hot shower and a change into warm, dry clothes, I sat in the living room snuggled in a blanket near Holly and sipping green tea.

"Where've you been the past few days?" I asked.

"At our parent's condo on the bay. We stayed there until yesterday."

"Where's Rachel?"

"She went home to talk to David."

"What's she going to do?" I asked, terrified of the answer.

"I don't know. One minute she loves him and the next she wants him dead."

"Well, she's angry."

"Yeah, but I think she wants it to work. It's not like they're dating. They're married."

I nodded in agreement. They should try to work it out. It's not going to be easy, but it was possible. I had seen couples overcome extramarital affairs and regain trust.

"That's what you should do, Marin." Holly said with the emphasis of a great idea.

"What?"

"You can counsel David and Rachel."

"No," I said, "I'm sure they don't want anything to do with me, let alone giving me access to their private marital life."

"Why not? If anyone can help them patch things up it's you. I'm sure they'll go for it. Especially if it were . . . pro bono." She carefully snuck in that last part. I looked at her like she was crazy, then she lifted her brow and pursed her lips as if to say, *do this or else.*

"Okay. If they go for it, I'll go for it."

Holly smiled. "What about James?"

I shrugged. "I don't even know where to begin with him."

"What if you explain everything? I mean you're not crazy, you were heartbroken."

"I doubt he would see it that way. Plus, he has his own issues with deception. He'll probably never trust another woman again, especially me." I frowned, knowing that getting James back would be a hopeless cause.

"You know that for sure?"

"Yeah, I'm pretty positive he wants nothing to do with me."

"Well, you'll never know for sure until you try. You care about him right?"

I nodded and my eyes stung with a fresh glaze of tears. My situation had come full circle, heartbroken, tearful, and pathetic.

"I think I'm in love with him." My heart pounded deeply as the words left my mouth and got caught in my throat. It was the first moment I realized just how much I cared about James.

"Then you have to go get him," Holly said, and she was right. If I wanted James back, I would have to go for it. Really go for it. I'd be taking a big chance, bigger than leaving Chad, bigger than playing James, and bigger than fooling myself. It was my true make it or break it moment, and I was ready because I believed in love. I stood for love—morning breath, movie-night in, grow old together love.

"Okay," I said. "I'm gonna do it."

Holly applauded, beaming, then tackled me with a playful hug. We sat side by side, our arms around one another, and our heads leaning together.

"Are we okay?" I asked.

"Yeah."

"You're a good friend, Holly. You have every reason to be angry with me right now, but instead you're here, helping me."

She released herself from our embrace and looked at

me. "Marin, you're my family. Yes, what you did was bad, but you're not a bad person. I know that better than anyone. You're going to have to do a lot worse to get rid of me." She pinched my cheek and I smiled. And in that moment, we were kids again and she was forgiving me for selfishly eating all of the good cereal. Just like that, we were back to being us.

The next day I took a basket of muffins to Rachel and David's house in an attempt to make amends. Rachel was home alone, dressed casually in jeans and a t-shirt with her hair in a messy ponytail. Her eyelashes were so thick and dark even without mascara that she appeared evening ready. She thanked me for the pastries and offered me a cup of coffee. We sat in her kitchen eating from the basket of goods while we cleared the air.

"I want you to know I'm not mad at you over any of this," Rachel said.

"You're not?" I asked.

"No. Why should I be? Besides, you're the one who told me not to go looking for trouble unless I was ready to deal with finding it."

"So why did you go looking for trouble?" I asked.

She sighed and looked away. "I always had the thought in the back of my mind and in the pit of my stomach, but I ignored it because I was so in love with him. I just needed to know for sure."

"Well now that you know, how do you feel?" I asked and waited patiently while she seemed to thoroughly consider her answer.

"I have so many feelings and don't know what to

think. I don't know what to think about love or marriage or trust"

"Yeah, but how do you feel?"

"I love David, despite everything. He's my husband. On the other hand, I don't know if I want to put up with it. The memory of it will never go away."

"I know how you feel. Looking back, I gave up because what we had wasn't worth fighting for, not because he cheated. I know I can do better."

"Yeah, I thought about that. Part of me feels like I can do better, but the other part of me feels like David takes good care of me. He makes me laugh, he helps me with the dishes, he even supports my scrapbooking hobby." She let out a little laugh and I joined.

"Those are important things too. Do you really want to give those up because of one mistake."

"No, not for one mistake, but how can I trust he won't do it again every chance he gets?" I watched her face turn sorrowful, tears wetting her eyes. She picked needlessly at her banana nut muffin. It broke my heart to see her like that, especially because I knew all too well what it was like, the racing thoughts, the sleepless nights, the decisions about the future. Her road was not an easy one, but I wanted to be there to see her through no matter what she decided. I couldn't let her go off the deep end and make the same mistakes I had.

"I don't know Rachel, but I want to help you find out. I want you and David to start seeing me a couple times a week for counseling. If you want to try, I can help you."

She let out a big sob and she covered her face with her

hands. "Really?" she asked through her tears. I nodded. She grabbed me tightly, and I held her while she cried on my shoulder. All I wanted was to hold her and take her pain away.

"Thank you," she said, and I smiled with relief.

It had been less than a week since my whole world shattered in front of me. Again. Already I was making headway toward putting it back together. Holly and I were in a good place. Rachel agreed to start counseling, and I was starting to feel more like myself again. The issue of James still loomed, but I planned to make an honest and humble attempt to tell him how I felt.

Later, I took a cab, a box of things he left at my place, and my timorous nerves to his apartment. Since his car was parked on the street, there was a good chance he was home. My hands shook as I walked up the stairs to the door and buzzed his apartment. I held my breath.

"Hello?" he spoke through the intercom. The sound of his voice made the shiver in my hands shoot throughout the rest of my body, and my heart pounded in my ears.

"It's Marin, can I come up?" I waited for his response, dreading the answer no. The intercom clicked on with a deep sigh.

"I don't want to see you right now." I closed my eyes and took a deep breath, trying not to get upset.

"I brought your stuff back," I said into the intercom.

"Just leave it on the steps."

He wouldn't even let me upstairs to his door, not even to shut it in my face. I felt defeated and decided to cut my losses, leaving the box of things behind me. When I reached the sidewalk I glanced up at the building at his window. We were physically so close, and yet so emotionally far away from where we were. I wasn't sure if I would have the courage to come back and try again, so I turned around, walked back up the stairs, and buzzed his apartment again. He didn't say anything.

"James, if you can hear me . . . " I started, gulping down my pride, "I want you to know that I'm sorry. I'm not at all proud of what I've done, and I don't intend to defend it." I let the intercom go for a moment. No response.

"What I did to you was terrible and there are no excuses for it. I think you deserve an explanation why." I paused and looked around. This was a private matter, but given that I was standing outside of the building, it felt public. And I was right. Standing on the sidewalk was an older couple just watching me, listening. They seemed to have no shame about it too. Old people get away with a lot sometimes. I gave them a humiliating glare, cleared my throat, and continued my plea.

"The reason is, I was heartbroken. I came home one night to find my fiancé having an affair. It destroyed me and everything I believed in. I thought that I would never breathe again. Then I found this stupid book that said all men cheat and lie about it. That it's in their nature and there's no exceptions. And I believed it. I believed it so much that I was determined to prove that his affair was in no way my fault." By then, a woman and her dog had stopped next to the old couple, everyone seemed to hang on my every word. As if pouring my heart into an inter-com wasn't mortifying enough, James' neighborhood wanted to humble me further. I sighed.

"So I used you. Unforgivably, I used you. After the camping trip, I decided to call it off. I had real feelings for you. I have feelings for you, but I couldn't carry on a rela-tionship that I started dishonestly. Then David cheated on Rachel and I got all fired up again, and then you found out. So what I'm trying to say is I'm sorry. I wish I could take it all back, because you are a great man, and I know now that you were faithful. I am so sorry I tried to dis-prove that. You deserve someone as amazing as you are, someone who would never doubt you for a second. And . . ." I started crying there in front of the old couple, the woman, her dog, some teenager on his bike, and the in-tercom.

"I wish I could go back, and I wish I could be that person for you." I let the intercom go so I could let out a sob. It was pitiful, but my attempt was honest and com-plete. I pressed the intercom button one last time. "Goodbye James. I wish you all the best."

I rushed downstairs past the crowd that assembled to watch my confession. My feet couldn't carry me any fast-er as the wind dried my tears. When I got home, Holly and Telly were waiting for me with coffee and my favorite blueberry scones. I skipped both and instead curled up on the couch to mope.

"What happened?" Holly asked.

"He wouldn't even see me. I had to apologize over his building's intercom while the neighbors watched. It was humiliating." They expressed wide eyes and pouted lips.

"Do you think he heard it?" Telly asked.

"I don't know. It doesn't matter. It's over. He won't even see me. I'm alone again." I leaned into Holly, sobbing. Telly sat on the other side next to me and put her arm over my shoulders. It broke my heart to think that I had ended up at the same bitter end where I started six months earlier.

"You're not alone, Marin," Telly said.

Holly lifted my chin so I could see her face. "You have us," she said. I was touched, fortunate to have such amazing friends.

"I love you guys," I said.

"We love you too," they said.

The three of us huddled together on my couch, grieving the things we lost and grateful for the things we still had.

20

Comes Around . . .

IT WAS A TUESDAY MORNING when I awoke suddenly from a dream about James and I walking in the park. Nothing special or unique, but it felt so real. At one time, it was real. I closed my eyes and tried to return to the dream, wanting to have another moment with him, but it was gone. My waking remnants of the dream made me miss him even more than I had in those last few weeks since I attempted to clear things up with him. Since then, I had resisted the urge to call or stop by his apartment. My heart skipped a beat, every time someone knocked on my door or called my phone. I always hoped it was James, but it never was.

It was a quiet, cool October morning. A morning like that should've felt peaceful, but instead it felt empty, lonelier than ever. Holly had moved back into her own apartment, which had been a difficult adjustment. I had less in my life to keep me distracted from the pain I felt and the pain I caused.

To cope, I busied myself with work, taking on more patients and working later hours. Unbelievably, Andy still counseled me, putting me through an emotional boot camp. It was a rare, yet effective style. His style. He helped me understand my insecurities about my family, about what happened with Chad, and about myself. I made good progress—his words, not mine. But that's the thing about therapy, the patient is really the only one who knows when they're ready to move on.

On my way to work, I got my usual call from Telly.

"What's up, girl?" she asked with excitement.

"The usual. What's going on?"

"Same. So listen, why don't you and I get all dressed up and go out tonight. I can't even remember the last time we went to a bar together," she said.

"No, I can't. I have to work. Plus the marathon's coming up soon, and I don't feel like going out drinking," I said, which was the truth.

"Marin, you've been working like crazy lately. Can't you get out of it and go out with me? Please!"

"I'm really not in the mood, Tell."

"I get it. You're in a funk. I'm trying to help you out of it. Come out with me for one hour. If you feel the same then we can go back to your place and watch reruns of *The Golden Girls*."

"You're the only person I know who still watches that show."

"Whatever, are you coming or not?" she said.

I knew she wouldn't stop until I said yes. "Fine, but

just for an hour."

That evening I left work around six, giving myself plenty of time to get ready. It was the first time I had been out with Telly in months. We'd slowed down on the bar scene after I was "settled" with James and she was settled with Will. Now, since we were both newly single, it seemed perfectly natural to venture out again, if not just for a couple of hours of needed attention. Though, the only man's attention I yearned for was James', and I didn't think that would change anytime soon.

Telly picked me up around eight and we headed back to Bleeker, the bar where I'd met Anderson.

"Here, Telly? Can't we go somewhere else?" I didn't want to risk running into Anderson again. Ever.

"No, this is a great place to meet decent guys. It'll be fun." Telly's definition of a decent guy was one who was good looking and well off with the emotional and physical attention span of a week. It wasn't my scene and I was uncomfortable long before we entered the bar.

I scoped out the place for Anderson and, of course, James. Every tall, sandy blonde-haired guy I caught a glance of looked like him for a moment. I needed a drink. Telly nursed her single Tartini, while I quickly downed a double martini.

"Try not to look so sad. You're scaring the men away," Telly whispered.

"Sorry, I miss James," I pouted.

"I know you do, but it's time to move on. Remember, casual relationships are the way to go. It's nearly impossible to get hurt."

"Is that why you dumped Will?"

"No, I left Will because I missed going out like this. I'm not ready to give up the chase, the new feeling, the freedom," she said.

"Don't you think you'd be more fulfilled knowing that someone loves you and wants to be with you after the newness fades away?" I asked.

"I don't look for fulfillment in other people, especially not men. Marin, we've talked about this. Do you think I changed my mind just because you regressed back to your old belief that relationships are the key to everlasting happiness?"

"I guess I'm realizing that we're all different. Some of us are not monogamous relationship people and some of us are. I was stupid to think I could convert. I'm a relationship person and I think James is too. I wish I'd realized it sooner."

She gave me a sour face and our waiter arrived with fresh drinks.

"From the gentleman at the bar," the waiter said. The man waved to us from the dim lit bar. Telly smiled flirtatiously and waved back.

"Oh, I am liking his little bits of salt and pepper," she said. I sighed irritably. Andy was the gentleman sending over drinks. He picked up his Jack and coke and approached us.

"Hi, Marin," he said and glanced sensually at Telly.

"You two know each other?" Telly said. I glared at him as if to telepathically say, *don't you dare.*

"Telly, this is Andy from work," I said.

"Andy . . . I've heard so much about you," she said as she shook his hand. One of my worst fears was that the two of them would meet. They were attractive, smart, and successful with an appetite for sex. Yep, they were birds of a feather and something was bound to happen. Something bad.

"Good things I hope," he said.

"Well, mostly good." She flirted and I rolled my eyes. Could the night get any worse?

"I'm gonna go back. I just saw you here and wanted to buy you ladies a drink," he said, and I felt instantly relieved.

"No, you should stay," Telly offered, and when she asked a man to stay, he stayed.

"I guess I can stay for one drink."

He sat down and inched closer to Telly. She edged a little closer to him too. I wasn't in the mood to go out, but I was in even less of a mood to watch Telly and Andy flirt in front of me only to imagine him taking her home. Yuck!

"I'm gonna go. It's been about an hour, and I wanna go home," I said as I stood and grabbed my purse.

"I'll take you home," Telly said.

"No, you stay. I'll call you tomorrow."

"Are you sure?" Andy asked.

I nodded and hugged Telly goodbye. I thanked Andy for the drink, which I quickly downed before heading outside to find a cab.

The next morning, Telly didn't call on my way to work, and I resisted the urge to call her thinking I might risk Andy answering the phone. I shuddered at the thought.

Ten minutes after I arrived to work, Andy was in my doorway.

"It was good seeing you last night," he said. I glanced up briefly and continued the work I'd barely started.

"Yeah, you too." He came in and sat on the edge of my desk.

"I like your friend, Telly. That girl is something else," he said with a satisfied smile.

"Spare me the dirty details, please. She's my best friend."

He scoffed. "Hold on, you think I took her home?"

"Didn't you?" I asked, instantly regretting not staying or making her leave with me. Telly and Andy together? It was all too weird.

"No." He looked offended, which wasn't easy to do. "I know my moral compass doesn't always point north, but I still have one. We're colleagues, but you're also my patient. I can't go around screwing my patient's best friends. It wouldn't be right."

"So you two didn't sleep together?"

"No, but I did get her card. As soon as you're done with therapy, I'm going to call her," he said, backing out of my office and taunting me by flashing her business card. I threw my pen at him, but he blocked it with his shoulder.

"It's a joke, Marin. Lighten up okay?"

"It's not funny," I yelled after him.

I worked steadily until noon when Holly met me at my

office for lunch. We went to the deli down the street for our usual salad, panini, and iced tea.

"Rachel told me she and David are seeing you today."

I nodded.

"Good, I hope it's going well."

I smiled at her tight-lipped, both of us knowing I couldn't tell her anything about David and Rachel's sessions or progress.

"So now in light of everything, what do you believe about the secret lives of men?" she asked. It was a tough question.

"I don't know," I said. "I don't think we'll ever know. But I also think we have to have faith in those we love and hope it works out. After all, love itself is a leap of faith."

She gave me a slanted smile but agreed. I could see her faith had been tarnished by the acts of David and Chad.

"Do you think there are any good men out there?" she asked.

"Yeah, I had one." I dropped my head.

She lifted my chin with her hand. "You'll have one again. I promise."

I smiled at her and she returned it, both of us innocently hoping for something good.

When I returned to the office, it was time for my therapy session with Andy. He was armed with his usual notepad, even though he almost never took notes and spent the majority of the time talking.

"So what do you think?" he asked, which took me by surprise. He also never asked my opinion in our sessions.

"About what?"

"About your progress."

"Overall, I feel better. At the same time, I'm afraid that I'll be notoriously suspicious of the next guy I'm with. I mean, how could I not be?"

"I think the question is why would you be?"

"Because of my past experiences." Duh!

"But don't your past experiences also prove that there are many trustworthy men?"

"I guess so." He had a point.

"Okay then, innocent until proven guilty. Marin, you can't live your life waiting for the other shoe to drop. It's not good for you, and it's not good for any of your future relationships. Guys hate that shit." He kneeled in front of my chair and looked into my eyes. "You have a choice. You can choose to worry and be suspicious or you can choose to be happy. So which is it?"

It was one of the most basic ultimatums in therapy, and one of the most effective. I had control of my own thoughts and fears. I had control over whom I dated and whom I chose to trust. I had control over my own happiness.

"I choose to be happy," I said, and I meant it.

"Great." He stood. "I think we're done here."

"What?"

"Yep, I'm releasing you from care," he said.

"Is this because you wanna call Telly?" I asked.

He smirked. "I'm not going to call your friend." *Thank God.* "Or am I?" he said, and I gave him a little shove.

"Kidding," he said putting up his hands to surrender. I

questioned him with my eyes, but he didn't flinch. Instead, he opened his arms.

"Now come here and give me a hug." I embraced him with a friendly and final hug. "You're a good girl, Marin. Don't ever change."

I smiled at the notion, feeling like I had finally found myself again. I turned back just before I left his office.

"Andy?" He looked up. "Thank you," I said with a smile.

"Anytime." He returned the smile with a wink.

The afternoon passed as usual and at four o'clock David and Rachel arrived at my office. They settled on the couch and updated me on the home assignments I had given them the past week. Everything seemed to be going well, but it was the beginning and they had a long way to go.

"I don't want to be that kind of husband." David remarked about his indiscretion.

"I know," Rachel said with tears in her eyes.

"I think you've made it clear to Rachel how sorry you are. Now you have to gain her trust back. That means being honest about who you are and what you're doing," I said, and he nodded.

"Rachel," I said, and she looked up. "Do you believe in second chances?"

"Sometimes."

"I know you're here now, and I know you're working on this at home. However, this is only going to work if you open up and really give David a second chance to prove that he can be a faithful husband."

"I'm trying, but in the back of my mind I keep thinking it's going to happen again."

"Rachel, I'm going to tell you something that my therapist told me." She looked curious and wiped her tears with a tissue. "You can choose to worry or you can choose to be happy. So which is it? Are you going to continue worrying, or are you going to give your husband a second chance?"

Rachel stared at me and then at him. She placed her hand softly on his knee.

"I'm going to give him a second chance."

He pushed her hair out of her face and gave her a grateful smile. "I love you," he told her.

"I love you too." Then he kissed her with what looked like all of the gratitude in his heart. I knew that he was thankful for her kindness. If only James could do what Rachel had done. Not that David or I really deserved it, but a second chance was all we really wanted.

After their session, I began packing my things for the day. I looked out my window and saw David and Rachel walking hand in hand. Somehow I knew they would make it through, giving me hope that somehow I would make it through too.

Sunday was race day. It was still dark outside when my alarm went off at five-thirty. I switched on the lamp and stared at the ceiling for a few minutes. Anxious thoughts about the run ahead consumed my mind. I breathed in deep and bent my leg to stretch my knee. It felt a little tight, but I hoped after a warm up it would loosen. Closing my eyes, I tried to imagine how the day would play out. I imagined myself running on the Golden Gate Bridge while the sun glistened off of the water and Telly and Holly cheered me on. I reveled in the thought of boldly crossing the finish line, feeling triumphant with my arms raised high. Then I thought of James, how he would miss it, and how much I missed him.

Seven a.m. marked the start of the US Half Marathon. When I arrived it was packed with participants, volunteers, sponsors, and supportive friends and family. My girls were nowhere to be found among the sea of faces that surrounded me. I signed in, took my tag, number 1011, and attached it to my white, running jacket. My buzzing nerves turned my stomach while I waited for the marathon to begin.

Between my nerves and the crowds, my breathing became fast and shallow. My eyes began to well with tears. I rushed toward a nearby clearing to pull myself together. In that moment, I was alone. No Telly, no Holly, no James. I looked out onto the bay and slowed my breath. I closed my eyes, trying to imagine a place of calm, thinking about the lake that James took me to on our camping trip. Trying to recall the soothing sounds of the water, the birds rustling in the trees, and the wind that picked up the leaves. I exhaled. I remembered how it felt to catch all those fish even though it was only my first time and I held onto that feeling.

I opened my eyes. The race wasn't about my friends, it wasn't about James, it wasn't about proving something or disproving something. It was about me and what I could do on my own. The race was about to start so I took my position and waited. I shook out my arms and adjusted my ponytail. While I waited, I noticed my shoelace had come untied.

Before I could finish my double knot, a familiar voice called out, "Marin!"

I stood and looked behind me. My brother, Michael, made his way over. He wore shorts, a long sleeved St. Jude t-shirt, and a tag that read San Francisco US Half Marathon- 1171. I beamed as he approached.

"What are you doing here?" I asked.

"Supporting St. Jude's, of course." I just smiled. "Besides, chicks love it," he said as he waved to someone in the crowd. I looked in the direction of his wave and saw Jennifer and the kids standing on the side in support. All wore matching St. Jude t-shirts. I waved to them too. The crowd started counting down and we were moments from race.

Three. Two. One!

Michael looked at me. "Come on, Marin, let's kick this race's ass!"

I nodded. The race was so crowded that we began at a walk. It wasn't long before the crowd separated and we were able to begin our run. Michael and I ran side by side to the bridge. It was just as I imagined. The morning sun glimmered on the water, there was a cold breeze that prickled my cheeks, but felt amazing on the rest of my body. I focused on my breathing and the finish line. As we made our way across the bridge and through the streets, I thought about the past six months and how many amazing moments passed me by because I was too preoccupied with my obsession. I was glad to be out of it. And running the marathon with my brother and all those people, I realized, that moment was mine.

Michael and I were nearly at the finish line when my knee began to ache. I kept my focus and tried to push through the pain. The closer we got, the more it hurt, and the more I wanted to stop. I hissed at the stinging in my knee and the tired muscles in my legs. *Almost there.* Then, I saw Holly and Telly near the edge cheering me on. I grinned as they waved me to finish. With their encouragement, I pushed harder and made it to the finish line. Right as I lifted my arms in triumph, I felt a tug at my foot, and lost my balance. Fighting to stay upright was no use, I tumbled to the ground and felt the grit of the asphalt scrape against my knee.

I lifted myself, gripping my knee in pain. My undone shoelace was the culprit. I'd never finished the double knot when Michael found me before the race. *Dammit!* Then the pain was superseded by a sense of humiliation. I really had to learn to be more graceful and tie my shoes properly.

Before I could think on it too long I heard, "Are you alright?"

I looked up and saw a face that matched the familiar voice. It was James. Surely I had hit the ground so hard that I was hallucinating, but whoever it was helped me to my feet. My eyes focused on him again.

"Marin, are you okay?" he asked. It was James. I couldn't believe it. What was he doing here?

"Oh, God," I said. It was by far more humiliating than

the time I had fallen in front of the office building and the intercom apology put together. It was my karma. The universe always knew how to get back.

"We have to stop meeting like this," he said.

"This is so embarrassing. Please, you don't have to help me," I said, trying to limp away.

"I don't mind," he said and placed my arm over his shoulders.

"You should mind. I don't deserve your help. I'm a terrible person," I said, tears flooding my eyes.

"No, you're not. You did a terrible thing, but you're not a terrible person." He walked me to a nearby bench. My knee was scraped, dirty, and bleeding. I couldn't look at him, so I gazed down at the blood seeping through my skin. Just as before, he had a small duffle bag with a first aid kit, and he went right into mending my knee.

"How are you?" he asked.

"I've been better." I sobbed.

"Yeah, me too." He wiped my knee with some peroxide and my skin tingled from the touch of his fingers. I shut my eyes trying to restrain the rush of emotion. Then, he lightly blew on my scrape. It was so undeservingly sweet.

"What are you doing here?" I asked.

"I came to see you," he said.

"You did? Why?" My heart jumped at the idea that he wanted to see me again. I wasn't too hopeful in case he came to tell me off.

"Despite everything . . . I miss you." I dropped my head and let out a cry, relieved by his words. Even though

I was thrilled he missed me, it made me feel even worse about what I had done to him.

"I missed you too. I'm so sorry, James," I cried. He put on the band-aid and lifted my chin.

"I know." He said, wiping a tear from my cheek with his thumb. "I've had a lot of time to think about this, and I get it. I went a little crazy too when Vanessa did what she did."

"Probably not that crazy," I said.

"No." He chuckled. "Not that crazy." I felt flushed at the thought of how I had behaved. I had my reasons, but in that moment they seemed silly and stupid.

"I just need to know one thing," he said still kneeling down in front of me. I looked at him and his crystal blue eyes. "Was it *all* a lie?" he asked.

"No," I shook my head, wiping new fallen tears. "All of the things I told you about me were real. The walks in the park and the night in the woods. It was all real."

He sighed deeply, and I held my breath.

"Good. I hear you're helping David and Rachel put things back together."

"Yeah. She wants to give David a second chance."

"I want to give you a second chance too," James said, looking like my own fairytale prince.

"Why?" I asked.

He stood up and held out his hand. I took it and he helped lift me from the bench. I didn't care that my knee was throbbing, or that I had fallen in front of all of San Francisco, only that James was there and he was giving me another chance.

"Because . . . I love you," he said.

I smiled. "I love you too."

It felt so good to tell him and even better that he felt the same, even after everything. We stared at each other for a moment, thinking how crazy it all was. He leaned in slowly and I lowered my eyes to watch his mouth as I had done so many times before. My heart leaped as he kissed me, like it was the first time. I shut my eyes tightly and relished in the moment with him. My stomach fluttered and I was so thankful to have him back. I loved him, I trusted him, and I wanted to be happy with him. Finally, I could start over, for real this time.

We pulled back and he leaned his forehead against mine.

"Now what?" I asked.

"Now, let's get you some ice cream." We beamed at one another. He took my hand in his and led me away from the marathon. I glanced back and saw Telly and Holly huddled together cheering me on. As I turned forward, I looked up at him.

"What flavor are you gonna get this time?" I asked.

"I don't know, but I think I'll try something more adventurous."

Hello Reader!

I really hope you enjoyed spending time in Marin's world. If so, you'll love the rest of *The Marin Test Series*. Available now!

I hope you'll connect with me on social media. You can find me here:

Visit at www.amandaaksel.com
Like on Facebook: www.facebook.com/amandaaksel
Follow on Instagram: www.instagram.com/amandaaksel
Follow on Pinterest: www.pinterest.com/amandaaksel

XXO-Amanda

Acknowledgments

I am deeply grateful for the support and encouragement of my husband, family, and friends during the pursuit of creating this novel. For that, I want to say a sincere thank you.

A special thank you to my publishing partners, Sara and Heather. Without them this work would still be unpublished.

And Chantell, my lobster, I couldn't have done this without our friendship.

AMANDA AKSEL

Amanda Aksel loves anything that's smart, sexy, and funny. She's the author of *The Marin Test Series* and *The Londonaire Brothers Series*. You'll often find her writing novels with an adorable maltipoo on her lap, pretending to be Sara Bareilles at the piano, watching reruns of *Sex and the City*, or sprinkling a little too much feta on her salad.